IMPLOSION

Joe Connor

Published by Argyle Fox Publishing

argylefoxpublishing.com

Publisher holds no responsibility for content of this work. Content is the sole responsibility of the author.

ISBN 979-8-89124-016-2 (Paperback)
ISBN 979-8-89124-015-5 (Hardcover)
ISBN 979-8-89124-017-9 (Ebook)

ARGYLE FOX
PUBLISHING

BOOK 1
IMPLOSION

To the Reader

May your imagination complete the story where the author could not.

CHAPTER 1
PAUL

You've done this a thousand times before. You can do it with your eyes closed.

Paul took a deep breath and stepped up to the football, kicked it on the sweet spot, and blasted it into the net in front of him. The kick was strong enough to go fifty yards. One more like that and Roswell would get the win.

"Come over here, Lewis!" shouted Coach Estep. "We've got one last drive. Looks like Devan might get it to around the forty-yard line. Got a fifty yarder in you?"

"No problem, Coach," Paul said. He was already three for three on the night with two kicks from inside the thirty-five and one from forty. He ripped a fifty-yard field goal during warm-ups, but this was the biggest football game of his life.

It was the state semifinal, and Roswell trailed by one. The school hadn't been to a state final in twenty years, and Paul could be the one to take them there. With ten seconds and one time-out remaining, Paul's best friend, Devan, was supposed to run for a few more yards. Then Coach would call a time-out before Paul kicked the field goal.

Devan and Paul were the only sophomores playing varsity for Roswell High School this season. Paul was on the team because he could kick. He played competitive soccer from age six and always played up a year or two. He wasn't big or strong, but he kicked with perfect technique.

Devan, unlike Paul, was a complete animal. His dad was an NFL Hall of Fame running back, and his mom ran track in college. Put simply, Devan won the gene pool lottery. He towered over the other sophomores, standing six-feet tall and weighing nearly 180 pounds. His muscles were like iron, and his teammates swore he could run through a brick wall. He had more than half of the big D1 colleges offering him scholarships as a sophomore, and he was popular at school.

The snap was clean. Quarterback and school heartthrob Chase Thomas handed the ball to Devan. Paul crossed his fingers as Devan ran through the line. Devan pushed ahead before taking a big hit and going down near the thirty-five yard line. As if he won the game, Devan leapt up to celebrate.

The referee placed the ball on the thirty-eight yard line. Coaches and players screamed for a time-out.

Paul did the math in his head: he needed to hit a forty-five yard field goal instead of a fifty. He relaxed. This would be his career record. Despite the pressure and deafening crowd, he was confident he could do it.

Coach Estep patted Paul on the back. "Take us to the final, Lewis," he shouted. "You've done this a thousand times. You'll be a hero after this. No different than in practice."

A little different than in practice, Paul thought. *There aren't usually thousands of people watching.*

Family and classmates stood on the bleachers, cheerleaders chanted on the track behind him, coaches from both sides screamed at players who dripped sweat and breathed heavily, some of whom were bleeding. Roswell was playing their archrivals, Milton. It had been a hard-fought game nobody expected to be this close. Milton had won state twice in the past five years.

The game clock showed four seconds, and the play clock was at thirty-five seconds as Paul jogged onto the field. Devan ran off the field and patted Paul on the back as he passed by. "You got this 'orse," Devan said in a thick Jamaican accent. He switched to a proper English accent and insisted, "You're money, mate."

Paul's nerves eased a little, and he smiled confidently.

Devan and his dad were the only people who called Paul 'orse. Though Devan was born and raised in America, his parents came from Jamaica to attend college in the US. In Jamaica, a horse—or a 'orse—was someone who worked hard. Really hard. Paul was also born and raised in America. However, Paul's dad was from England. He came to America just before the European war broke out eighteen years ago. Longtime neighbors and best friends from childhood, Paul and Devan always called each other 'orse or mate. None of the other players used these nicknames, but Paul and Devan didn't care.

The teams lined up for the kick. A Milton player with facial hair stood directly opposite Paul, panting and glaring as Paul stepped off the kick.

"I heard about you, thirty-two," the Milton player growled. "You're a fairy soccer player who thinks he can play football with the big boys. You haven't got enough muscle in those skinny legs of yours to score from forty-five."

The Milton players laughed.

"Not just a soccer player," another player shouted, "but the son of British coward. He's got coward's blood in him, that boy. Wants to turn and run like his old man."

Paul eyed the referee, expecting a penalty flag. Instead, the ref smirked.

Paul stared at his taunters without flinching, determined not to show his nerves. He stood only five foot six and weighed a meager 120 pounds, but Paul wished he played in the game for real so he could hit those giant jerks. His frustration and anger built with each breath.

Paul glanced to the sidelines. His kicking coach smiled, closed his eyes, and took a deep breath. Paul did the same. Every practice, Coach Clarke encouraged Paul to channel his energy and emotions into a single kick. From Paul's perspective, his kicking coach was more into mental strength than actual football. The coach spoke constantly about channeling the energy within your body, taking every emotion and focusing on a single action. For Paul, that action was kicking field goals.

It seemed an odd approach, but Coach Clarke helped Paul use his anger, frustration, joy, and excitement for more powerful kicks. Coach Clarke believed when people channel all their energy into a single object, they accomplished more than they thought possible. "If people realized how much power was within them," he often told Paul, "they could move mountains."

Paul took in the mountain before him. He took a deep

breath and focused on channeling his anger and nerves into the kick. But it wasn't enough. The Milton players' laughter and taunting overwhelmed him. Paul caved.

"Your momma didn't care what kind of blood I had when I was with her the other night, thirty-seven." Paul's teammates laughed, encouraging him to scream more. "And you, twenty-four"—Paul shook his head—"you been doing your homework and heard about me? Our coach never mentioned anything about number twenty-four. No one knows you."

"Tone it down, kicker!" the referee yelled.

Anger blurred Paul's concentration. "They started it!"

The referee wagged a finger at Paul.

Focus! Paul drowned out the sounds around him and harnessed his nerves and anger. He got into position and took a final deep breath.

The snap was high, but Reece pulled it down. Paul's heart pounded as Reece set the ball, laces slightly left. In an instant, Paul connected with the ball and followed through powerfully. It was a good kick. Paul knew it as soon as it left his foot. End over end, the ball sailed through the goalposts.

Before it landed on the ground, Reece jumped on Paul, knocking the breath out of him. Soon, Paul was under a sweaty dog pile. Cheers and laughter swelled as players ran from the sidelines and jumped on top. Devan scrambled to pull Paul from the bottom of the pile. The two embraced in a bear hug. Then Devan and another player hoisted Paul onto their shoulders. Fans rushed the field, chanting "Roswell!"

Coach Estep met the Milton head coach mid-field. As the pair reached out to shake hands, two Roswell players dumped a cooler of Gatorade on Coach Estep. He squealed as the blue liquid and ice drenched him.

Hordes of students jumped around the Roswell players, with Paul at the center. Paul saw Finley Matthews draw near. He'd had a crush on her since the first day of school. Blood raced to his head. Her long blond hair, normally pulled up for soccer, was down. Her brown eyes sparkled and met Paul's for a brief moment.

The rush of scoring the winning field goal, the bright lights, and the euphoric atmosphere were getting to Paul. He imagined Finley walking toward him and waving. Paul lifted a hand to wave back. He blinked twice. It wasn't his imagination. Finley was making a beeline for him.

Paul leaned forward to greet her as Chase Thomas, quarterback extraordinaire, pulled Finley into his arms. Paul saw number four—Chase's number—painted on Finley's cheeks. His heart sank. Chase and Finley were dating.

He didn't have time to feel sorry for himself. The coaches called the players over to line up and shake hands. Paul went to the back of the line behind Devan. His eyes were peeled for Milton's thirty-seven and twenty-four, sure they'd be fuming.

It was twenty-four that came to him first. When they shook, his hand swallowed Paul's. He pulled Paul closer and squeezed like he wanted to break him. Hatred pooled in his eyes. Paul tried to pull away but couldn't escape the solid grip. Twenty-four squeezed harder. Pain shot through Paul's hand. It felt like his knuckles would break. There was no time to channel energy. Instead, Paul stepped hard on twenty-four's toe and dug his cleats into his bones. The Milton player shoved Paul away, cursing him out.

Paul ducked, avoiding a wild swing aimed for his face. Before twenty-four managed a second shot, Devan pushed him to the ground.

Number twenty-four scrambled to his feet and charged. Devan stood his ground, and the sound from their collision echoed as Milton's thirty-seven tackled Paul from the left. Though caught off guard, Paul twisted on the way down and somehow landed on top of thirty-seven. Paul straddled the confused player, eager to release his anger and frustration with something besides field goals.

Paul slammed his right hand into thirty-seven's face. "You stupid"—left hand—"fat idiot!" Right hand, left, right—Paul's hands cracked against the opposing player's jaw. "Tell me I've got cowards blood now!"

Devan and twenty-four grappled to the left as players from both sides rushed the scene and joined the brawl. Coaches from both sides ran in to break it up. Coach Estep reached the scene first, heaving Paul off the Milton player as Paul got a final kick into thirty-seven's ribs. Blood dripped down thirty-seven's face, as Paul blurted out every British curse word in his repertoire.

Coach leaned in close to Paul. "I'm going to shout at you for a second to make it look like you're in trouble," he whispered, "but I'm proud of you, boy." He looked hard at Paul, winked, and made good on his promise. "What the hell is wrong with you, Lewis! Don't be starting fights like that after we've won a game and embarrass the entire school!"

Paul was too shocked to hear the screaming. Proud? Wasn't a coach supposed to keep his players from fighting?

"Do I need to report your kicker, coach?" The Milton head

coach walked toward them, fury in his face. "That boy"—he aimed a finger at Paul's chest—"should be suspended!"

"I'm dealing with it," Coach Estep said. "Heat of the moment thing. It's our first state final in twenty years. My guy got a little excited, and I'm sure your twenty-four doesn't want to make a big deal of getting knocked around by our sophomore kicker, does he?"

The Milton coach grimaced.

Coach Estep smiled at Paul and nodded toward the Milton coach. "Apologize, Lewis."

Paul looked at the Milton coach with confusion in his eyes. "Sorry, sir."

The Milton coach cocked his head, measuring whether to accept the apology or press the issue. Behind him, the fighting died down, and the teams separated.

"Okay, okay," he finally said, "I'll let it go this time. But don't ever pull that crap again. If you sort out that temper of yours, you'll make a good football player." He nodded and shook Coach Estep's hand, murder in his eyes. "Good game, Coach, and good luck in the final."

Coach Estep grabbed Paul by the arm and led him toward Roswell's locker room. The pair walked through crowds of staring students.

"Way to go, Lewis!" one student yelled.

"Even our kicker beats up on Milton!" another shouted.

Paul's dad sat rigid and alone in the middle of the bleachers, scowling. He ignored his son and addressed Coach Estep. "Everything okay, Coach?"

"Sure is, John," Coach replied. "Nothing to worry about. We'll talk later."

16

CHAPTER 2
PAUL

Paul followed Coach Estep past clothes on pegs and open bags on the floor next to discarded tape in the empty locker room. Coach stepped into his office, let Paul enter, then closed the door behind them. He walked around the desk, settled in his big leather chair, and smiled.

Paul stood in his pads and green jersey. His helmet was somewhere on the field, abandoned during the fight. Paul's legs shook under his weight. A nervous foreboding replaced the adrenaline that sent him into a rage.

Coach rested his elbows on the arms of his chair, his fingers interlaced. The light shone off his bald head. His arms bulged in his tight white t-shirt.

"Did you see the look on his face?" Coach chuckled. "I've been waiting five years for Milton's coach to look at me like that. Lewis, I'm so glad we have you on this team. You are money, son!" He laughed again. "I'm sure you'll have to serve a detention for this, but don't worry about it. That was awesome!"

There was a knock on the door. Another muscular man with a shaved head scowled at Paul through the window.

Coach waved him in.

"I want to apologize for my son losing his cool back there. We've spoken about this before." John squinted at his son. "He needs to do bet—"

"Don't worry about it, John," Coach Estep interrupted. "Those boys deserved a good beating, just like their coach. They were talking trash to Paul the whole game." He lowered his head and leaned across his desk toward John. "FF talk about you English fellas. Those prejudice slurs are becoming common language and between you and me, I don't like it."

"Thank you, Coach. That means a lot." John grinned and turned to his son. "What did they say to you, mate?"

Paul looked to the ground, embarrassed.

"Coward's blood and stuff like that."

"That's nothing new. I've told you it's not worth fighting over."

Paul's face grew hot as the insult echoed in his mind.

"It wasn't just the insult," Paul said. "In the lineup, he squeezed my hand—hard! I tried to pull away, but I couldn't, so—so I stamped on his foot."

Coach Estep howled. John wasn't smiling anymore.

"Squeeze it back harder then!" he yelled. Stronger, tougher, better. It was his MO.

Paul swiped a tear.

"Come on, John," Coach said. "That boy was big—even for a senior! Paul didn't stand a chance in a straight battle of strength. He had to do something. He had to play to his strengths, so he fought with his mind, not his muscles.

18

Important for football players to know when to do that. And," he eyed Paul, "where did you learn to punch like that, son?"

"We have a punching bag at home," Paul answered. "Me and dad work out together."

Coach slapped the desk with both hands. "I like this family more and more!" He reached a hand out. "Great to have you both on the team."

John shook the hand and focused on his son. "We'll talk when we get home," he said. "Great kicking by the way— your longest kick in a game."

A tear snuck down Paul's face as his teammates entered the locker room behind him, shouting for joy.

"Dry your eyes, son." John nodded. "Go celebrate with the team."

Coach motioned for John to take a seat. John rested his hands on the chairback instead.

"The coaches have a little meeting in this office after the game," Coach said. "I'd like you to join us."

"I'd love to, but my wife is waiting outside. She's gonna be worried sick about Paul. I need to tell her he's okay."

"Do what you gotta do," Coach said.

"Thanks," John replied. "And great win tonight."

Paul and his dad walked out of the office together.

"Hello, sir," Devan said through a smile.

"How many times do I have to tell you to call me John?" John punched Devan's arm. "You played great tonight, Devan. Paulie, can you ride home with Devan's parents? I need to get your mum and little sister home. She got really tired towards the end of the game."

19

Paul gave a thumbs up, and his dad turned to leave. As he did, a handful of Roswell players turned their backs, a sign that they didn't appreciate his lack of support for the current president.

Paul gritted his teeth.

"Chill 'orse," Devan whispered. "It's not the time to pick another fight."

Chase, the quarterback, glared at those who turned their backs to John. "Turn around, boys!" he yelled. "You can think how you want outside of football, but this team will not have players disrespect a parent like that." He looked at John. "Sorry, sir."

"Thanks, Chase," he said, "you're a good lad. Great game tonight."

Chase ran his hand through his wavy blonde hair and gave a flawless, white smile. Paul wanted to hate Chase for his good looks, perfect grades, and dating Finley, but Chase was too nice. Paul couldn't help but like him.

Once John left the locker room, Chase headed to Paul. All eyes were fixed on them. Chase shook Paul's hand and spoke in a loud voice.

"Well done, Lewis. We wouldn't be going to state without you." He looked meaningfully at Paul. "I'm glad your dad came to our country."

"AMEN!" Devan patted Paul on the back. "Win as a team, fight as a team. That championship is ours, boys!"

With that, the team unleashed a singular shout of triumph, followed by high fives and fist pumps.

"Quiet down boys!" Coach Estep raised his wristwatch as he stepped into the crowded locker room. "Principal

Hennessey wants to say something to you all."

On cue, a two-foot hologram of Principal Hennessey's torso and face projected from Coach's watch into the center of the room.

"Congratulations, student athletes, you have done your school proud. Be sensible this weekend—stay out of trouble and come back next week, raring to go. I'd love to see that trophy back here next semester." He paused, waiting for the players' applause to die down. Then, he finished: "USW for all."

"USW for all!" repeated a handful of enthusiastic players.

Coach nodded at the principal. The hologram disappeared.

"You played excellent tonight, gentlemen." Coach was calm and poised. "I know what happened with those Milton boys and all that trash talk, and I want you to know this—a team that is divided along any lines cannot be at its strongest. If we want to win state next week," he said, "we need to play our strongest. I'm not here to tell you what to believe, but when you put on that green uniform, we are all on the same team. If one of our players is insulted, you stand together. If one of them is attacked, you fight for him. No exceptions."

Players shuffled their feet uncomfortably and stared at the floor.

"Seniors, listen carefully." Coach eyed the boys who turned their backs on John. "You have one final game with me as your coach. We've been together four years, and I desperately want each of you to leave this school with a championship ring." Coach admired an imaginary ring on his right hand. "But if I hear any talk like what I heard from

21

those Milton players tonight, the person guilty will not play next week. We are a team. I will not coach players who bring division."

Paul's breathing caught. If the wrong people heard what Coach just said, there would be trouble.

"Am I making myself clear?"

Half-hearted mumbles echoed around the locker room.

"The world is a crazy place," Coach continued. "Some of you may be soldiers this time next year. But believe me, no matter what the future holds and no matter how far you travel, you will always look back on this time. High school football is the best time of your life. And if we stick together for one more week as a true team, we can win state. Then you can always come back home to Roswell and see your name on our school wall as a champion."

Coach pulled a football out of a bag and spun it three times.

"Tonight's game ball could go to a few people," he said. "Devan, you ran for over a hundred yards. Chase, you led well, and your passing was exceptional. How about young Lewis getting us the winning points?"

The locker room erupted, as those who turned their backs on John stood stone-faced.

"But tonight's game ball goes to big Tommy Harper. He did all the dirty work that the fans and media won't remember. Blocking for your runs, Devan. Protecting you, Chase, play after play. And I didn't see it with my own eyes, but Tommy—I heard you punched Milton's thirty-seven after the game, sticking up for young Lewis!"

The team shouted in approval. Coach yelled over them.

"Principal Hennessey has told me that you and Lewis both have to serve detention on Monday after school for fighting. But I'm giving you this game ball tonight and letting you know how proud I am of you."

Coach handed the ball to Tommy, who stood half a foot above him. The team patted Tommy on the back as the coaches followed Coach Estep into his office.

"He's right, fellas." Chase walked to the middle of the locker room and held up a hand. "One more week and we'll take state! But tonight, it's Friday. So, we party like a team and watch big Tommy bear dance for us with the game ball."

Tom obliged, wiggling his hips with the game ball above his head. The locker room erupted in laughter, as Chase waved his hand for quiet.

"We've got permission to be at Tyrone's house until two," he said between laughs. "If you don't know where he's at, ask him before you leave. Do not show up if you don't have permission! We don't need to get shut down again."

Players danced and joked as they hit the showers, left the locker room, or relived their favorite moments from the game. A whiff of body spray bulldozed Paul's senses. Gagging on the smell, he sat down next to Devan and reminisced on the season.

The only sophomores on the team, they started the year as outsiders. Being the son of NFL hall-of-famer Demaro Jones wasn't enough to earn respect for Devan. Politics weighed too heavily. When Brother Swanson ran for election to lead every church in the American empire, Devan's dad openly spoke out against him. Demaro believed faith institutes needed more freedoms and that the United States of North

America shouldn't force its beliefs on other nations. Brother Swanson and his supporters disagreed. This made life difficult everywhere for Devan, including the football field.

Things started to change when Devan ran through half the starting seniors in a single play during the first practice. After that, he was taken more seriously.

Unfortunately for Demaro, President Hudson won reelection. Supported openly by Brother Swanson, President Hudson's reelection stripped Demaro of much of his social standing. All his NFL sway was tossed in the trash. Immediately after winning his third term, President Hudson declared it was God's call for America to spread democracy and Christianity to the world. "By peace where possible," he said, "but by force, if necessary."

In the three years since, the country grew accepting of the President's ambition. He longed for the fruition of Prophet Stacey Lee's vision of a United States of the World (USW). President Hudson claimed that people with coward's blood were more common since his reelection. "Coward's blood" originally described Europeans fleeing the European war. Many of these so-called cowards moved to America by marriage. Others had friends in high places or crossed borders illegally. All longed to escape Europe's destruction. Now, anyone who didn't support the USW supposedly had coward's blood running through their veins. Hudson's most ardent supporters even claimed that anyone who didn't align with Lee's manifesto were too scared to fight for America's divine destiny.

Because Devan's dad opposed the president, Devan wasn't allowed to play football his freshman year. When he was granted permission to play the following year, he had a bone to pick. After crushing skulls one play after another, Devan proved he belonged on the team.

Paul wasn't so lucky. Being part British made it difficult to get respect from the team, despite his many field goals. He trained one-on-one with his kicking coach, mere yards from the rest of the team, but they were in different worlds.

"Everyone's gonna love you now." Devan patted Paul on the back.

"Maybe," Paul said, "but I'm still just a kicker. I want to play in the game for real."

"Those guys out there are pretty big, Paulie. You need to put on a few extra pounds before you take them on."

Paul grunted. "Did you not see me beating up on those seniors after the game?"

"Sure did, brother," Devan laughed. "But getting a few punches in and playing four quarters are two very different things."

Paul bit his lip. The fire inside begged to come out and play again.

"I could wrap 'em up!" he said, forcing himself to remain calm. "I get you from time to time!"

"Come on bro, let it go." Devan toweled his face dry. "You're a great kicker. Let that be enough. We wouldn't be in the state final if it wasn't for you. And hey, let's enjoy tonight."

"I wish," Paul said. "I doubt our parents will let us go."

Devan's jaw dropped in mock surprise. "First time in twenty years the school's gone to state. They have to let us go! I don't care that we've never been asked to a post-game party before. This is different. Listen," he said, "when we get in the car, tell my dad that your parents are letting you stay at the party 'til twelve."

"You guys coming?" Chase walked toward Paul and Devan. "To Tyrone's house—you coming?"

Devan flashed a grin to match Chase's. "We'll be there," he insisted. "Our parents can't say no."

"Well," Chase said, "the team wants you there. Just make sure you get permission from your parents. I don't want it canceled again. Let them know there will be alcohol for the seniors, but Reece's parents will be around."

Devan saluted. "Aye, aye, Captain!"

Chase saluted back half-heartedly and smirked. "You picked up a lot of yards tonight, Devan. It's nice to know I can give my arm a rest and we'll still get down the field. And hey, great kicking tonight, Lewis."

Big Tommy bounced the game ball off Chase's head and caught it.

"Let's go, Chase." Big Tommy waved the ball at Paul and Devan. "See you later guys."

Devan and Paul waited a few minutes, then left the locker room. Outside, Demaro waited in the crisp, cool air. He wore a big brown coat, green gloves, and a hat with the Roswell 'R' on front.

"My two favorite players!" he yelled in his thick Jamaican accent. "You must be da last ones out. You boys were fantastic tonight. Couldn't be prouder! Come on—your modder is in the car waiting for us. I been in this country a long time, but my body still don't like this cold."

"Well done, boys," Devan's mum said as they got into the car.

"Thank you, ma'am." Paul eyed Devan, signaling with his eyes for Devan to ask his dad about the party. Devan opened his mouth, then closed it.

"What you boys so quiet for?" Demaro asked. "I expected you to be all fired up after a game like dat."

Paul nodded to Devan again. Devan turned away and looked out the window.

"Devan is scared to ask if he can go to the party at Tyrone's house tonight," Paul blurted out.

Devan hit him in the arm playfully. "Chase wants the whole team together," he said. "Reece's parents will be there."

Devan's parents looked at each other in silence, squinting and licking their lips. Finally, his mum spoke up.

"I don't know, son. Didn't one get canceled when some underage kids got drunk?"

Devan stammered. "Some of the seniors will be drinking, but they definitely won't let us get away with it. Besides," he said quickly, "those kids who drank too much weren't football players."

"And what about girls?" Demaro asked. "You boys are both sixteen now, so the network won't tell me what you've been up to."

"Come on, Dad." Devan rolled his eyes. "You shouldn't want to know that. Anyway, there aren't any girls that I really like."

"Don't tell Cristina that," Paul whispered.

"Anyway," Devan said loudly, "what did you all do before anyone got tracked by the network? Weren't you eighteen when you got married? That's only two years away for me!"

"Watch yaself, young man." Demaro spoke in a sharp

tone that caused Devan to roar with laughter. "Your modder couldn't keep her hands off me when we were fifteen. She would have definitely been in big trouble if the network was around back then."

Juliet slapped her husband on the leg.

"So, I can go to the party?" Devan asked.

"We'll talk about it at home," Demaro said.

"Come on, Dad," Devan pleaded.

"We'll talk at home," he repeated. As he drove, Demaro reminisced on his college days.

"My, my, how things have changed. We were some of the first people to get the watch back in college you know. It was brilliant to have completely free internet, phone calls and anything else on the network was free. Back then, no one watched anyone. The government didn't track your every move." During Demaro's rookie NFL season, the league first required players to get the neck chip and permanent watches. Some players left the league, refusing to wear it. They tried striking, but the league wouldn't budge.

"Once the nation saw us pros wearing the watches," Demaro said, "all the young kids wanted one."

Little by little, more people came around to the idea. When everyone with a criminal record was required to get a watch, civil war became a real threat.

Those days, however, were long past. Paul's generation never knew life without watches and forced access to the network, twenty-four seven. Now, every baby born was required to wear one. Those who promoted the watch had data on their side. There was no crime anymore and very little sickness.

As they neared their neighborhood, Paul's right hand began to swell. Demaro slowed down and pointed at some younger kids playing flashlight tag in their front yards.

"Okay Paulie, we're here," Devan's mom said. "Talk to your mom about the party and ask her to give me a call once she's decided."

"Will do, Mrs. Jones. Thanks for the ride." Paul stepped out of the car and looked into the backseat. "Hopefully see you soon, Devan."

CHAPTER 3
PAUL

When Paul opened the front door, his younger sister, Hope, ran toward him.

"Great kick, Paulie!" she screamed. "That was amazing!"

"Thanks, Hope." Paul hugged Hope in her pajamas, as she squeezed him with all her might.

"Woohoo!" Paul's mom, Hannah, scurried to the kitchen. She wrapped her arms around Paul, squishing Hope. "Way to go, Paulie—you won it for the team!"

"Mom, you're squashing me," Hope yelled with a giggle.

"Sorry, baby," replied Hannah.

From the hallway, John gave a barely noticeable smile. It was the same smile he gave when Paul won the soccer championship or was kind to one of his sisters.

With his mom's arm draped around him and Hope clinging to his side, Paul walked to his dad.

"Well done, son!" Paul's dad shook Paul's hand, sending pain shooting through Paul's knuckles.

"Ow!" Paul yanked his hand away. "Guess I'm still tender there."

John lifted his son's hand for a closer look. He tilted his head in thought. "It's good it's bruising," he said. "Means it's not broken. Let's get some ice on it."

"Come on, Paulie, I got you some dinner ready," his mother said. "Okay, Hope, off to bed straight away. You were almost asleep at the game." Hope kissed her mom and dad on the cheek before giving Paul a big hug.

"It's fun having a big brother who kicked the winning field goal," she whispered. "Come tuck me in, Momma."

"I'll be up in ten minutes, baby. Go brush your teeth and get in bed, and I'll be up."

As Hope ran off, Hannah explained that Hope couldn't sit still when Paul had the chance to kick the game-winning field goal. Paul grinned, thankful she survived multiple heart surgeries over the past year. Thankful she had so much love and kindness.

John handed an ice pack to Paul. The throbbing pain eased as Paul placed the ice pack onto his right knuckles. He let out a sigh of relief.

"So," John said, "did he deserve it?" He looked at Paul's knuckles and placed a glass of chocolate milk on the table.

"Yeah," Paul said between gulps of chocolate milk. "He was talking trash every time I went on to kick. Kept looking at me like I was dirt."

Hannah handed Paul a plate of food. "That's no reason to hit him, Paulie."

"He said I had cowards' blood," Paul said, "and he nearly broke my hand in the lineup."

31

Hannah raised an eyebrow. She exchanged a look with her husband.

"Well," she said, "why didn't the official throw a flag?"

Paul rolled his eyes. "You know most officials aren't gonna call fouls for that, Mom." Paul held his hands up and turned to look at his dad.

"I'm glad you stuck up for yourself, mate, but"—John was stone-faced—"it's better for everyone if you just let those things slide. Try to fit in as best you can."

"Try to fit in!" Paul raged. "I don't even have a British accent. I was born in North Carolina. The only way I could fit in more is to not have an English dad. Or maybe we could start going to church every week. That'll probably help."

John shifted his weight and scowled. Paul squirmed on his stool. Hannah cleared her throat to break the tense silence.

"I don't want to talk about politics," she said. "I'm going to tuck Hope in."

John flipped on the stove to make tea. Paul pushed his plate of food away and stood up.

"Where are you going?" John asked.

"For a run," Paul said. "I don't even get a real workout on game days."

John held up a hand. "Don't go too far, mate. I'll have a cup of tea waiting for you when you get back."

Paul took his ear buds out of his coat pocket and dropped the coat on the floor. He opened the front door and paused a moment before slamming the door shut.

Outside, he looked up to the star-filled sky. There was a slight chill in the air. Despite the temperature, he took off in his football pants and sleeveless shirt.

"Time my run," he called out, while placing the ear buds in his ears.

"What time would you like to run tonight, Paul?" came the robotic response.

"Two miles in twelve minutes."

With that, Paul took off, grinding his teeth. He hated putting up with so much just because his dad was British. He'd have been dead if he fought in that dumb European war—along with his mom and older sister, Jude.

Why did people think they were cowards for saving their families? Paul wondered. "Play techno playlist," he said. The music pulsated and helped him run faster. Anger incited him to run harder. Paul approached the neighborhood kids still outside playing.

"Great kicking tonight, Paulie!" one of them shouted.

The others turned and raised their arms in the air. "Paulie! Paulie! Paulie!" Some of the older kids ran beside him. A few sprinted to keep up.

Paul gave a thumbs up and panted. "You ready to start really running now?" he asked.

The kids' eyes shone at the challenge.

"Let's go, then!" Paul kicked into high gear, leaving all but one boy in his wake. A few seconds later, the last boy gave up with a scream of defeat.

Paul's lungs and legs burned, but he kept running faster and faster. When he rounded the corner, he slowed down to check his watch. He'd already finished a mile in five minutes and thirty seconds. If he kept this pace, he'd complete two miles within his twelve-minute goal. Paul's anger subsided as the techno music pushed him onward.

He exhaled heavily as he considered how they treated his dad after the game. *It's not his fault people treat us like that,* Paul thought. *They're the idiots—not Dad.*

Nearing his house, he looked at his watch—one point nine miles in eleven minutes, forty-six seconds. *Close enough,* he thought, then told his watch, "Run finished." The timer stopped and the music quieted down.

"You're out for a run?"

Paul turned at the voice. Devan walked toward him, shaking his head.

Paul shrugged. "I got angry at Dad over what happened tonight and needed to run off some steam."

"Well, get ready for the party," Devan said.

"You're allowed to go?" Paul asked. "I haven't even asked my parents yet."

"Don't worry bro." Devan waved off Paul's concerns. "My mom already spoke to yours. My Mom's taking us, and your dad's going to pick us up."

Any remnant of anger washed away. It would be their first Friday night party. Both were sixteen, which had significant cultural implications.

"We can kiss girls now," Paul said. "This is awesome!"

"Who's gonna wanna kiss your ugly self?" Devan teased.

Paul held his arms high in the sky. "I'm the hero tonight," he said. "Remember?"

Devan clasped hands with Paul, then turned to go home. Paul threw open the front door to his house, breathing heavily and sweating. He took one step up the stairs and was stopped in his tracks.

"Paulie!" his dad called from the kitchen. "Come in here, mate."

Paul obeyed. A hot cup of tea sat next to a plate of food. He wanted to shower and get to the party, but the smell drew him in. He sat in a chair and took a huge bite of roast.

Between bites, he looked at his dad. "Can I get some water, please?"

John poured a glass of water and set it on the table. Paul downed the whole glass, as his dad watched, willing Paul to look up.

Eventually, it happened. Paul looked up. The two locked eyes for a moment before Paul looked away. "I'm sorry, Dad. I'm better after running it off."

His dad patted him on the back. "How's your hand?"

"It's fine." Paul twisted it and winced. "Not too painful."

"Me and your mother have decided you can—"

"I know. Devan told me." Paul sipped his tea. "I really am sorry about before, Dad."

"It's all right, son. Most people aren't USW fanatics, but we do have to be careful around those who are. Just try and go with the flow." His dad rubbed his chin and took a sip of tea. "For everything that's wrong with this empire, it's still probably the best place to live. After the incident in history class and now this, people will be watching you."

Paul swallowed a bite of bread. Then swallowed again. "I'll try and hold it together," he promised. He sipped his tea, then sat quietly as the drink warmed up his insides.

"War is inevitable son," John sighed. "You're old enough to know that. Whether we start it or another empire, it's coming. But I want you to have as normal a life as possible

35

before it comes." He tapped on the table and whistled. "Enjoy yourself tonight. Don't do anything stupid, but have fun."

***

Sixteen to kiss, seventeen to drink five units of alcohol, eighteen to drink all you want, and nineteen to have sex. It was the law. Premarital sex was frowned upon, but not illegal.

At nineteen, residents could come off their parents' credit score. However, children who lived in the same house as their parents remained connected to their parents' credit score. The abundance of rules made it hard to remember how to get and maintain a good credit score. Most important was staying out of trouble and openly agreeing with the government's ideology for a free, democratic world.

Any time a rule was broken, the network picked up on it, and the rule breaker's family paid the price. People with low scores received fewer benefits from the government and performed mandatory community service.

Kissing underage wasn't too serious an offense, but repeated offenses put a family's credit score at risk. Same with excessive drinking. But sex underage led to serious trouble. Last year, two juniors had sex and got expelled from school.

The morality rules had gotten stricter in recent years, and sex outside of marriage—for minors and adults—affected credit scores more than ever. The government backed their laws with studies showing people are happier in committed, monogamous relationships. These rules also protected against disease and helped maintain optimal mental health.

Teenagers often threatened to take off their watches and

remove the chips in their necks. But no one did. Taking off a government-mandated watch was one of the most serious crimes. Offenders went to prison, no questions asked. Rumors claimed that prisoners got multiple chips implanted, which provided even more control. The government then used this control to perform all sorts of crazy experiments. No one knew if it was true, as few went to prison.

***

Paul felt awkward talking to his parents about girls, but they weren't fazed. His parents were laid back when his older sister, Jude, had boyfriends in the past, but they didn't like her current one. Steve, a freshman at Georgia Tech, was last year's valedictorian at Roswell High and one of the smartest people Paul knew. He loved the Freedom Fighters. Also known as the FF, *Freedom Fighters* was the common name for the United States of North America's military. Steve already signed up to join the forces after graduation.

Paul liked the idea of joining the military, but he wanted to play in the NFL first. This was unique among his classmates. Unlike former generations, being part of the FF was cooler than being a professional athlete.

Paul turned the shower to the hottest temperature and undressed as the steam filled the room. He rubbed the condensation from the mirror and flexed, moving his body into different positions to get the best lighting in the mirror. He wasn't bulky like Devan, but he was cut—especially around his abs. As he looked in the mirror, he pictured all the girls at school ogling him. In his mind, he walked past them all to reach Finley Matthews. The pair shared a class and spoke at a few secret soccer games.

A decades-long school tradition, the secret soccer games featured the school's best sixteen soccer players—eight guys and eight girls—as selected by team captains. These scrimmages were a hot commodity at school, and everyone wanted an invite. Paul quit the school soccer team to play football, but he still played club soccer. Thanks to his dad's coaching during his early years, Paul remained one of the best soccer players in the school. As a result, he was one of few people invited to play.

The secret games were more of a social gathering than actual practice. You learned the location the night before—if you got selected. No coaches were present. The games took place during summer break and were always shirts versus skins.

The boys on the skins' team took their shirts off, and the girls played in their sports bras. No one knew when the first shirts-and-skins game took place, but it was tradition now. As with most of his life, Paul was an outlier for the secret game. He was the first rising sophomore to play. Few rising juniors even got an invitation. The exclusivity of an invitation was an instant reputation boost—most of the time.

Some soccer players hated Paul. He was too young. Besides, he chose football over soccer. The code of the gatherings, however, required the best soccer players get invited. Paul didn't mind players not wanting him in the game. It made him feel better when he juked or tackled them. The games were friendly for the most part, but a few of the seniors roughed up Paul a couple times. Paul took the beatings without fighting back. He knew acting out could revoke future invitations.

At the end of the last game, as everyone was high-fiving and shaking hands, Finley hugged Paul, while wearing only her sports bra. Her vanilla perfume left Paul with a memory he relived countless times.

Looking in the mirror, he practiced speaking to Finley. "Do you fancy getting a milkshake after school?" *Ugh*, he thought, *I sound like Dad—way too British.* "If you need to practice extra for soccer, I can help you out." *No, that sounds arrogant.* "Do you want to go to prom?" *I can't ask her that. I'm a sophomore.* "How are things with you and Chase?"

He was searching for the right words and reprimanding himself when his watch beeped. It was Devan. *Be there in five.* The brief text pulled Paul from his daydreaming. He jumped in the shower and speed-washed, then brushed his teeth in the shower to save time. In less than five minutes, he was dried, dressed, and ready to go.

"You've not even done your hair mate," John said as Devan's car pulled up in the driveway. "You're not going out like that." He ran upstairs and shouted, "I'll get you some gel."

"Serious Dad?" Paul groaned.

"I am serious, do not leave! You'll thank me later." Paul rolled his eyes and sighed again as he stood alone with his mom. His mom stood in front of the door. She walked past him, opened the door, and shouted,

"Two minutes, Juliet!" Closing the door, she turned around to Paul, put both hands on Paul's cheeks and pulled his face to hers.

39

"Listen to your mother," she said. "I know you try to act all tough in front of us talking about girls and I don't mind a little joke, but my next few words are very serious. A young woman's heart is something not to be played with. If I ever hear that you have treated a young lady disrespectfully, you'll be grounded till college. I have raised you better than that."

No sooner had Hannah stopped speaking than she patted Paul's cheeks and beamed her beautiful, affectionate smile that always made Paul feel warm inside. He couldn't help but smile back. He knew she was right. He wanted to treat girls the way his mom would approve.

Paul grabbed the door handle as his dad grabbed him from behind. Paul squirmed as his dad smeared gel in his hair and sprayed him with cologne that was popular twenty years earlier.

"Come on, Dad!" Paul fanned at the spray.

"Quick picture before you go, Paulie." His mother played with her watch and brought up the hologram camera. Picture taken, Paul squeezed out of Hannah's grip and ran outside.

Devan cackled as Paul waved to his parents from the car.

"Looking good, player," Devan said. "The girls won't be able to keep their hands off you." Juliet quickly turned around and gave Devan a terrifying death stare.

"Young man, I don't care what the law says you can do when you're sixteen. If I smell perfume or see lipstick on you when you get home, you're grounded for life." Paul laughed out loud. Juliet quickly turned to him with darting eyes and said, "You too, Paul!" Then, in the sweetest voice possible she leaned out her window and shouted to Paul's parents, "See you later, Hannah. Bye, John."

40

Paul's parents waved back as he and Devan laughed under their breath to one another.

CHAPTER 4
FINLEY

You look so good!" Beth cried.

Finley squinted at the mirror, scrutinizing herself. "You think so?" she asked. She rolled the sleeves up on her unbuttoned light-blue plaid shirt. A white tank top hinted at her belly and danced above denim daisy dukes. "Should I wear boots or sneakers?"

"Boots, I think." Beth took in her friend. "Yeah—definitely boots."

Finley tossed a pair of boots beside her bedroom door.

"And now that I think about it . . ."

Finley turned to her friend.

"Those shorts are pretty short, Finn."

"I thought you said I look good?" Finley pouted.

"You do—really good. But you're with Chase now," Beth said. "He's the kind of guy most girls think about being with forever, not someone to play around with."

"We're seventeen, Beth. My mamma regrets getting married so young. She says we're supposed to have fun while we're still young." Finley smiled in the mirror and took a sip of wine. "Anyway, Chase will go off to college or the FF next year and probably forget about me."

Beth grabbed Finley's hands. "Most of those FF soldiers marry when they join. Chase isn't dating you just for fun. He's serious. You're the first girl he's ever been out with. I think—"

"You think what?" Finley asked.

Beth bit her lower lip. "I think he wants to marry you."

"Beth!" Finley blushed and sat down crossed-legged on the floor. "He didn't even try to kiss me last weekend, and that was our sixth date. I want to know what it's like to kiss someone before I marry them."

"Well," Beth said, her eyes dropping to the floor, "I'd like a boy to hold my hand."

"Oh, Beth." Finley reached toward her friend.

"We've been friends for more than a decade," Beth said. "Tell me the truth—would you date someone like me?"

Finley sighed. "You're one of the smartest kids in school," Finley said. "On top of that, you're gorgeous. Your olive skin, your long, straight, jet-black hair, your enchanting brown eyes."

"That's not all I am," Beth said.

Finley squeezed Beth's hand. "You're more than Persian," Finley said. "You belong here, not Persia. I'm glad your family stayed."

"I am too. But—"

"But nothing!" Finley said. "You're just as American as me. It doesn't matter if you don't go to church. Me and Mamma only go on Independence Day and Lee Day anyways."

"But at least you go," Beth whined. "My parents refuse to go, and it kills our credit score. Everyone knows what we are, and it's only a matter of time before people like us die out here. Only a Muslim will marry a Muslim, and most of them moved back to Persia!"

"Come on, Beth. Plenty of boys like you."

"Not enough to marry me." She raised sad eyes to Finley. "And I've put on weight since quitting soccer."

"You're not big at all! Even if you were, some boys like curvy women." Finley smiled and slapped Beth lightly on her hips. "They're fun to grab hold of. And if you want to get married, just go to church."

"My parents would kill me!"

"They'll kill you if they see that!" Finley pointed at a tattoo on Beth's left foot, a circle with one straight line down the middle with two branching from it near the bottom. Finley had a matching one on her right foot. They were outdated symbols of peace. The pair got the tattoos a year earlier as a quiet act of rebellion.

Tattoos were legal, but you needed parental permission before age eighteen. Finley bribed the tattoo artist by promising to go on a date with him. She never made good on the deal.

"Mom still hasn't noticed." Finley walked across the room and poured a glass of wine. She held the bottle out to Beth. "You sure you don't want to try some?"

Beth shook her head. "I told my parents I wouldn't. You going to start going to church with Chase?"

"Let's talk about something else. I'm sick of religion." Finley stuck out her tongue and made a gagging sound.

"Doesn't Chase keep asking?" Beth asked.

Finley shrugged. "Not really. I mean, I go enough to fill the quota. It's just a bunch of songs about America and us being God's chosen people. Then someone talks for ages. You should go if you love America so much," Finley said sarcastically.

"Don't you love America?"

"Course I do!" Finley said. "But the church stuff is way too intense. Anyway, if you could be with any boy in school, who would it be?"

Beth's forehead wrinkled as she contemplated her answer. Finley leaned toward her, but Beth never spoke.

"Come on," Finley said, "we're best friends. Please!"

"Well, I have two I kinda like."

Finley dropped to the floor, crossed her legs, and scooted close to Beth.

"You have to tell me!"

"Don't tell anyone," Beth said.

Finley crossed her heart and pretended to zip her mouth shut.

Beth pursed her lips. "Okay, I trust you," she said. "Devan—from the football team."

"Oh yeah," Finley giggled, "he's cute. Let's talk to him tonight."

"You know how nervous I get around boys."

"Have a glass of wine then to settle your nerves," Finley raised her glass and smiled. "It's impossible for your parents to know now that you're seventeen."

"Okay," she whispered. Finley let out a squeal of delight and jumped to grab Beth a cup of wine. Beth swished the wine in her mouth and swallowed.

"Yummy!" She smiled and took another sip.

"Wine, tattoos." Finley wagged a finger. "You're a real rebel now, Beth. What do you like about Devan?"

"He's really strong, but he's only a sophomore."

"So what if he's a sophomore?" Finley sipped her wine. "I used to have a crush on a sophomore—Paul Lewis, Devan's best friend."

"The kicker?" Beth asked.

"Yes, the kicker." Finley laughed. "But I know him from the secret soccer games. You could have come to those with me if you didn't quit playing."

"Soccer's your thing, Finley. Plus, I was never as good as you. Why Paul?"

"He's really cute and a little edgy. Did I tell you what he did in our history class?"

"What happened?" Beth asked.

"Mr. Wilby mentioned something about people refusing to defend their country and being afraid to fight. Without even raising his hand," Finley said, "Paul shouted out, 'You don't know what you're talking about!' Mr. Wilby was shocked, and Paul stared him down like he was ready to punch him!"

Beth's eyes widened. Her glass rested against her lower lip. "Then what?" she asked.

"Principal Hennessey came and took Paul out of class. Before he left, Paul shouted something about history books not telling the whole story and that Mr. Wilby shouldn't talk about people he doesn't know."

"Did he get in trouble?"

"I heard someone say detention for a week. Whatever punishment he got, he hasn't spoken in class since." Finley ran her tongue across her teeth. "Then this other time, we were playing soccer. Rachel was having a really bad day, but she wouldn't say why. The senior boys were teasing her, and she started to cry. Ben Chadwick said some nasty things and made everyone uncomfortable. Then out of nowhere, the soccer ball smashed Ben in the face! Paul ran up and said it was an accident, but . . ." Finley sipped her wine and smiled. "After the game, I saw Paul checking up on Rachel. He's got a sweet side to him. But I like how he's a little crazy."

"He definitely looked crazy punching that big Milton player tonight!" Beth exclaimed.

"I know," Finley agreed. "It was hot, right!"

"Finley," Beth slapped Finley's arm. "You're supposed to be with Chase!"

The two giggled and took long drags from their wine glasses. A loud beep from Finley's watch vibrated warning her she was close to her limit of five units of alcohol. She sighed. It beeped again. A quick look, and she grabbed Beth's arm.

"Come on, Beth—drink up. They'll be here in five minutes."

Finley's mom, Denise, looked up when the girls passed through the living room. She was in her pajamas drinking wine, eating chips, and painting her toenails scarlet red.

"We're leaving, Mom," Finley said.

"Girrrrrls, you look so good!" Denise grabbed the couch to keep steady on her feet. "I know the party finishes at two, but take as long as need coming home. I don't care if the government send me any messages. You're young," she said with a wink, "and should be allowed to enjoy yourselves."

Finley kissed her mother's cheek and jumped when her mother pinched her bottom.

"Good night, Ms. Matthews," Beth said through laughter, then shrieked when Denise squeezed her bottom as well.

"Both you girls are fire tonight!"

"Mom!" Finley yelled. "Beth's family doesn't do things like that." Beth still looked flustered, but Finley couldn't help but laugh a little.

"Beth's pretty much family anyway."

"Thanks Ms. Matthews."

"You're welcome sweetie," she replied. "Bye, girls. Have a great night. Be yourself and don't change for anyone."

"Bye, Mom," Finley groaned walking out the door. Finley always liked taking the stairs to stay healthy, even though they lived on the nineteenth floor. Her mom always took the stairs and looked like she was barely twenty at thirty-six. Finley figured that could be part of her secret, so she picked up the habit from her mom.

Nineteen flights later, Beth had to catch her breath at the bottom. Chase waited outside beside his black sports car. Big Tommy climbed out of the front seat to get in the back.

"No way, Tommy." Finley held up a hand. "You're too big to be in the back of this little car. Beth and I will ride back there."

"You sure, Finn?" Chase smiled mischievously. "I'd like you to ride up front with me."

"And I'm happy to ride in the back with Beth," Tommy said with a sheepish look.

Finley shook her head and climbed in beside Beth. She mouthed "He likes you" to Beth and pointed at Tommy. Beth lowered her head with embarrassment. Chase placed a finger on the dash display. The engine came to life, and church music grew louder in the speakers.

"Please, not this Chase," Finley pleaded.

"This is such a good one Finn." Chase eyed Finley in the rearview mirror. "You don't even like the beats?"

"It's not what I want to listen to on my way to a party." *Or ever*, she thought.

Chase switched the music to a mainstream rock song. Soon, the four of them nodded their heads to the beat.

As the song came to a close, Tommy turned abruptly. He looked at Beth.

"I just want you to know how wrong I think it is the way people—the way people think about Muslims." He spoke quickly, his tongue nearly stumbling over every word. "I mean," he continued, "you're just as much American as any of us. You're really smart and they shouldn't be allowed to deport people as pretty as—"

Tommy froze. His face reddened. He wiped sweat that was forming on his brow.

"Jeez, Tommy," Chase said, "how many beers have you had?"

"I know my limits," Tommy said. "You gonna join me for one at the party, captain?"

Chase shook his head. He didn't drink alcohol—ever.

CHAPTER 5
FINLEY

C hase pulled up to a gated community, and a guard
approached the car.

"Hello, sir," Chase said.

"Chase—how you doin', son? I watched the game. You
guys did great!" The guard pushed away from Chase's car and
waved him through.

"This place has security guards?" Finley wondered out
loud.

"Not security." Tommy grinned. "He's a guy who does
things for people. He fixes things and is also a doctor—stuff
like that."

As they drove through the neighborhood, Finley's mouth
fell open as they passed huge mansions with beautiful flowers,
trees, and water fountains. Tasteful lighting highlighted the
beauty of it all, and picture windows displayed sparkling
chandeliers inside each house. One house had four garages.

"This is it," Chase said.

"It?" Finley said.

"Well, not *it*," Chase said. "This is my house."

Finley gawked. Her two-bedroom apartment would fit in Chase's house ten times over. She shrank in her seat at the thought. As Chase pulled into the driveway, Finley's stomach lurched.

"Chase," she blurted, "we're not meeting your parents, are we?"

Chase picked at his teeth. "Don't worry, they're out of town."

"Phew," Finley let out a sigh of relief. An awkward silence followed before Finley stumbled into another sentence. "Sorry, I didn't mean it like that. I just thought . . . and with the house being so big. I wasn't prepared to meet your . . . What do your parents do?"

Tommy and Chase laughed.

"Don't worry, Finn. They're in D.C. I wouldn't have sprung that on you without any warning. We're just going to park the car here. We'll walk to Tyrone's house. It's just round the corner. I thought it might be nice to walk a little."

"Wait," Tommy said. "You don't know who Chase's uncle is?"

"It doesn't matter." Chase's eyes bulged threats at Tommy. "I'll tell you another time. I'm glad you don't know."

Finley shrugged. "What are your parents doing in D.C.?"

"They're friends with the president," Tommy joked.

"For real?" Finley asked.

"They are friendly with President Hudson and work closely with him," Chase said.

Finley's stomach ached. *They definitely won't like me when they find out who my mom voted for in the last election,* she thought. Then she thought of Beth and gave her a sympathetic smile. Last year, it was President Hudson who "helped" Muslims return to Persia. Finley squeezed Beth's arm as they exited the car.

They walked in silence. Chase kicked a rock and cleared his throat. "I know what you're thinking, but my parents are different. Not everyone who works with the president wanted to send those with different ideologies back to their original empires."

Finley gave Beth's arm a friendly squeeze, and both girls relaxed. Chase grinned and asked Tommy to walk ahead with Beth so he could speak privately with Finley. Tommy reached out an arm, and Beth took it willingly. Her eyes sparkled as she walked away on Tommy's arm. Chase slowed his pace to get some distance from Beth and Tommy. Then he talked slowly.

"I didn't want to tell you about what my parents did," he said, "or what kind of house I lived in, Finn."

Finley scanned the area as she matched Chase's pace.

"There's a lot of girls that like me just for that reason," Chase continued. "They like the idea of marrying someone whose dad is high up and has a lot of credit. I was surprised you didn't already know honestly. After our first date I figured out you had no idea. I liked that."

"The soccer girls told me your dad was into politics, but I just kind of ignored them. It didn't really interest me."

Chase grabbed Finley's hand and slowed their pace even more. He gnawed at the inside of his cheek.

Oh no! Finley thought. *He has something to say. I hope he doesn't start getting super serious about our relationship already.*

"Finley," Chase said, "you're the most beautiful girl in school." The pair took three slow steps. "But that's not the only reason I want to be with you." Two more steps. "I'll tell you why one day, but my grandma said something about . . ." He paused, took a few more steps. "Finley, you know I'm serious about my faith, this nation, our calling. Some people do the right things to get good credit, but I really believe in it. I don't want you to come to church for me, but—"

"Oh, don't worry," Finley cut in. "I won't."

Chase nodded. "Then Grandma was right." He shook his head. "I only want you to change if you really believe it. But I need you to know, I'm not dating you just for fun."

Finley's heart skipped a beat. She was only seventeen. *Aren't I too young to be a wife?* she wondered. She looked into Chase's eyes and knew he believed every word. *Does he love me already?*

Finley stopped walking. She turned to Chase and took hold of both his hands. As she gazed into Chase's eyes, he fidgeted. She pulled closer, their faces inches apart, their hands between their stomachs the only distance between them. Finley guided Chase's hands onto her hips and edged even closer. She tilted her neck back and pursed her lips. Her heart pounded as she closed her eyes.

This is it, she thought, *my first kiss*. She moved her lips ever closer. *He won't like the taste of wine on my tongue, but he'll get over it.*

Chase's hands left her hips, and he pulled back. Finley's face flushed red. Her stomach swirled. She stepped away and longed for Beth to be closer, to comfort her in her trauma.

"I'm not ready for that yet, Finley."

53

Finley held back tears. She folded her arms and walked after Tommy and Beth. Embarrassment quickly turned to anger. *Can't be seen kissing a girl from a family with bad credit*, she thought. *His daddy wouldn't approve.*

Chased caught up with Finley and grabbed her hand. She pulled it away, lowered her head, and stomped on.

"Finley, I'm sorry," Chase said. "I'm just not ready, and I don't think it's fair on you. Our youth leader says we should wait to kiss until we get engaged."

Finley glared at him and kept walking.

"Finley," Chase plead.

She stopped to face him. "That's a load of crap!" she screamed. "You church guys have high morals but look down on others who don't hold the same standard. One second you talk about marriage, and—and then the next you won't even kiss me!"

"It's because I really like you, Finley. I didn't want to do that until I was sure you were as serious about me as I am with you."

Finley slammed a foot into the ground and clenched her fists. She looked up into his eyes and felt her heart flutter. She was angry, but Chase was still handsome.

"Ready, Chase?" She buried her attraction with anger. "When a girl places your hands on her hips, closes her eyes, and tries to kiss you, it means she's ready!"

She stormed off. Chase followed. They neared the party. The front garden was lit up, and people hung out near the entrance. Music streamed from inside.

"Finley," Chase called from behind, "give me a break. I've never done that before. I was nervous."

Finley turned to yell at him one more time but stopped. Chase looked pitiful and embarrassed. His head dropped. *He's too good*, Finley thought. *Perfect student, perfect athlete, perfect Christian patriot boyfriend.*

Then Chase's eyes concentrated on her legs. Finley pulled back her shirt to reveal her stomach and moved her hips to one side, making her body appear curvier. Chase's eyes widened before he turned away. Finley rolled her eyes. She took off her shirt and tied it around her waist. She blew a kiss at Chase and moved toward the party.

"Finley, what are you doing?"

"Give it a break," she shot back.

Beth and Tommy stood outside the front door, talking to some volleyball players. A black car pulled up and Devan Jones stepped out of one side. Finley focused on the guy who stepped out of the other side—Paul Lewis. His loose-fitting clothes made him look skinny, but Finley remembered his rock-solid abs from playing soccer together. He walked through a line of football players, giving handshakes and high fives.

I bet he would have kissed me, Finley thought.

Finley waltzed through the middle of the group and pulled Beth inside without a word. The music thundered. The dim room pulsated with dancing. A few of Finley's soccer teammates waved her over to dance, but Finley just waved.

She headed straight for the alcohol machine and allowed her face to be scanned.

"You're at your limit, Finley Matthews," stated the machine's polite, female robotic voice. "You must wait another three hours before consuming any alcohol. Would you like to speak to someone to help control your level of alcohol consumption?"

"A little help, Beth?" Finley said.

Beth stepped forward. The machine scanned her face.

"Three units, Beth Yousefi. What would you like to drink?"

Beth looked at Finley for an answer.

"White wine," Finley said.

"White wine, please," Beth echoed.

A list of choices appeared on the screen, and Finley tapped Chardonnay. A small door opened on the machine. Beth grabbed the wine and took a quick sip before Finley yanked it out of her hand.

"Bottom's up!" Finley tilted the drink and finished it with a single draft. She wiped her hand across her lips as her watch beeped. "Of course," she said. She rolled her eyes and tilted her watch so Beth could read the message: *Your mother has been notified you are over your drinking limit.* Beth covered her mouth. Finley used to look at her mom the same way. Then it became normal. Finley always promised she'd never become like her mom, but this was different.

"I tried to kiss Chase."

"What do you mean—tried?" Beth asked.

Finley grabbed Beth's hand and walked them into the backyard. Football players and cheerleaders swam and played pool volleyball in a huge, heated pool next to a man-made waterfall. A few cheerleaders gave Finley dirty looks as she and Beth settled down at a free table. Half-yelling through slurred words, Finley told Beth everything that just happened.

"What are you going to do now?" Beth asked.

Finley shrugged. She reached for a wine glass that wasn't there and frowned.

"There aren't many guys with that kind of self-control," Beth said. "At least you know he won't go off with other girls if he's with you."

Finley waved off Beth's comment. "Those cheerleaders keep looking over here."

"They're jealous of you, Finn." Beth smiled. "Everyone knows Chase really likes you."

"I don't know why."

Beth furrowed her brow.

"He could be with any girl," Finley continued. "Why doesn't he pick one who's . . . someone who goes to church and wants to build America and—and, and everything?"

"Hey look!" Beth pointed at the sky deciding to drop the subject. "We've got a great view of Elysium from here. It's so incandescent."

Finley looked at sky's bright glow. The asteroid looked like an oversized white star.

"Scientists say it's a special type of rock or mineral we don't have on earth," Beth said excitedly, "and that's why it glows like that. But it's just a reflection of the sun's light really. Just like the moon. It's so cool!"

Finley yawned. She checked her watch and licked her teeth.

"Finley," Beth said, "this is a once-in-a-lifetime thing. For an asteroid to come within three thousand miles of earth very rarely happens. We're lucky to be alive right now."

"Hello, ladies. Mind if we join you?" Tommy held two soda bottles and had a goofy grin.

"Sure." Beth blushed.

Tommy put the soda bottles on the table and sat down. Chase silently sat beside Finley. Finley felt heat rise in her face. She scanned the pool area. No one was paying them any attention.

Tommy gasped. "Dude!" he yelled. "Look at Elysium tonight. I haven't seen it shine that bright for a while."

Beth's eyes widened. She looked from Tommy to Elysium and back again.

"You know, I saw a conspiracy theory about it the other day," Tommy said, "but it's already been taken off the network. Some people think it's gonna hit us!"

Chase tilted his head to see Elysium, then said dully, "It won't come within two thousand miles of us."

Tommy leapt to his feet. "I know that's what the scientists say, but this guy I heard reckons the material the rock's made of might be attracted to the earth's gravity or something."

"There is no scientific evidence behind that claim," said Beth.

"Don't listen to anything Big Tommy says. He's been hit one too many times in the head making sure Chase doesn't get hurt." Devan stood behind the group, laughing at his own joke.

Paul relaxed beside Devan and locked eyes with Finley. Something stirred inside Finley. Paul looked away.

"Whatever, Devan," Tommy said. "It probably won't happen, but think about it. If that thing hits us, half the world would be gone."

"Half the world's gonna be gone soon enough," Devan said, "especially with our wonderful president leading this great nation." He raised a hand in mock salute.

"President Hudson is chosen by God!" Chase shot back.

"He ain't Jesus, Chase!" Devan said. He pinched his eyes with his fingers. "My bad, guys. But some senior boys were talking trash to me and Paul again when we showed up. I'm just annoyed at everything." He opened his eyes and forced a chuckle. "We should be celebrating football tonight, and those guys are talking about taking over the world."

Paul was rigid, his arms crossed, his lips tight.

"Did you get hurt in that fight, Paul?"

Paul shifted in his seat and relaxed when Finley spoke to him.

"Nah," he said, "not really. They started it. Hurt my hand a little though."

"That's because you smashed his face up, bro!" Devan slapped Paul on the back. Paul stared at Finley, as his body's tension melted away.

Tommy pulled a chair next to Beth's, so they could talk about Elysium. Chase got recruited to officiate the pool volleyball game as both teams trusted him to tell the truth.

Paul and Devan pulled up a seat and sat down next to Finley.

Finley sipped on her soda. *This night is turning out to be pretty fun*, she thought.

"Hey!" a harsh voice yelled. "You dating a Persian girl now, Tommy?"

Drew Humphries sneered, surrounded by the other guys who turned their backs on John in the locker room. He tipped his hat, careful to show the USW logo emblazoned on front. Paul grimaced. Beth slumped.

Chase stayed seated by the pool and rubbed his cheek thoughtfully. "Come on now, Drew," he said. "Not now, dude."

"We're not dating," Tommy stammered. "But if we were, what's wrong with Persians?"

Butterflies buzzed in Beth's stomach.

"I don't care if she's Persian," Drew said. "I don't care if she's Arabic, Russian, from China or Mars. As long as she's part of that false Islamic ideology, there's no place for her in this country. And soon," he continued, gulping his beer, "the world."

Chase was on his feet. "Remember what coach said tonight. Besides, you don't even know Beth."

Drew scoffed. "You're our captain on the field, but you can't tell me what to do off it." The guys beside Drew nodded in agreement. "And screw what coach said," he said. "You know war is coming, and people like Beth will officially be enemies then."

Finley imagined knocking the smirk off Drew's face. The volleyball game went silent. All eyes were on the scene Drew orchestrated. Feeling their eyes, Beth shriveled up and looked at the ground. Finley opened her mouth to speak up when—

"Go to Hell, Drew." Paul's eyes burned with fire. He popped his neck to the left, then the right.

Finley stared, her mouth agape. Devan stood beside Paul and announced that he had Paul's back. Chase backed away as a crowd of people gathered around.

"What did you say, kicker?" Drew yelled.

"I told you to go to Hell," Paul repeated. "And if you turn your back on my dad again, I'll send you there."

Drew leaned back and howled. "You haven't got it in your blood to fight in a war. You're just like your daddy." He spit on the ground for emphasis.

Paul cracked his knuckles, then sprinted at Drew with murder in his eyes. Gasps and cheers fed the nervous energy. Drew dropped his drink and raised his fists, but there was no need. Big Tommy grabbed Paul and restrained him.

"Hold it there, Paulie," Tommy said. "Now's not the time."

Paul lunged and lurched to get free, but Tommy only tightened his bear hug.

Drew put his hands on his knees and bent down. "Aw, he's cute! Let the little kicker come over, Tommy. I'd love to see him try and hurt me."

Tommy shifted his arms to keep his hold on Paul. Finley put an arm around Beth who watched the scene in dismay.

Chase approached Paul and Tommy. He lowered his head and spoke calmly, quietly. "Let it go," he said. "They all graduate at the end of the year anyway. Get into it, and it'll turn out worse for your families."

Devan took two confident steps when Tyrone's father called out.

"Hey!" he yelled. "Break it up, everyone. What's going on?"

Tommy held Paul in a head lock. Devan stood nearby, ready to fight.

Tyrone's father shook his head. "I'm not surprised to see you in the middle of this, Lewis. You guys better leave before anything happens. Your parents don't need more checkups from the government. I thought you knew that."

Tommy released Paul. Paul made a beeline for Drew, but Tyrone's dad stepped between them.

"I don't care if you scored that field goal," he said. "I'll report you right now if you don't leave."

"Fine!" Paul stormed past Tyrone's dad, barged into Drew with his shoulder, and kept going. As Devan followed, Drew moved out the way. The crowed did the same.

Finley held Beth and imagined Paul protecting her. Beth's shoulders shook in Finley's grasp. She was crying.

"Okay, everyone—back to the party!" Tyrone's dad yelled. "Let's get back to celebrating Roswell's win."

The crowd slowly dispersed. Beth and Finley wanted to leave. Chase and Tommy left to get the car. As they were leaving, Tommy and Chase stopped to talk with Drew and his friends. The conversation was short, and it ended with Chase shaking hands with Drew. Tommy kept his hands in his pockets as Drew held out a hand to shake.

Two cheerleaders walked over to Beth and Finley. Tia and Ginny were the seniors every boy in every grade wanted. They wore towels over one-piece swimsuits.

"Oh, Beth," Tia asked. "I'm so sorry that happened. But you know it's only going to get worse unless you start coming to church."

Finley flinched. Beth licked her lips.

"Your parents probably won't change," Tia continued, "but you shouldn't let that ruin your life like it has theirs. Would you like to come to church with me on Sunday? You should come too, Finley."

"Why would I want to go to a church?" Finley snapped. "So I can be like Drew? No thank you." Her watch beeped.

"Gotta go, girls," she said sarcastically. "Chase is out front with the car."

Finley snatched Beth by the arm. As the two rushed away, Beth looked over her shoulder.

"Thanks for the invite," she called out, "but it's not the right time for me."

They walked back through the house where the party was back in full swing. To their horror, Drew was at the front door, drink in hand and surrounded by his boys like he owned the place.

"Just keep hold of me and walk a little faster," Finley told Beth. The girls dropped their heads and walked past the boys quickly without stopping, hoping they wouldn't be noticed. They got past them and were walking over to where Chase was waiting with the car, but before they were five feet past Drew, he shouted out.

"Bye, bye Persia." The people around him laughed. Finley stopped in her tracks as Tommy got out of the car to open the door for Beth. She nudged her forward to Tommy, turned around, and walked directly back toward Drew.

Chase lowered the window and shouted, "Get in the car, Finn!"

Finley wasn't sure what she would say or do when she got to Drew, but she was done with him. As she walked, she stared into his eyes and was repulsed that he was actually checking her out. His eyes were all over her body making her cringe.

When Finley was face to face with him, he smirked and said quietly, "Had enough of Chase, Finn? Why don't you come hang out with us instead?"

63

His friends laughed again.

"Sure," Finley smiled back. "Chase is a bit too goody-goody anyway isn't he? I'm right at my limit, but I could do with another drink." She winked.

Drew handed Finley his beer, and his grin grew even bigger. She despised him! He was arrogant, and it was time somebody wiped that smirk off his face. She took his cup, put it to her lips, took a big gulp, and then spat the beer all over his face. She threw what was left in the cup over his clothes. Then, dropping the cup she turned around, wiped her face, and strutted back to the car, swaying her hips with attitude.

"Sort out your girl before somebody else does Chase!" Drew screamed, his face dripping with beer. But everyone was laughing at him. Finley got to the car, opened the door then turned around to Drew and blew him a kiss.

"Sorry, dude, you kind of deserved that," Chase said.

For being such an awful night, it turned out surprisingly satisfying for Finley.

CHAPTER 6
PAUL

$\backsim\!\!\bigcirc$

Alright, mate—160 on your last set. Let's see if you can get five reps!" John slammed his hands against his thighs. Paul lay back, squeezed the bar and took a deep breath. Euro trance music blared as butterflies fluttered in Paul's stomach. The government banned lyrics that didn't glorify the empire, so John made up words as he went along—something about two people dancing and getting together.

He interrupted his on-the-spot lyrics and boomed at his son. "You got this, mate!" he shouted.

Paul held his breath and pumped out five, struggling a little on the final rep. Bar racked, Paul sat up. His dad patted his back and demanded one last round of push-ups.

Paul exhaled slowly.

"'Til you fail," his dad said.

Paul dropped to the floor and started pumping them out. His arms and chest burned. Eight reps in, his legs shook, and his chest seized up. Gritting his teeth, he managed two more push-ups before failing on number eleven. He collapsed, his chest slamming to the ground, his breaths coming heavily.

Saturday-morning workouts had two benefits. First, games were easy on his body, and Paul thrived on pushing his limits. Second, he liked working out when all the other players were asleep. It made him feel like he was catching up to them.

His dad reached to turn down the music as Devan entered the open garage door.

"You guys started early today."

"Hiya, mate," John said. "How are you feeling after last night's game?"

"Not too bad. Thank you, sir."

"John," Paul's dad replied with a smile.

"Not too bad, John—just a few bumps and bruises. Nothing serious." Devan glanced at the bench and counted the weight. "Whoa—160? How many reps you get, Paulie?"

"Five." Paul stood up from the bench and stretched. "But it was my last set."

"Decent," Devan said. "Is that your record?"

Paul nodded. Devan dropped to the bench with swagger and shook off the concern all over John's face.

"I got this, John." Devan relaxed on his back and knocked out ten reps with ease. It frustrated Paul to watch. He worked out twice as hard as Devan, but he was still no match for Devan's natural strength. It had been like this since they were kids. They grew up in the same neighborhood as best friends and played on all the same sports teams growing up. Devan had always been the strongest and fastest of the two, but Paul worked harder and was technically better at throwing and kicking.

John cocked his head. "My turn." He settled onto the bench. "Now, I am a little tired after our workout, but let's see what I can do." He pumped out ten and pretended to struggle on the eleventh, saying, "Gotta beat Devan." With a grin on his face he pumped out nine more like it was nothing. He picked up his water bottle, grinned, and left Paul to put the weights up.

"Dude," Devan said, "your dad's a beast!"

Paul shrugged and started racking weights.

"Look at the messages I got last night." Devan held his wrist out toward Paul. "Lucy said she was looking for me all night at the party."

Paul switched his watch on to receive calls. He always turned it off during workouts. Devan gave him a hard time about it, but Paul was a focus fanatic.

"Came over to tell you—we got extra tickets to the Bulldogs' game today," Devan said. "You wanna come?"

Paul straightened his back. "Seriously?" he asked. "That's awesome! Let's put these weights away and ask."

As Paul and Devan entered the kitchen, they were greeted by smells of crispy bacon and greasy sausage. Thanks to mandated meat rations, Saturday was the only day the Lewises ate breakfast meat.

The rationing began the year Paul's parents got married. Government officials explained that the rations helped the environment. Dietitians pushed to make rations mandatory for its health benefits. People with good credit and high health scores could eat meat three times a week. Lower scores in either category resulted in less meat. The Lewis family members were all very healthy, so they got the full amount.

Along with the bacon and sausage, Hannah cooked eggs, beans, mushrooms, toast, and pancakes. At the other end of the kitchen, John blended a protein smoothie. He poured the pink drink into a glass, handed it to Paul, and looked at Devan.

"Do you want some, mate?"

"Sure," Devan replied.

John poured another glass and handed it to Devan.

"How are you?" Hannah asked.

"Good, thanks, ma'am."

Paul's mom grinned. "Hannah is fine, Devan."

"I'm good. Thanks, Hannah."

Hope bounded into the kitchen and threw her arms around Devan. He gave her a big squeeze in return.

"You played really good last night," she said.

Devan thanked her and asked about her first full week back at school.

"I was tired yesterday," she said. "I nearly fell asleep before Paul won the game for us."

"A year in and out of hospital will do that to you," Devan said. "But that bicuspid aortic valve disease can't stop you."

Hope nestled into Devan's neck and squeezed tight.

"Oh, hey," Devan said, "my dad has two extra tickets to the Bulldogs' game today. He's speaking at the alumni pre-luncheon in one of the suites. He wanted me to ask you guys to come."

"We'd love to!" Paul turned to his dad. "Can we?"

"That sounds fun," he replied. "I'll go with Paulie, and you"—John motioned to his wife—"can have a girl's day with Hope."

Hope clapped, and her eyes lit up.

"Then it's a plan," said Hannah. "And Paul, share your bacon and sausage with Devan. You know our rules—your guests, your rations."

Paul chugged his smoothie and grabbed his plate. He took a long moment lamenting his now-divided portion of bacon and sausage. But his sorrow left when he sat down at the table to two fried eggs—a tiny bit drippy, three hash browns—burned just a little to give them a perfect crispy taste, baked beans, mushrooms, two slices of toast, and a never-ending stack of pancakes in the middle of the table.

As they ate, they discussed the upcoming Bulldogs' game and the pending arrival of Paul's older sister, Jude.

"She gets in Monday from college," Hannah said. "The same day we leave to get Grandma. Then, Jude heads back Saturday morning after the game, and Grandma wants to go to church with us on Sunday."

Paul moaned and rubbed one hand across his forehead.

"Oh, come on," Devan said. "I go every week bro. Church ain't too bad!"

"Your church is different though," Paul said. "It's just in somebody's house."

"It's still church though." Devan shrugged. "Just without all the crazy politics."

Breakfast went silent. Paul's parents glanced at each other. His father wiped his mouth and forced a smile.

"You know you're safe to say that here, Devan, but be careful speaking like that around others," John said.

Devan swallowed hard and whispered, "Yes, sir." He cleared his throat, took a sip of orange juice, and continued.

"You guys should come to Dad's church."

"That sounds fun," said Hope. "I'd like to go to Mr. Jones's church."

"I'm not sure, princess," John said. "How's your dad doing after starting it up, Devan? We didn't sit together at the game last night, and I've not seen him for weeks. It's been going about a month now, right?"

John looked uncertain. He'd heard an FF soldier attended and wondered why. Devan explained it was necessary to have the soldier there for his dad to maintain his credit score.

"He records the sermon my dad shares. He takes notes on everyone who attends," Devan said, "and then stays around to chat at the end of service. He's a pretty nice guy, actually."

When he first came to America—before Paul was born, John was very vocal about his belief that the American government should have done more to help refugees from the European War. He was a popular professional soccer player for Atlanta United at the time, so lots of people heard what he said, and some didn't like it. He was fired from the team not long after, started having issues getting money from the bank, and the government even had someone follow him around.

He never told Paul exactly what happened that changed his mind—only that it wasn't worth getting on the government's bad side again. Since then, he'd had a steady job in business, worked his way up the ladder, and always made sure his family kept up appearances.

John coughed. He opened his mouth just as a light whistle sounded. "Tea's brewed," he said, then picked up the pot and started pouring.

"You know," John said, sipping his tea, "when we go get Grandma on Monday, it's supposed to be the day Elysium is closest to earth. We'll have a great view from the mountains."

***

"How was the game?" Hannah whispered. Lounged on the couch, she pressed a finger to her lips and pointed down at Hope who was sleeping on her lap under a blanket.

Paul gave a thumbs up. "Bulldogs won by a touchdown," he whispered, "with only forty-five seconds on the clock."

"How was the fancy dinner?" his mom asked.

"Really nice," John replied. "Demaro did a great job speaking. Those people love him—a Bulldog legend. The coach spoke to us, trying to get Devan to commit already." He patted Paul firmly on the shoulder. "Heard about our boy kicking the winning points last night as well, didn't he, mate?"

"Yeah, he knew me as a kicker," Paul said. "Next season"— he clenched his fists and flexed his pecs—"he'll know me as a defensive player."

***

Paul was almost asleep when his dad came in to say good night.

"That was a fun day, eh?"

"Yeah," Paul said. "I want to play in a stadium like that. Is that what it was like playing in England?"

John closed his eyes. "Similar. English people are"—he

opened his eyes, which oozed sadness—"English people *were* crazy about football."

"Tell me about it, Dad."

"It's getting late, son."

Paul begged for a story. "You never talk about it," he said. "I just want one story—please?"

His dad sighed deeply. "Well, I never played in the top league—wasn't quite good enough, I suppose. But the lower divisions were the real heart and soul of English football anyways. Kids would support the teams their grandfathers watched as kids. It ran in people's blood throughout generations. I played my best days at Stockport, right next to Manchester. Would have been nicer if I'd played for United or City."

"You stilled played professional though."

"The crowds were loud—really loud!" The sadness in his eyes disappeared. A smirk stretched across his face, stripping away years of exhaustion. "Grown men singing and chanting songs about the clubs and players they loved. The best games were when we played a local team like Oldham, Macclesfield, or Rochdale. Those games got intense. I scored the winner in one of those games. It was the last day of the season, and we clinched a place in the playoffs. The crowd went nuts! When the final whistle blew, they rushed the field and lifted me on their shoulders. Just like you last night."

Paul's heart warmed. "And the playoffs?" he asked.

"Lost to Luton. Got battered three nil. I'm glad we got beat though. I went out that night in London with some of the lads to drown our sorrows, and that's where I first met your mum. And the rest," he said dramatically, "is history!"

He kissed Paul on the forehead and pushed off the bed. At the doorway, he turned.

"Great workout this morning," he said. "You're getting strong, son."

***

After a solo Sunday morning workout, Paul came into the kitchen. His parents were drinking coffee and deciding whether to go to church. John said they needed to clean the house and mow the yard before Grandma came to visit, but his mom insisted they could do that in the afternoon. Eventually, John won the argument with a promise to attend church next week "If the Falcons win today."

After breakfast, Paul and his dad began raking leaves.

"Hey there, neighbor! I heard about your winning field goal." Kelvin Stewart, the Lewis's neighbor, waved. "Well done!"

Paul thanked him. His dad grinned and leaned on his rake.

"You working on the bunker again, Kelvin?"

"Sure am." He ran a wrinkled hand through his white hair. "We won't have time to get to SafeCities when China attacks. You know that, John."

John shook his head in agreement, then got back to raking.

That afternoon, Devan came over to watch the Falcons game. The Falcons won easily, which meant the whole family was going to church next week when Grandma was in town.

After Devan left, Paul finished his homework, then

retreated to his room. On the way there, he stopped at Hope's bedroom. She sat on the edge of her bed, engrossed in a book.

"Psst!" Paul said. "What are you reading?"

"The scriptures."

Paul tiptoed to Hope's bed and plopped down beside her. He rubbed her back with one hand and squeezed her gently with the other. "You really believe in this stuff?"

"I think so."

Before her surgeries, Hope argued with Paul—a lot. Not anymore. She seemed like a new person. She was kind and content, as if she'd had a change of heart. Technically, she had.

"People who like them books don't seem to like people like Dad," Paul said. He spoke softly. "I used to like church when I was younger. Dad said they used to read the Bible in England, but everyone got rid of it before the war."

"Maybe it would have helped them in the war." Hope smoothed a wrinkled page in her Bible.

"You sound like some of the guys on my football team." Paul put his elbows on his knees and leaned forward. "Anyway, why would English people like it? Doesn't it say everyone will be American in the end?"

"The manifesto is the only one of the three books that talks about America's call to the nations." Hope turned to the front of the book and pointed at the table of contents. "I think the Bible is the most important one. It's really old—like thousands of years old. It was written way before we were even a country. The Declaration," she continued, "is the next oldest. That changed humanity forever. I like the lines in it:

'All men are created equal!' Lee's manifesto, the one about how everyone should act like Americans, came last."

Paul grinned. "I remember learning that for religion class at your age. When's the test?"

"I don't have a test," Hope said. "I'm just reading for fun. I want to know about God more and if he's really in these books."

"How do you know God's a *he*?"

Hope squinted her eyes. She stuck her tongue out of one side of her mouth, then moved it to the other side.

"I saw some stuff when I was sick—when I was in the hospital. But—well . . . I'm not ready to talk about it."

Paul spent the rest of the evening absorbed in video games. When he settled into bed, he checked his watch one last time. There was a message from an unknown number.

Thanks for sticking up for Beth Friday night. That was pretty cool. See you in class tomorrow.—Finn

CHAPTER 7
PAUL

Paul woke up to his mom shouting up the stairs. He checked his watch: seven twenty-nine. His family's home network wouldn't be on until eight—thirty more minutes before he could respond to the text from Finley. His watch dinged for the government's daily morning message.

Breaking news: EN-99 is ready. Glory to God for supplying us with the latest technology in warfare. USW for all!

Paul rubbed his eyes and reread the message. *Weapon?* he thought. *What new weapon?*

He sprinted through his morning routine, obsessively checking his watch, desperate to respond to Finley's message. He got dressed and devoured two pieces of toast, some cereal, and a glass of orange juice before eight o'clock. He sat at the table and stared at his watch, willing the time to pass.

"Everything okay, Paulie?" Eight o'clock was one minute away. Hannah leaned against the kitchen countertop and gave Paul a questioning look.

"Just need to respond to a message I got last night."

"Oh yeah," she said. "Who from?"

"Just a friend from school."

Hannah cocked a curious eyebrow but said nothing. At eight, every watch in the house beeped and vibrated with incoming messages, emails, and alerts that came through since the family network shut off at nine the night before. Paul skipped through his messages and found the only one that mattered.

Sorry for not responding last night, he wrote. *Didn't see your message until our network was switched off. Those guys are jerks!*

He hit send and dropped his arm to his side. He tapped a finger on his leg three times, then moved his arm where he could see his watch. No response. He put his arm back down, then raised it again repeatedly. His heart thumped. Three more minutes passed—still nothing.

She must be getting ready for school, Paul thought.

Hannah cleared her throat. "You sure everything's okay?" she asked.

Paul's heart raced as he realized he'd been holding his breath. He inhaled deeply through his nose to calm himself like his kicking coach taught. *Channel the energy to something positive.* "Yeah, I'm fine. "He stood up, grabbed his lunch off the counter, and kissed his mom on the cheek. "Thanks, Mom."

Ten minutes left to catch the bus, Paul walked into the living room, where his dad watched the news. On the television, FF soldiers fired what appeared to be laser guns. Paul gave a double take. *Laser guns?*

"Look at that new weapon, mate. Looks like something from an old movie my granddad used to love. Hey, honey!" John craned his neck toward the kitchen. "Come look at this. This is what the government's message was about this morning. Looks like a gun from that old movie, *Solar Wars!*"

"Do you mean *Star Wars?*" Hannah shouted back.

"That's the one." He leaned forward in his chair, mesmerized by the green laser beams flashing from the FF soldiers' guns. "Hudson's pretty excited about it," he said. "Guess it won't be long until our chosen president invades those other empires to 'set them free' now he's got these."

Just then, Paul's watch beeped. It was Finley! *See you in class* was followed by a smiley emoji. Paul returned a thumbs up emoji and sighed with relief. He turned around to see his mom watching him intently.

"Are you sure everything's okay?"

"Yes," he said through a smile. "See you later. Bye, Dad."

"Paul," Hannah said, "remember—we won't be here tonight. We're going to get Grandma."

Paul had totally forgotten. He was so consumed with responding to Finley's message.

"Oh yeah," he said. "Have a good trip. See you Wednesday."

"See if you can get a ride home with Devan after practice," Hannah instructed. "I'm not sure Jude will be back in time to get you. She said Steve's coming over to watch Elysium with you all."

"Okay," Paul responded, walking out the door.

It was a crisp, fall Georgia morning. A little cold this early, but the sun was shining. It would be warm again by noon. The trees displayed vibrant yellows, reds, and oranges, made all the more beautiful courtesy of Finley's text message.

As Paul walked to the edge of the driveway, he wondered why Finley texted him. *Did she have an argument with Chase, or was she just grateful and wanted to be friends?* Before Paul could decide on an answer, Devan showed up and the bus lumbered down the street.

"Morning, bestest friend."

"What?" Devan looked confused.

Paul lifted his watch to show Devan Finley's message. Devan's eyes bulged, and he sat up straight.

"Nice going, bestest friend. What period do you have class with her?"

"After lunch."

"Cool, make sure you have a mint or some chewing gum. Actually"—Devan pulled a box of mints from his backpack and dropped a few in Paul's hand—"put these in your pocket. Make sure you use them after lunch."

Paul scanned the parking lot as the bus pulled up to school. His heart leapt at the sight of Finley, then sank. She was getting out of Chase's car. She wore a long-sleeve white shirt with a black puffer vest, tight blue denim jeans, and black boots.

"There she is, bro." Devan poked Paul on the arm. "Go speak to her."

Paul pointed at Chase.

"So what? Chase didn't stick up for Beth the other night, did he?"

They stepped off the bus and walked toward two FF soldiers at the front doors. Students crowded around them for

79

a better look, while teachers waved students inside without success. Everybody crowded closer for a look at the soldiers. Some kids held their watches out to take selfies with them.

"Everyone, straight to the auditorium!" Principal Hennessey's voice boomed over the loudspeaker, startling the starry-eyed students. "Do not go to homeroom this morning. Go straight to the auditorium for a special assembly. Tardy students will receive detention."

Paul and Devan pushed their chests out and stood tall as they walked past the FF soldiers decked out in their official uniforms—black and white body armor with the FF logo over the white breast plate, black boots, checkered armor on the arms, legs and fingerless gloves, black berets, and sunglasses. Each soldier held what Paul recognized as the new EN-99 weapons.

As they filed past the soldiers, the students gawked. Some guys around Paul were saying how cool they looked, others were impressed with the weapons, and a cluster of girls giggled about how hot they looked.

The commotion continued at the entrance of the auditorium, where two more FF soldiers stood at attention. These soldiers wore the same distinct uniforms but were noticeably different. They were females.

Now, the boys ogled and the girls straightened up. FF soldiers had to be fit and strong, and the tight FF uniform confirmed these two women fit the bill. One had blonde hair and blue eyes. The other had fire-red hair and matching lipstick.

Paul was sure the soldier with fire-red hair and bright red lipstick smiled at him.

"Dude, they are hot! Where do we sign up?" Devan smirked.

"We have to be eighteen. And your dad wouldn't let you anyway."

"My dad loves America, just not the way the church is," he said with a whisper.

"You'd rather be in the FF than the NFL?" Paul asked Devan as they filed into the auditorium.

As they sat down, a strong hand from behind patted Paul on the back. Paul's heart skipped a beat.

"Morning fellas—exciting way to start the week we become state champs, eh?"

Paul turned and felt his stomach lurch. It was Chase. Finley held his arm and smiled. Paul's pulse quickened.

"Yeah," Paul agreed, lowering his voice to prevent any cracking. "Morning, Finn."

Microphone feedback meant Principal Hennessey was at the front. The student body stood for prayer, the national anthem, and the pledge of allegiance. Hand on his heart, Paul quoted the words he said every school day since kindergarten:

I pledge allegiance to the flag
of the United States of North America
and to the republic for which it stands,
I will answer the call of our forefathers
to fulfill the destiny we have been chosen for—
to bring democracy and freedom to all,
one empire under God, indivisible,
with liberty and justice for all.

"Now," Principal Hennessey said after the announcements, "will the varsity football team please stand up?"

Paul and Devan stood. They shook each other's hands, then turned to do the same with Chase. Students cheered and applauded as Principal Hennessey continued.

"Congratulations on a hard-fought game Friday night. I expect all students to come out and support us this Friday night as Chase will lead the team in the State championship." Principal Hennessey paused here as the students roared. "Now," he called as the commotion died down, "please take your seats."

He didn't mention me! The winning field goal with no time left on the clock. Chase didn't even do anything special. Devan played better than him!

As Paul dropped to his seat burning with jealousy, the lights faded. A huge hologram appeared above the stage showing the United States of North America flag blowing in the wind. Patriotic music played in the background as the camera panned to President Hudson and Brother Swanson, flanked by FF soldiers armed with EN-99s.

Students oohed and aahed. Next was a barrage of historical images—pilgrims holding Bibles, founding fathers signing the Declaration of Independence, and George Washington raising a sword in victory. A baritone voice narrated the story as the pictures scrolled.

The upbeat tone took a dramatic shift. "Then Stacey Lee," the narrator continued, "anointed by God, revealed America's great destiny. She brought us into a time of free healthcare, education, and communication for all who chose it. She invited the poor and downcast into our land. But jealous empires, who hated to see the children of God rising up, killed our prophet." The music swelled as holograms

82

of the Mexican war flashed by, refugees ushered across the border and welcomed with their watches. The hologram of Mexican immigrants dissolved. Stacey Lee's face took their place. "But no one can stop destiny!" the narrator promised. "Soon, other nations around the world repented and joined our empire. Holy democracy began to take its rightful place in the world, and the United States of the World began!"

The narrator went on to explain how God validates the USW's development through medical advancements and environmental transformation. Holograms of pristine oceans, rivers, and forests were followed by a smiling John Sutton.

Paul leaned toward Devan and pointed. "That's Gizmo— one of my granddad's students. I met him a few times, but we haven't seen him since the funeral."

The video finished with floating holograms of Brother Swanson, church leaders, and President Hudson.

"Now God has chosen Brother Swanson and our president to bring to full completion democracy and freedom. They lead us to pursue this destiny at all costs. No call is higher, no mission greater. This generation has been chosen to build on the foundations of the great men and women who have gone before us. Now," said the narrator, "our chosen leaders have given us the weapon to rid the world of those who oppose freedom."

Persian Ayatollahs, Russian armies, and residents of the Chinese empire appeared above the stage. They stood defiantly for a brief moment before getting zapped away with a laser. They fell in agony, and a soldier appeared in front of an American flag, holding an EN-99 weapon.

"We introduce to you to the validation of our God-ordained destiny: the EN-99," the narrator stated plainly. "USW for all!"

The auditorium erupted. Paul stood and clapped and shouted support. As he did, he scanned the auditorium to ensure no one noticed it was an act.

It was easy to look convincing. The holographic film was powerful. He felt the allure of unquestioning patriotism. America was the greatest empire to ever exist. Paul celebrated that.

The applause carried on until two male and two female FF soldiers took to the stage. The crowd went silent as a huge target got rolled to the left of the soldiers.

The taller of the two men took aim at the target and fired his EN-99. A green laser shot from the gun. The auditorium of students let out a collective gasp as the laser hit the target. But nothing happened. The soldier changed the gun's settings. He fired nonchalantly. A red laser blasted the target into a pile of fiery rubble. Two men rushed the stage to extinguish the flames. The soldier who fired the shot walked to a microphone.

"The EN-99 can fire green or red lasers. Green," he said, "only stuns humans and leaves them unconscious for a short time. Red, on the other hand, kills and destroys anything it hits. This weapon needs no bullets or electricity. It runs on human energy and fires as fast as you can pull the trigger."

He held the gun with both hands and took a step backward. The blonde female soldier moved to the microphone.

"This new weapon was designed by beloved scientist and patriot John Sutton, who has done so much for America's destiny already. In his own words about the weapon's power source—" She pressed her watch and a small hologram of John Sutton appeared. The soldier grinned as the hologram spoke: "EN-99 stands for the ninety-nine percent of unknown energy that runs through each one of us. We have now discovered the way to harness this energy and channel the power into a single beam of energy. The power of the weapon lies within the one who possesses it." Mr. Sutton disappeared, and the soldier lowered her arm. "This is the weapon we are revealing to the world that all FF soldiers will use," she said. "The US has even more powerful weapons fueled by this latest technology. However, we cannot show you those today."

She walked to the side of the stage as Devan's mouth dropped. "More weapons?" he mouthed.

The other two soldiers stood at the microphone. The male spoke first.

"We are not here just to show you this new weapon," he said. "President Hudson has declared from this day forth that anyone seventeen years and older can now be a member of the Freedom Fighter family." The junior and senior class roared with excitement. "Settle down, guys—you can't leave with us today," joked the soldier. "You still need parents' permission if you are under twenty-one."

Finally, the redhead had her turn. "We would love for you to join us," she said softly. "War is inevitable, and it's your destiny as Americans to set the other empires free from evil tyrants. USW for all!" She raised her arm high with a clenched fist.

"USW for all!" repeated the students.

The assembly released, and Paul pushed through the herd of students to science class. Beth huffed and took the spare chair beside him.

"I don't care if they take away all our family credit," she said. "That was a horrible presentation. I have family in Persia, and they're not evil people."

Paul flinched at the words, but there was no reason. Pegged an outsider by some, he sat in the back of the classroom by himself. No one heard what Beth said.

"I don't care anymore," she continued. "You agree with me, right? This religious empire stuff is insane."

Paul shrugged.

Beth groaned. "Not you, too? I thought you stood up to stuff like that."

"I do," Paul whispered. He gave a forced smile to a group of students who were suddenly watching him. "No one should be forced to be American, but even your family knows American ideologies are better than Persian ones. Otherwise, they would have moved back there. I've seen the documentaries on how they treat women over there."

Before the words left his mouth, Paul doubted them. He knew it was wrong to force people to join the USW, but he'd rather America win the pending war than another nation. Beth hung her head. The group that was watching Paul earlier ignored them now.

"Surely when this war starts, you'll want America to win?"

"Yes," Beth admitted. "But America is not a religion. This isn't what God wants!"

Mrs. Spencer called the class to attention. Paul's grade

86

was on the line. He forced himself to focus, which helped him forget about the assembly. Toward the end of class, the teacher reminded the students of Elysium.

"Tonight is when it will be in its closest proximity to earth," Mrs. Spenser said.

Paul was actually looking forward to watching Elysium tonight with Jude and her boyfriend. Even though his parents were skeptical of him, Paul liked Steve. Visions of asteroids faded as Paul considered the upcoming game. He imagined himself as a star defender. Just as he pictured himself causing a game-winning fumble, Beth handed him a folded sheet of paper. Paul opened it.

You won't tell anyone what I said, will you?

Paul's face burned with shame. He twirled his pencil, then wrote:

I don't care what religion you are, and I won't tell ANYONE what you said.

He held the note out toward Beth.

"Paul and Beth!" Mrs. Spenser called. The class turned to view them. "Are we passing notes at the back of class? That's not like you, Beth," Mrs. Spenser said as she walked toward the back of the classroom. "I wondered why you sat all the way in the back today."

Paul's heart sank as Mrs. Spenser snatched the note. Beth's eyes watered. Mrs. Spencer opened the note and read it silently to herself. She looked Paul in the eye with unexpected compassion.

"I need you two to stay behind after class, please." Mrs. Spenser stuffed the note in a pocket and walked to the front of class. "It appears we have two love birds in our class.

Maybe you can have a romantic evening watching Elysium together this evening."

Some students laughed. Others let their mouths drop open. Paul breathed a sigh of relief.

The bell rang and students emptied the room, leaving Paul and Beth alone in the back of the classroom. Mrs. Spencer motioned them to her desk.

"You two"—she glanced through the open classroom door—"need to be more careful. If the wrong people see that kind of note, it would be very bad for your families." Mrs. Spencer pulled the note from her pocket. She tore it into tiny pieces, which she dropped into the trash. She poured a half cup of coffee on top of the scraps. "It's better for you two to keep your heads down for the next few days. Don't make a fuss. Go along with what's happening."

As students entered the classroom for next period, Paul and Beth started to leave. Mrs. Spenser grabbed Paul by the arm.

"I just told the class you two were together," she whispered. "Maybe try pretending like it for a while."

Beth slid her clammy hand into Paul's. Her body was rigid and tense.

A crowd of students in the hallway pointed and laughed as they exited. Others turned their noses up and looked away. *A Brit with coward's blood dating the only Muslim in the school.* Paul smirked at the thought. *This will spread through the school in a heartbeat.*

Beth squeezed Paul's hand tighter as the laughs continued. He squeezed back.

"Where's your next class?" he asked.

Beth looked at him. Her brown eyes complemented her olive skin. Her beauty caught Paul by surprise. He felt something stick in his throat. Fortunately, he didn't have to speak any more. Beth took over.

"Math," she said. "Walk together?"

Murmurs and whispers followed their every step. Paul didn't remember the hallway being so long.

"In here," Beth said. She stood on her tippy toes and gave him a kiss on the cheek. He blushed. She giggled and said, "Bye babe."

Stunned, Paul froze. Beth leaned in closer. "Thank you."

It wasn't at all romantic, yet somehow, Paul knew instantly that a special bond of friendship had begun between them. Instantaneously he was blown away by how beautiful she really was without any hint of having a crush.

He turned around, heading to his next class. To his surprise, Finley Matthews was standing looking at him. To say she looked shocked was an understatement.

"Beth!" she gasped.

Beth giggled and bit her lower lip. "I'll tell you in class, Finn—it's nothing."

Finley didn't acknowledge Beth's response. Instead, she made a beeline for Paul. Without any warning, she punched him viciously in the face. Not a slap, but a full-on right hook to the jaw that knocked him back a little. Paul tried to act tough, but it hurt.

"What the hell, Finn?" he gasped, massaging his jaw.

"Finley!" Beth yelled. "Stop."

"Finley Matthews!" yelled the math teacher. "Detention, tonight! In the classroom immediately."

CHAPTER 8
FINLEY

‿‿◦⟋‿‿

Finley's morning was not going well.

It started with her mom freaking out about their bad credit. If things didn't get better, Denise swore, they would have to live with her sister in North Carolina again. This was followed by an awkward car ride, as Chase went on and on about Friday night at the party. Finley fumed at Chase for not sticking up for Beth. Chase defended his actions, claiming he was trying to bring peace and help the team.

Then came the assembly. Afterward, Chase had the audacity to not only defend it, but celebrate it during first period religion. As soon as the bell rang, Finley stormed away without speaking a word.

As the halls filled, Finley's pace increased, anger building with every step. *How can he support what we've just seen? Those people don't want to set the nations free, they just want power. Am I the only one who sees it?* When she turned the corner, what she saw took her over the edge. In front of the whole

90

world, her best friend kissed the boy Finley had a crush on.

Finley shook. Her teeth clenched. *She's supposed to my friend!* she thought. *I told her I had a crush on him! She knew I messaged him just last night to say thanks! I spoke to her for hours about what to do. Now this?*

As Paul faced her, he gave a smile—a sly, deceiving smile. *Does he like her?* Rage pulsed through Finley's veins.

"Beth," Finley gasped. Rage fogged her senses. Beth watched as Finley punched Paul square in the face. Pain shot through her hand.

"What the hell, Finn?" Paul rubbed his jaw.

"Finley!" Beth yelled. "Stop."

"Finley Matthews!" yelled the math teacher. "Detention, tonight! In the classroom immediately."

Finley took her seat and tossed her backpack on the floor. Beth hurried to her side.

"Finn, that was a . . ."—Beth lowered her voice—". . . show. He needed to hold my hand," she said hurriedly. "I gave him a kiss as a thank you. I don't even like him that way!"

Finley gasped. Her red, angry face changed to a red, embarrassed face.

"Finley! Are you trying to get sent to the principal's office?" Ms. Shaw smoothed the front of her plain, green blouse. She took a long, slow breath and closed her eyes. When she opened them, her countenance had softened, along with her voice. "Today's been a very eventful morning," she said, "and it seems all of you are a little too excited. Let's have a surprise quiz in silence."

The class groaned in harmony as they opened their

tablets and clicked the quiz link. Finley's pounding heart was matched only by her throbbing hand. Distracted by Beth's giggles and the vision of Paul's post-punch face, Finley struggled through the quiz. She finished just before the end of class and relaxed. Lunch was next. All would be well.

In the hallway, Beth burst into laughter. Finley wanted to be angry, but Beth's laugh was contagious.

"So," Finley said through laughter, "why'd you kiss him?"

Beth pulled a compact from her purse and checked her makeup. "You really like him, don't you?" she asked.

Finley's jaw dropped. She grabbed Beth's arm and held her close as they walked toward the cafeteria. "I do," she admitted coyly. "But I didn't realize it until I saw you kiss him. I guess I still have a thing for him."

Beth guided them to where they used to eat lunch together, prior to Finley and Chase becoming an item and Beth joining computer club.

"I'm supposed to meet Chase for lunch," Finley said.

"And I'm supposed to be in computer club," Beth replied. "Seems we'll have to miss."

The sun hung high above, warming the friends as they sat on the grass. Twenty yards away a group of guys played basketball. Beth explained to Finley why she and Paul had to act like a couple.

Finley twisted her hair. She lifted her face to the sun and said it may not matter much longer. "Mom says she may be moving to my aunt's in Charlotte again."

Beth covered her half-eaten sandwich and placed it in her bag. "Dad talked about moving back to Persia after the news this morning." She wiped away a tear.

"I'm so sorry, Beth." Finley set her lunch in the grass. "I've been so caught up in all my drama. I'm a bad best friend."

"These are scary days," Beth said. "I don't even know if I fully am Muslim, but that doesn't matter."

One of the boys nearby took a shot. The ball bounced off the rim. Finley ate her hummus and coleslaw sandwich, filling the air with the scent of vinegar.

Lunch passed in knowing silence. When the bell rang, Finley helped Beth to her feet.

"See you after school," Beth said.

"Not today." Finley punched at the air.

"Oh yeah—detention. Well, see you tomorrow then. I'm watching Elysium with my family. Call if you need anything."

Finley hugged Beth, and the two made their way inside.

"By the way," Beth said, "you looked pretty bad ass when you hit Paul."

Finley's nerves grew with each step closer to history class. *Paul Lewis will be in there*, she thought. *Don't beat around the bush. Just go straight over to him and apologize.*

She took one step inside the history classroom, and her stomach sank. Across the classroom, Paul sat alone, touching his jaw gingerly. He eyed Finley with suspicion. Finley walked directly to him.

"I'm sorry—so sorry, Paul." Finley fidgeted a moment before stuffing her hands in her pockets. "Beth told me what you did for her, and I think that's really sweet. What I did—I kinda lost it back there."

Paul grinned.

"I'm really, really sorry! How can I—"

"It's fine." Paul reached into his pocket. He placed a mint

93

into his mouth, crossed his arms, and examined Finley.

Just as the silence grew awkward, Devan arrived.

"Watch out, Paulie!" Devan ducked behind Paul and held onto him like a shield. "Don't let Mayweather get you again."

Paul laughed and raised his hands in defense.

"Mayweather?" Finley asked.

"A famous boxer," Paul said. "He never lost a match."

"That's because," Finley joked, "he never fought me."

Paul held both hands up in defeat.

"Okay, class," called Mr. Wilby, "take your seats."

Finley slid into a desk next to Paul.

"You takin' my seat, Mayweather?" Devan raised his fists.

"Yes," Finley replied confidently.

"Mr. Jones, please take your seat," demanded Mr. Wilby.

"It's taken," Devan replied.

"Then find another one, sir."

Devan moped to the front of the class. Paul craned his neck toward Finley.

"Why did you punch me?"

"I thought Beth was going behind my back with you."

"Behind your back?"

Finley covered her mouth in shock. She grew hot all over. She grunted.

"What?" Paul asked.

Finley looked into Paul's deep blue eyes. Butterflies bounced in her stomach.

Think, Finley! she told herself. *Think fast!*

Paul shook his head. He slumped down in his seat and faced Mr. Wilby.

"I used to have a crush on you."

Paul turned and watched Finley, but she dared not look back.

"Used to?" Paul asked.

At the front of the classroom, Mr. Wilby produced a hologram of a map of Mexico. He explained that Mexico was once an independent nation before becoming a prosperous state within the USNA.

"Stacey Lee was considered insane in her younger days by some, but as you are all aware, it was through her manifesto that people began to see the complete destiny of America. When she invited all Mexican citizens who desired abundant life the opportunity to immigrate to America free of charge, millions showed up at the border."

Finley, like everyone else in the class, had heard this story since infancy, but she needed to know it in even more detail for the upcoming exam. It was impossible for her to concentrate though, sitting next to Paul after what she had just said. Even though she was feeling uncomfortable she didn't regret saying it. Mr. Wilby continued.

"Many of Lee's opponents thought this would be the end of America, but as she prophesied, no criminals, drug cartels, or gangs entered. They couldn't live as criminals wearing the watch, so they stayed in Mexico."

Finley turned her neck slightly, pretending to stroke the side of her hair, hoping to catch a glimpse of him. Paul was facing the front of class trying to listen, while she stared at him with butterflies fluttering in her stomach. Suddenly, he turned to look at her. Finley faced the front of class embarrassed, her heart pounding as she smiled to herself.

"And," Mr. Wilby continued, "on the day of her liberation speech welcoming the first redeemed nation to our empire, President Lee was tragically shot and killed."

Finley turned to looked at Paul again. He was looking back at her. Her heart skipped a beat. The world stood still, and the lecture became white noise. Neither blushed nor looked away. *Does he like me back? Can he feel all this energy exploding between us or is it just me?*

They didn't know it, but class was almost over. They had been staring at each other for longer than they thought. The spell broke when other students began packing their tablets. Finley hadn't even taken her tablet out of her bag. Devan approached them with a scowl.

"Dude!" he said to Paul. "I was so bored! I nearly fell asleep, but I couldn't. Wilby's eye was on me the entire time."

"I thought it was interesting," Paul said. "Class seemed to fly by."

Chase leaned into the classroom and waved at Finley. He nodded at Devan and Paul. "What's up, sophomore superstars? Ready for practice today?"

"Sure are," Devan answered enthusiastically.

"No can do," Paul said. "Detention for me and Tommy— remember?"

Chase stood upright. He reached for Finley's hand, as she chuckled.

"Looks like I'll be there, too," she said.

CHAPTER 9
FINLEY

It was my fault, Chase—seriously." Finley sighed. "He didn't do anything wrong. I was having a moment, and I punched him. I'm done talking about it, but thanks for caring."

Chase tilted his head to the side. "Fine. Do you still want a ride home after practice?"

Finley thought for a moment.

"How else are you going to get home—walk?"

"Why don't we get a bite to eat after practice?" she suggested. The thought of going home to her mom during one of her episodes did not sound fun.

"I've got that thing with my dad tonight."

Finley threw her arms in the air. "Fine," she snapped. I'll just walk home. It doesn't matter."

A cluster of students walked by, one playing a trumpet.

Chase moved toward Finley.

"Are you okay, Finn? Look, we don't have to talk about it right now, but I'm really sorry your mom's having a hard time again. I'm sure it will work out. It'll just take time."

Finley cringed. *I should call it off with him*, she thought. *We're too different.*

"I really like you, Finn." Chase took both Finley's hands in his own. "I know we come from different families, but I'll never force you to believe the same as me. Sometimes people in church get it wrong, but Jesus never does."

"Maybe."

They stopped in front of detention, and Chase leaned forward and kissed Finley on the cheek. He'd never done that before. Nobody had ever done that before. A warm rush ran through her body.

"See you after practice," Chase promised.

Finley watched Chase walk away. When he turned the corner, she giggled a moment, but stopped abruptly. Paul sat at a desk, one hand holding his chin, the other draped across the desktop. His eyes were locked on Finley.

She sat opposite of Paul and Tommy. The only other student was David Finnigan. He sat at the very back of class, slouched down and wearing his trademark sadness. Rumors kept most people away from David. He allegedly burned the American flag once. Some said he suffers from bipolar disorder—a disease that was eradicated 100 years earlier—because he refused immunization.

The rumors started when word got around that he didn't live with his parents. They were in jail, so he stayed with an aunt. This happened a decade earlier. But incarceration was rare, so it was major news. According to released government documents, David's parents got convicted of trying to destroy their watches and chips.

"Stand and recite." The detention teacher stood at attention as a hologram appeared with passages from the Stacey Lee manifesto. Finley read the words along with the narrator. Paul and Tommy followed suite. David folded his arms and stood in silence.

After ten minutes of recitation, the teacher swept a hand over her watch. The hologram disappeared. The teacher inserted her earbuds and pressed a button on her watch.

"I'm covering detention today. What is it?" She paused. "I'll be right there." The teacher grabbed her bag and rushed out the door. "Mr. Milner," she yelled from the hall, "please cover this detention. I have an emergency."

The teacher's voice faded as a janitor entered the classroom. He was clean shaven and had leathery skin and long, grey hair tucked under a nondescript blue ballcap.

"Well hello, young 'uns. They must be desperate if they letting me cover." He gave a toothy grin and leaned against the teacher's desk. "I had to write lines in detention when I was your age. What do they have you do nowadays?"

Tommy shifted in his seat.

"We normally recite something from Lee's manifesto," Paul replied.

"Well." Mr. Milner drew out the word, turning the single syllable into three, four, or five. "We won't be reciting any of those lies while I'm here."

The students froze. His words were blasphemy, cause for losing substantial credit. David howled from the back of the classroom. He doubled over and clapped his hands.

"Never knew our old janitor was a rebel," David laughed. "How long have you been part of the resistance?"

"The rebellion ain't real," objected Tommy. "And I should report you for calling the manifesto lies."

"Go ahead, son." Mr. Milner picked at his fingernails. "The world may be over tonight anyway, one way or another."

Paul sat upright. David stood up and began pacing.

"Elysium is probably gonna hit us," Mr. Milner said, "and I've heard a rumor that there'll be an attack on the Pentagon tonight. And if both of those don't happen, I've heard that China has their nukes pointing directly at us ready to launch."

"You read about that conspiracy, huh?" Tommy leaned back in his desk chair.

"Sure did, and it's gonna happen. Mark my words."

"You're nuts, old man." David paced angrily. "Elysium won't hit us. You don't know anything about the rebellion. My parents got put in prison for being connected to it."

"Your parents must be good people."

Paul slammed his hand on his desktop. "You're gonna end up in prison for saying stuff like that!"

"Maybe I will," Mr. Milner said. "But I'm an old man now. I've kept my mouth shut for too long. I have to speak what the Lord wants me to!"

Finley winced.

"I'm leaving," David said. "You're just another religious nut!"

"Walk outta that door," Mr. Milner said, "and that GPS tracker will go off, young man. Someone will probably take me away soon anyways. Sit down and listen. You might learn something from an old man."

David hesitated, then sat down. Mr. Milner sat on top of

a desk, his feet resting on the seat in front of Finley.

"Tell us then," Finley challenged. "Tell us what we should know."

Mr. Milner looked at her with wise eyes and a kind smile.

"Yes, ma'am. I should have shared this long ago, but I was always afraid. After seeing that assembly this morning and the possibility of disaster tonight, what do I have to lose?"

"Your life, I suppose," Tommy chimed in.

"Fair enough." Mr. Milner removed his hat and set it on one knee. He cleared his throat and licked his lips. "Did you know Lee had people killed in her early days to get that manifesto in schools?"

"She brought real freedom!" The veins on Tommy's forehead throbbed visibly. "No empire is greater than ours. And you're lying about Prophet Lee. She would never have done that!"

"Craig Milner. Come with us please."

Two male FF soldiers from the morning assembly stood in the doorway. Their EN-99s reflected the overhead lights.

"You guys are faster than you used to be," Milner said. He set his hat back on his head and eased his way off the desk and onto his feet.

"Talking about an attack on the Pentagon raises flags in the system, Mr. Milner." The taller soldier approached Mr. Milner. "Please come with us to answer some questions."

Mr. Milner tipped his hat, and the pair of soldiers grabbed the aged janitor. Mr. Milner complied without a struggle. At the door, he turned and winked.

"Free yourselves from the deception, children," he said. "Free yourselves."

"That guy was nuts!" Tommy yelled.

Finley felt behind her right ear where the network chip was embedded.

"Don't worry," David said. "They don't listen to all our conversations."

"What do you mean?" asked Tommy. "*All* our conversations?"

"Do they listen to us when we're at home?" Paul asked.

David sat on the desktop where Mr. Milner had been. "If they listened to us in private, they would have taken my auntie by now, I'm sure. But in public buildings, they track every conversation. Lets them catch people speaking out against the government. Say the wrong words in a short time frame, and you get flagged. Once you're flagged, someone starts listening. Keep at it, and you get taken away. I've never seen it that quick though."

"They'd only take them away if they were a danger to society," Tommy argued.

"They think anyone who doesn't agree with Lee is a danger to society!" The room went silent. David lifted both hands, palm up. "And they're probably still listening."

"I don't believe it," Tommy blurted out. "Even if they do listen, they wouldn't do it unless it was for our own protection."

"Tell that to my parents," David said calmly. "They organized a group protest during Hudson's first election. That's all they did, but that's all they had to do."

Tommy, Paul, and Finley turned pale. David kicked the side of the teacher's desk.

"The night before they got arrested, my parents broke off

our watches and cut out their chips." He began pacing the room. His eyes glazed over. "I was only seven. They pinned me down and held a scalpel to my neck. I was terrified, but I did what they told me to do. I remember Mom shouting at Dad, blood dripping down her neck. 'We've gone too far. Stop it, Rob!' Dad raised the scalpel to slice my skin, as the FF rushed through the door and saved me."

Finley whimpered. Paul and Tommy shuffled uncomfortably. David stopped pacing. He settled back into a desk and sat stone faced. First Paul and then Tommy started to speak, but then stopped.

"If they're listening, they'll be here for me soon. I'm not supposed to talk about that to anyone except my aunt and counselor. I'm sick of holding it in though." He dropped his head to his desk." Everyone thinks I'm crazy anyway."

The classroom door opened. Principal Hennessey walked in with a fake smile and jittery urgency.

"Sorry about all the drama, students. Mr. Milner has been taken in for questioning. You'll just have to finish detention without a teacher." He looked at his watch. "You have exactly four minutes and twelve seconds left. But David, you don't have to wait that long. Your aunt is here early to pick you up."

David stared through Mr. Milner with dead eyes. "My aunt's not here," he said dully. "She went out of town. Should have just had the FF come get me."

Finley's heart raced.

"David," Principal Hennessey said, "it's just your aunt. You don't want to make a scene like last time, do you?"

David moved robotically from his seat.

"There's a good lad," Principal Hennessey said. "And to answer your question, Mr. Lewis, the government does not listen in on conversations in the privacy of people's homes." He flashed a malicious smile. "Don't you think your father would have been arrested by now if that was the case?"

Principal Hennessey left with David by his side. The remaining students sat in stunned silence. Four minutes later, their watches beeped simultaneously, signaling the end of detention. Finley followed Paul and Tommy toward the football field.

"The janitor was definitely crazy." Tommy spoke as slowly as he walked. "But David . . . What if—"

Paul massaged the chip in his neck. "Why would he lie like that? He had nothing to gain from it."

If the janitor and David got taken away for what they said, Finley thought, *they could do the same to Beth.* She gasped. The boys glanced at her and kept walking.

"We'll see," Tommy said. "For now, we need to focus on practice."

Finley settled onto the bleachers that overlooked practice. Linemen and running backs, tight ends, and nose guards sprinted, juked, and collided on the field. Finley's eyes followed their movement, but her head was far from football.

Do they really keep us safe or are they controlling us? The credit system sucks, but we don't have crime or sickness. Maybe the government really is taking care of us. Her thoughts jumped from fear to acceptance to appreciation, then started over. It was too much to untangle. *They hate people like Beth. But it's only a few people like Drew Humphries who are really mean to her. She'll be fine. But her family doesn't feel safe.*

Finley inserted her ear buds, closed her eyes, and cranked the volume to drown out the sound of football practice and the drama of a crazy day.

CHAPTER 10

PAUL

Chase, Drew, and Big Tommy talked in hushed tones. Tommy was more animated than them all, but it was obvious they were talking about something serious. Suddenly, all three turned to look at Paul. He spun away from them and awkwardly put his shirt on. Drew shook hands with Tommy and Chase and left the locker room. Paul took his chance.

"Hey," he said to Tommy, "my dad can't pick me up tonight and Devan's going out with his dad. You don't drive home past the rec center, do you?"

"Sorry, man." Tommy zipped his bag. "Chase is giving me a ride home."

"No problem, Lewis—you can jump in with us. I'll be driving home that way." Chase held up a finger and walked toward the coach's office.

Paul thanked Chase and stepped outside. The fading sun threw dazzling oranges and reds across the sky.

"Hey, Paul."

After all the yelling at practice, Finley's soft voice startled Paul. She had a bandage around her right hand.

"How's the hand?" he asked.

"Fine, thanks." She stroked the bandage. "How's the face?"

Paul laughed. A couple senior players walked by, hooting and hollering. They jokingly pushed Paul. Paul gave a fake laugh and pushed them back—harder. The locker room door opened again.

"Let's roll!" Chase grabbed Finley's unbandaged hand. He looked over his shoulder at Tommy and Paul. "How was detention?"

Paul and Tommy exchanged knowing looks with Finley.

"It was . . . interesting."

"Tommy thinks detention was interesting? How?"

"We'll talk in the car," Tommy said.

Chase held the car door for Finley as Tommy and Paul climbed into the back.

"How's your hand, Finn?"

Finley held her hand up, and Chase kissed it like Prince Charming. Paul's stomach twisted. *What a creep!* he thought. Chase started the car and pulled away from the school. Soon as the school was out of sight, Paul slapped the back of Chase's seat.

"Lee was a liar," he began. "Her manifesto robbed us of true freedom. God doesn't exist. Religion in this country is a man-made invention to control people. We should join the revolution and fight the FF!"

Chase spun in his seat. "What the heck is wrong with you, Lewis? Get out of my car!"

"Make me."

Chase jumped out of the car and slung open the rear door. He grabbed Paul and pulled. Paul didn't budge. Chase jerked and twisted Paul's arm. Paul held his ground.

"I've been sticking up for you all season, Lewis. All this time, you really are full of coward's blood!"

Big Tommy ran around the car and pulled Chase off Paul.

"What are you doing?" Chase kicked at Tommy. "Get off me!"

"Give it a minute," Tommy said through his teeth.

Chase panted. He still held Paul, but he stopped pulling. Two cars slowed down. Tommy released Chase and gave a friendly wave. The cars kept moving. Chase pushed away from Paul. He slammed the rear door shut and returned to his seat.

Chase's knuckles whitened as he gripped the steering wheel. He pulled the car to the side of the road and made eye contact with Tommy in the rearview mirror.

"It's not what you think," Tommy said. He went on to explain everything that happened in detention.

They sat in silence for what seemed like an eternity but was only a few uncomfortable moments.

"So, Lewis is testing out what Principal Hennessey said?" He squinted. "He thinks some government officials care about what high schoolers talk about, so they listen to us all the time?"

"I know it sounds crazy," Tommy said, "but—"

"Is that what you're saying?" Chase demanded.

"Yeah." Paul peered out the side window. There were no

blue lights. No government officials trailed them. "I thought they'd be here by now."

Chase rotated his hands on the steering wheel and pulled back onto the road. "They're telling the truth. The government doesn't listen to people's private conversations. My dad told me. They listen to everything in public buildings and transport, but not homes or this car." A green sedan passed to their left. Chase gave a half wave. "The FF won't be coming."

Finley giggled nervously.

"Told you that old man was crazy," Tommy said.

"Yeah," Finley said, "but what about David?"

"David Finnigan?" Chase sounded disgusted. "He was taken from his parents when he was a baby. They were on drugs or something. When they finished rehab, they got him back. First thing they did was try to kill him. Dad thinks they did something worse." Chase breathed in through his nose. "He's convinced they were part of a rebellion or something."

"Why have you never told me before?" Tommy asked, shocked his best friend would keep that from him.

"Dad told me not to gossip about it. He gets enough grief from other kids as it is. Don't go spreading more rumors."

"You're a good man, Chase," Tommy encouraged. Paul had to agree: Chase was a stand-up guy, even though Paul wanted to hate him for dating Finley.

Tommy's head was spinning. Before he could gather his thoughts, the car stopped outside his high-rise apartment. He stumbled out of the car and walked toward the building, scratching his head.

"I don't want to go home tonight," Finley said.

Chase reminded her that his dad made plans for them. He suggested Finley go to Beth's house.

"She's busy tonight," Finley said as they pulled up to Paul's house.

A bright red truck was parked behind the Lewis's minivan.

"Is that Steve Holmes's truck?" Finley asked.

"Yeah," Paul said. "He's dating my sister."

"I like Steve—not a good football player, but a good guy." Chase whistled. "He's probably gonna sign up with the FF if his parents let him. He was born to be a general."

"We worked on an assignment in science last year together. I haven't seen him since he left for college."

Paul pulled the handle and put one foot out of the car. *She doesn't want to go home*, he thought. *She's friends with Steve already, so it would just be like hanging out with friends to watch Elysium. I'm gonna ask her to stay.*

He tapped Finley on the shoulder.

"Why don't you hang with us tonight?" he asked. "My parents are out of town, and my sister Jude is back from college. We're eating and watching Elysium together."

Finley looked at Chase.

"You should go in, Finn." Chase looked at his watch. "I want to come in and say hello, but—"

"Then come in and say hello."

"I'd love to, Lewis, but I have to get home."

"Just say hi, and then leave." Finley gave a pouty face. "I want you to come."

Chase agreed. He parked the car. Finley and Paul walked side-by-side to the door.

"I'm sure Steve will be happy to see you, and Jude will

110

make enough food—probably veggie lasagna or chili because we're saving all our meat rations for when Grandma's in town." The words sprinted out of his mouth, trying to keep up with his heart beat. *Finley is coming into my house*, he thought. *Chill out. Slow down. Be cool.* "Yeah, it'll be a pretty chill night." He paused in front of the door trying to slow his breathing.

"So, are you gonna invite us in, Paul?"

Paul jumped. He forgot Chase was behind them.

"Sure," he stammered. "Come on in."

Jude rounded the corner in black yoga pants and a red, oversized University of Georgia hoodie. She flung her arms around Paul.

"Little bro, I missed you!"

Paul half-heartedly hugged her back, determined to act cool. Once Jude released him, Paul introduced Chase and Finley. Jude took a step back and looked Finley up and down.

"Love the outfit." Jude dramatically threw a kiss at Finley's clothing. "Classic, yet stylish."

Paul tossed his book bag at the bottom of the stairs and gently set Finley's next to his. They all walked into the kitchen, where Steve was overseeing the chili's progress. Finley and Steve greeted each other like best friends and jumped into a conversation.

As they talked, Paul handed out seltzer water. He lingered when handing one to Finley. She thanked him without making eye contact.

Soon, the conversation turned to the morning's assembly. Jude and Steve said they showed the same video at their colleges.

"I've been reading up on those weapons all day," Steve stated. "Everyone's saying it's a game changer. No empire will be able to match us now."

Paul scoffed. "What good are guns against bombs?"

All nuclear and chemical weapons were disarmed after the European war, but rumors circulated that many countries were rebuilding their nuclear and chemical arsenals.

Steve took a long drink of his seltzer water. "This war will be won or lost on the ground." He wiped his mouth with a sleeve. "Bombs are a real threat, but we have the best missile defense system and underground cities—SafeCities. If we do, I'm sure others do as well."

The first SafeCities were built after chemical weapons were dropped during the European War. The fallout motivated scientists to discover ways to exist without relying on the land for years at a time.

"Empires used to let each other inspect their nuclear sites before Hudson took over," Steve continued, "but other nations hate him because of God's call on his life. Soon as he was in office, the inspections ended."

"Maybe it's because we were building weapons." Jude raised an eyebrow and crossed her arms. "Maybe the inspections stopped because we stopped letting them inspect us."

Steve stirred the chili vigorously. "We had to!" he said. "How else do you expect us to react with the threat of Persia, China, and Russia building an Alliance? They've always hated the West. And now, they are more anti-God, anti-good, and anti-democracy than ever. I'm confident in our ability to defend ourselves from a nuclear attack and retaliate with such force"—he banged the stirring spoon on the side of the pot—"we can spread Christianity to the world!"

Finley furrowed her brow.

"Calm down, Steve. You shouldn't want war," Jude said. "Billions will die."

Finley agreed.

"Yes, war is terrible," Steve said without skipping a beat. "But it's the only way for our empire to fulfill its destiny. The four empires of the world are not just seeking power and glory. The coming war determines the culture and religion for our grandchildren and their grandchildren's children. If these empires don't repent and seek democracy within the USW, war is the only option."

Chase pumped a fist in the air. "USW for all!"

"USW!" Steve raised a fist. "And hey, you guys hear about that janitor?" He left the spoon in the chili and turned to face the others. "Guy was arrested at your school this afternoon. He's a suspected Russian spy. It's been all over the news this afternoon." Steve explained.

"That makes sense," Chase said. He scratched his neck. "I would love to hang out, but I have to get going. Let's hang out again tomorrow. I can drop Paul off after practice again, and we can continue this conversation."

"Let's do it," Steve said. "I'm hoping to join the FF after Christmas."

Jude's eyes saddened. She scooted past Steve to stir the chili.

"I think I might join," Chase said. "My dad wants me to go to college first though. I'm desperate to try out one of the new EN-99s."

"They're the path to our destiny, brother." Steve smelled the chili and smiled. "God has revealed to Gizmo the way to harness the human soul and activate its full power."

"Gizmo doesn't even believe in God," Jude bellowed in frustration.

Chase coughed. "John Sutton's an atheist?"

"He's not the only one," Jude said. "At Granddad's funeral, he said Hudson was one as well."

Steve laughed. "Oh, come on, Jude. Hudson is not an atheist! We've spoken about this."

"He uses religion to control people." Jude lifted the spoon from the chili and took a small taste. "That's why he and Swanson are so close."

"If people choose not to believe in God, that's their choice. But it's not fair to spread conspiracies about our president when he speaks openly of his faith. And brother Swanson is a great man!"

"I like him too," Chase laughed. Jude and Steve joined in, but Paul and Finley seemed to be missing something. Was it an inside joke? "I really do need to go now. Let's carry this on tomorrow."

Paul rushed upstairs to shower after Chase left, desperate to be as quick as possible so he could be back with Finley. Still dripping when he stepped out the shower, Paul wrapped a towel around his waist and checked himself out in the mirror before stepping out into the hallway.

"Not bad, Paulie," he said to his reflection.

As he stepped out the door he froze. His stomach knotted up. Finley was walking toward him. She stopped about five feet away. She wasn't sure where to look as Paul grabbed the towel around his waist, perturbed it may fall down.

"Looking for something?" he asked nervously.

"Bathroom?" she smiled.

"Well you can use that one now I've finished, or there's one in my parents' room down the hall."

Neither moved. Finley's eyes dropped slightly, glancing over Paul's half-naked body but quickly shot back up to look him in the eyes. Paul was unsure what to say or where to go. *Should I move or wait for her to go to the bathroom?*

"There's a bathroom downstairs you know."

"Steve was using it, and dinner's ready. You should hurry up," Finley said, raising her eyebrows.

"I'll be two minutes."

Still, neither moved. The energy between them was tangible. A mixture of nerves, temptation, and a little guilt flooded the atmosphere from within each of them. Paul covertly tried to tense his muscles.

"Waiting for something?" Finley finally asked.

"Just need to get by. My bedroom is right behind you."

Finley looked into the room with teasing eyes. Paul walked forward, stepping close to the wall so as not to touch her. Suddenly, penetrating pain pierced through his toe. He'd hit the spring door stop.

"Urrgghhh!" He groaned, lifting his foot as the spring boinged loudly. He stumbled toward Finley who was trying not to laugh. She put her hand out to stop him and touched his bare chest with the tips of her fingers. Paul tried to steady himself by putting one arm on her shoulder as his free hand instinctively grabbed for the towel. His heart stopped, a lump in his throat. Both froze, still touching one another.

Thank God my towel didn't fall, Paul thought. "Sorry!" he said with a nervous smile, pulling his arm back.

Finley kept her hand on his chest, which was still wet from the shower. Butterflies danced in the pit of Paul's stomach. They looked at one another and just like in history class, time stopped and nothing else mattered. Slowly, Finley traced her fingers down Paul's body onto his abs.

"You're a little bigger than I remember from soccer in the summer," she smiled. "Maybe I'll have to start working out with you. I'd like some abs like that."

Fireworks went off inside Paul. He thought about kissing her. *She's still with Chase,* he reminded himself. *It's not right.*

"Hurry up, Paul!" Jude shouted from downstairs. "Dinner's ready."

Finley jerked back her hand and smiled. Paul's eyes were glued to her as she quickly walked by him to the bathroom without looking back. He couldn't move. His heart pounded in his chest as he tried to catch his breath. *She's definitely still into me!* he thought, as he rushed into his bedroom and changed at record speed.

He stood at the top of the stairs waiting for Finley when she came out of the bathroom. His hair was still wet. So was the back of his shirt. Finley walked straight past him smiling and began walking down the stairs. She paused halfway down and turned around.

"Come on then," she called.

Paul smiled and followed, the atmosphere charged with passionate tension.

***

Hot black bean chili with corn chips—the perfect comfort food after a crazy day. Paul ate three bowls as he talked football with Steve and tried to eavesdrop on Jude grilling Finley about her relationship with Chase.

After cleaning up, Jude made hot chocolate as the others gathered around the backyard firepit. The temperature dropped as Steve worked on the fire. His meticulous firewood arrangement proved he'd been in the FF youth. Steve talked to himself as he positioned each piece of wood with precision. As he mumbled, Jude poked her head outside and told Paul to get jackets for everyone.

"Finley likes you!"

Paul stood in front of the hall closet, holding two jackets with one hand and grabbing a third with the other. As the words registered, his spine tingled.

"She kept looking at you when I was asking her about Chase," Jude said.

Paul stuttered and grabbed for another jacket.

"She's really pretty," Jude said. "Just do right by Chase. He really is a good guy."

Paul brushed past Jude without talking. She followed him outside, grabbing a jacket. The fire crackled as Paul took a seat next to Finley. He looked up at the sky of stars, which were outshone by Elysium.

That huge rock is closer than the moon. The thought left Paul's head as quickly as it arrived. *Finley is right here, beside me, at my house, and she likes me.*

As if reading his thoughts, she turned to Paul and peered into his eyes. She smiled and said loudly for everyone to hear, "It's pretty exhilarating to think how close that thing is. Being this close to complete destruction really makes you wonder."

"Scientists theorized it may be attracted to our planet like a magnet. I don't believe it or the conspiracy theories," Jude said. "The earth's magnetic field is kind of like an invisible barrier that protects us from lethal space radiation and the sun's solar flares. Without that field, we would have been gone long ago." She tilted her head back. "If the asteroid did come towards us tonight, it would be torn apart before hitting us."

"I say we nuke it to make sure it won't hit us," Paul said.

"There's no telling what would happen if we did that!" Jude said. "Besides, this has happened before. Do you not listen at school?"

Paul grinned sheepishly. *I'm sitting next to Finley!*

"Even if it comes at us, world governments all agreed to fire on it simultaneously. Apparently," Steve added, "emperors and presidents have their fingers hovering over red buttons as we speak."

"A common enemy." Jude sighed. "It's nice to have a common enemy, I guess."

"How can something so beautiful be considered an enemy?" questioned Finley.

Nobody answered. Steve broke a branch into pieces and set them into the fire. The fire sizzled and popped.

Finley's watch beeped.

"Ugh!" she groaned. "Looks like mom wants to come pick me up now."

Fifteen minutes later, Denise arrived. Jude stood and gave Finley a hug.

"You're welcome here anytime," Jude said.

Finley thanked her and slowly stepped toward Paul. He hesitated for an awkward moment. Then he held out his arms. Finley stepped into his embrace, giving Paul flashbacks to their last hug: on the soccer field, Finley wearing only a sports bra. The scent of Finley's hair snapped Paul back into the present. It was a slight coconut fragrance—not overpowering like other girls.

Paul felt Jude's eyes on him as Finley held him.

"I don't think I'll be with Chase much longer," Finley whispered. She squeezed Paul one last time and let go, leaving Paul breathless.

CHAPTER 11
PAUL

Paul's watch vibrated a second time. This time, he woke up. It was 12:48 a.m. *Why is the government sending messages in the middle of the night?*

Elysium has turned, the message read. *World empires are doing everything they can to destroy it.*

He shot up in bed, reread the message, and ran into Jude's room.

"Jude, get up!" Paul shouted frantically.

Jude stirred, then rolled over.

"Jude!" Paul shook his sister. "Check your watch!"

Slowly, Jude cracked open one sleepy eye. "It's happening." She leapt out of bed and rushed downstairs, Paul tight on her heels.

"Breaking news," announced a panicked television reporter. "Led by NASA's planetary defense system, world empires are working together to destroy Elysium. Our sources state that multiple empires revealed a storage of secret nukes set to fire. As you know, nuclear weapons shouldn't even exist." The announcer looked away from the camera. "But we are believing what the enemy meant for evil, our God will use for good."

A countdown in the bottom corner showed forty-seven seconds. Forty-six. Forty-five. Flashing images of nukes firing into space filled the screen. The announcer tightened his lips.

"Please pray," he plead as the TV showed another nuclear missile headed toward Elysium. "Impact is expected in twenty minutes. Governments are confident this will work and we will be safe, but please—if you can get to an InterCity station, they are taking people to SafeCities now. If you cannot do that, find somewhere underground."

"We have to call Mom and Dad!" Jude said. She looked down as her watch rang. "It's them."

"Put them on hologram," Paul demanded.

A small hologram of their parents' face appeared above Jude's watch.

"Hey, guys." John rubbed his neck and spoke softly. "I'm glad you're together."

Hannah was calm. She explained that Hope was still asleep, and their neighbor, Mr. Stewart, agreed to let Paul and Jude stay in his bunker.

Someone knocked. Paul rushed to open the door. Mr. Stewart wore a flannel shirt half unbuttoned. His unshaven grey whiskers aged him a decade. Paul scanned the sky. Elysium was three times the size it was earlier in the evening.

"Paulie, Mom and Dad want to say bye." Jude wiped a tear and held her watch steady to keep the hologram in place.

"I love you, son." His mother reached a holographic hand toward Paul. You'll be safe with Mr. Stewart."

A lump caught in Paul's throat as he said goodbye. *Is this our final goodbye?* he wondered. A tear in each eye clouded his vision. Yearning to appear strong, Paul refused to blink. The tears stayed in place.

"You're going to be fine, guys." John spoke with manufactured confidence. "Even if the nukes don't work, the chances of that thing hitting us are slim. And even then, it's not like in the movies where it always hits America. Stay with Mr. Stewart and look after one another."

"I've got enough supplies for a month. We'll be fine," replied Mr. Stewart.

Jude disconnected the call and cried openly. Paul rubbed her back and swallowed the lump in his throat. He focused on taking long, slow breaths to push back the tears.

"I'll put the kettle on," Jude said through tears. The British answer to any problem always started with a cup of tea. Jude, being one of the last living people to be born in England, felt it her responsibility to carry on some of these traditions, making her father very proud.

She was born in Manchester just before her parents flew to the US on one of the last flights out. Paul's granddad had appealed to one of his influential friends in Washington to get them on the flight. Days later, the vilest period of the war ensued. Chemical and nuclear warfare didn't just kill most of humanity in Europe. It wiped out almost all things needed to sustain life. The Russian empire acquired most of the spoils of the war. Only scientists ventured into Europe now, and always in full protective clothing. There were rumors of life, but nothing confirmed for eighteen long years.

***

Jude held her hot tea and scooted closer to Paul. It was 1:30 a.m., and all three—Paul, Jude, and Mr. Stewart—were wide awake and glued to the television.

Paul held his mug with both hands, squeezing it rhythmically to release his nerves. The tension was palpable, as the nukes would meet the meteorite any second. Paul thought of all the movies he'd seen where the world was saved at the last minute when the nations of the earth rallied together in a last-ditch attempt to save humanity.

The announcer put a hand to his ear and nodded.

"We're hearing the impact has been successful," he said. "Twenty nukes were sent up, and ten made impact. Praise God! Now, we're waiting for the explosion to clear up to confirm mission accomplished."

Jude let out a spontaneous cheer and jumped into the air.

"That," Mr. Stewart yelled, "that is how the US takes care of business!"

Paul grabbed his sister. The two laughed as the news reporter's expression transformed from joy to horror.

"As reported previously, Elysium received ten direct hits. Two bigger rocks remain, nearly a mile long each, along with thousands of smaller pieces. I'm being told Elysium—none of its pieces—has changed course." Still images of larger and smaller stones popped up on the screen. The off-camera broadcaster continued. "Scientists state Elysium continues toward Earth and now moves at twice the speed. Impact is estimated within ten to fifteen minutes. Experts believe the majority impact will be in the Middle East, but . . ."

"Quick—into the bunker!" Mr. Stewart ordered.

With no time to think and no time to feel, Paul jumped off the couch and started following Jude and Mr. Stewart, who pushed through the front door toward his bunker. Overhead, Elysium grew ever larger.

A swishing sound sped overhead. Paul ducked as a fireball slammed into the house next door. With a deafening explosion, the house burst into flames that engulfed the house instantly and lit up the night sky. Paul froze.

The Clarkes, he thought. *They're dead.*

"Paul!" Jude shouted.

Paul shook his head and chased Jude toward Mr. Stewart's back garden. Distant explosions shook the ground. Enflamed houses began dotting the horizon. *I thought we had ten or fifteen minutes.*

Gasping for air, Mr. Stewart waved Paul and Jude through the bunker entrance. Jude scurried down a spiral staircase that extended three stories belowground. Paul and Mr. Stewart followed. At the bottom, Jude pushed a steel door that entered on a living room. There were couches, a coffee table, and a wall-mounted television. A wide opening showed a small kitchen behind one couch, and multiple doors leading to other rooms and hallways.

"This is your bunker?" Paul took it all in.

Mr. Stewart shouldered the steel door closed. He hurried across the room and turned on the television. The screen was black. He turned it off and rubbed his hands on his pant legs.

"I started building this place over twenty years ago when the war in Europe started. Figured we'd be next. Never expected to use it for an asteroid though." Mr. Stewart smiled wearily. "There are two bedrooms. Jude, you take the one through the door on the left. The one on the right is mine. Paul, you get the couch."

The bunker trembled. Jude screamed and grabbed Paul's wrist. Paul pictured Devan's house.

"Don't you kids worry," Mr. Stewart said. "We're about three or four stories underground. One of the big ones will have to hit us to take us out. That said, if you haven't spoken to Jesus in a while, now may be a good time. I'm heading to bed. Help yourselves to anything you need. Good night."

How can he just leave us like that? Paul wondered. *He didn't even ask if we're okay.*

Jude sat down carefully on an antique green couch. A painting hanging on the wall rattled. Paul placed a hand on Jude's shoulder. She flinched, then turned her bloodshot eyes toward him. Tears ran down her cheeks.

"I don't know what's happening, Paulie." Jude trembled and gasped for air.

Paul put his arms around her. Without saying a word, he helped her stand up and walked her to her designated bedroom. Jude's muscles tensed as she hugged herself and shivered. Paul sat her on the bed in the spare room. Neither wore shoes, and the bottoms of their pajama pants were damp. Paul rubbed his feet rapidly on the carpet to warm them. Rumbles continued overhead.

"Need a drink?" he asked. No answer. "I'll just go get you a drink from the kitchen."

Jude clawed at his arm. "No!" she shouted. "Don't leave me. Please."

"Okay, I won't go anywhere." He sat beside Jude and

125

pulled back the sheet and blanket to her bed, releasing a musty smell. He dusted the sheets with his hand. "How about you lie down and get some sleep?"

Still shivering, Jude made her way under the sheet and blanket. He turned off the light, lay down next to Jude and again clasped her hand. Except for the small night light in the corner of the room, it would have been complete darkness. They hadn't laid next to each other in bed like this since they were kids. *I'll just stay with her until she falls asleep*, Paul decided. But the bed was soft and comfortable, and Paul felt safer being next to Jude though she continued to whimper.

He lay still, eyes open staring into blackness thinking of his family, wondering if asteroids had hit North Carolina. The moment was surreal, like a dream. Had he really been with Finley, sitting round the firepit just hours earlier? The rumbles began to slow down as Jude's sobs finally stopped and her breathing regulated. Paul was warm under the covers, the musty smell no longer bothering him. While most people were running for their lives or watching their houses burn to the ground above him, Paul Lewis drifted to sleep holding his sister's hand in complete safety thirty feet underground.

CHAPTER 12
PAUL

Paul awoke disoriented. The smell of freshly brewed coffee brought back the memory of the Clarkes' house going up in flames. He held a hand with rings on three of five fingers. *I'm in a bunker below the ground,* he told himself. *Jude is lying next to me. Elysium hit us.*

His stomach churned. *Did Mom and Dad make it to a bunker? Was Devan's house in flames?*

No rumblings broke the silence. It was over—for now.

Jude stirred. The nightlight reflected off her bloodshot eyes and tear-stained face. He had to be brave for her. That's what his dad would want.

"It really happened then? I was hoping it was a dream—a nightmare." She scrunched her face and shook her head. "What time is it?" She raised her watch. It was blank. The network was offline.

"Mine's offline too." He shook his wrist. "That's never happened. How long have you been up? Have you spoken to Mr. Stewart?"

"No, I haven't. I heard him getting coffee though." She rolled on her back to face the ceiling. "I'm not sure how long I've been awake. I've kinda been in and out of sleep all night. I think it's the morning though. I really need the bathroom."

Paul poked Jude's belly. She almost smiled but gave a stern look instead as she hopped out of the bed. Mr. Stewart was at the kitchen table, sipping a cup of coffee.

"Good morning, Mr. Stewart," Paul said.

"Morning?" he mused. "It's almost lunchtime. You two hungry?"

Jude held her stomach. "Can I use the bathroom first?"

"Go through that back door, first door on the left."

At Mr. Stewart's suggestion, Paul helped himself to a cup of coffee. He added creamer and two spoonfuls of sugar and sat across from Mr. Stewart, who was absorbed in a book. Paul drank slowly and tried to think of something to say. Mr. Stewart read, unfazed by Paul's presence.

The oddity of Mr. Stewart's silence grated on Paul. *I'm sixteen and desperate for answers*, Paul thought, *and he's just sitting there reading that book. What is his deal?*

By the time Jude returned, Paul was halfway through his coffee and worked up. Jude entered with a skip in her step.

"Can I get some coffee please, Mr. Stewart?" she asked.

"Sure you can, sweetheart." Mr. Stewart looked up from his book. "It's a fresh pot. Creamer's in the fridge, sugar's in the white bowl there."

"Thank you," Jude said pleasantly. "And thanks for getting us last night."

Mr. Stewart nodded and returned to his reading. Jude sat down with her coffee and hummed. *She's acting like Dad,*

Paul thought. *She's either in denial or she just gave herself the world's best pep talk in the bathroom.*

"What's the plan then?" Jude asked, oblivious to Paul's frustration.

Mr. Stewart laid his book on the table and tipped his coffee cup to get the last drop.

"Well," he said, "I'm going to give it a couple more hours before I go up to take a look around and see if the air's breathable. I don't know what it's going to be like, but if I can, I'm going to start helping people."

"How?" Paul snapped.

"I used to know this book inside out, but I'm a little rusty now." Mr. Stewart raised the book so Paul could read the title: *Homeopathy and First Aid.* "I was a doctor in a former life, and it seems like the Lord isn't finished with me healing a few more people."

"Great!" Jude said. "We'll come and—"

"We need to find Mom and Dad!" Paul spat.

Mr. Stewart patted the cover of his book. "I agree—we should find out where your parents are and how they're doing. However, we need to find out what the damage is first." He scratched his belly and yawned. "From what I heard last night, we've been hit by a bunch of smaller asteroids that broke off from the big one when it was nuked. It lasted for around ninety minutes. Somehow, they got hurled to Earth at a faster speed than the scientists expected. Hopefully the big ones missed us."

"And my parents?" Paul asked.

"Everything's going to be . . . fine," Jude said.

"Well, it's sure going to be different," Mr. Stewart said,

"but the Lord's kept us alive, and we'll do the best we can with whatever it's like up there. Hopefully the network will be back up soon and we can get an idea of the destruction."

"Everything isn't going to be okay though, is it?" Paul breathed heavily. "And why did the Lord protect us and not the Clarkes? And they're not the only ones! For all we know, every house in our neighborhood got blown up last night."

Jude focused on Mr. Stewart's finger, as it tapped the table. Paul stood up and glared at them both before storming into the bedroom.

Hannah told him he got his audacity and skepticism from his dad. That he needed to work harder keeping it under control. His dad said it was in their blood. He made fun of the way Americans were swept away by charismatic speakers and the emotional hype they fabricated. "British people would never go for this," he'd say when one of Hudson's speeches was on TV. It had been passed down to Paul.

The night around the firepit seemed so distant, beautiful, harmless. Paul pictured Finley beside him, talking about Elysium as her eyes sparkled in the firelight. *Finley!* he thought. *Where's Finley? Is she dead?*

He left the bedroom and yanked on the metal door leading to the stairs and the world above.

"Where you going?" Mr. Stewart lounged on a couch and pushed back a cuticle. "It could be uninhabitable up there. There's probably a lot dead, and I don't know if your friends and family are part of that."

Paul's chest tightened. He shuffled his feet. His eyes danced around the room, landing everywhere except on Mr. Stewart.

"Sit down, Paul, and listen to an old man for a second."

Paul suddenly felt shame for the way he'd spoken earlier. He should have shown more respect to the man who had saved his life.

"I know what it's like to lose the people closest to you. My twin boys were freshmen in college. They played football, like you. Died in a car crash. My wife went into depression and passed away a few years later." He patted a wall. "God is still good no matter how you feel. If you're alive, he has a purpose for you. Took me seven years to build this bunker. I believed it would save someone one day, and it's going to. But I refuse to let this bunker be the salvation of a boy who gives up hope."

Paul swallowed. He lifted his head and caught Mr. Stewart's eyes. Something stirred in the pit of Paul's stomach. Mr. Stewart's words had almost awakened something inside of him that had been sleeping. But Paul didn't know what. Hearing those words made him believe he had been saved for a purpose.

"Believe me, son, it's going to be real hard for everyone," Mr. Stewart said. "At times you'll be scared and want to act like a little boy and run your mouth off. But believe me, you have been saved for a purpose. So start acting like it."

He focused on his breathing and thought over Mr. Stewart's words. *He's right*, Paul thought. *I can't give up. My family may still be out there. I was saved for a reason.* "Yes, sir."

Mr. Stewart grabbed a pencil and notebook and walked to his bedroom. Alone in the living room, Paul spoke aloud to God for the first time in years.

"God, if you're really there, I'm not sure why you sent an

asteroid to earth, but will you help me do what you saved me for? Even though I do love America, I really don't like church and the empire stuff. Thanks for Mr. Stewart and how he saved me and Jude. Please make sure Mom, Dad, and Hope are okay. Grandma, too, and Finley and Devan. Oh, and Beth, she's Finn's best friend. And God, I really like Finn."

When he opened his eyes, Jude was in front of him with her arms crossed.

"Finley will make a pretty good sister-in-law one day." She giggled and dodged the pillow Paul threw at her. "Hey! Your secret is safe with me."

***

The three of them wore sky blue HAZMAT suites and gas masks. Each had old-fashioned communication systems in their ears. A wire dangled down, connected to a mouthpiece.

Mr. Stewart slowly pushed on the door. Glimmers of daylight lit up the stairwell, and Mr. Stewart stepped outside. Paul and Jude held their breath.

"Looks like it's safe to come out," Mr. Stewart said through the headset.

Paul held an arm out, allowing Jude to go first. Outside, the back of Mr. Stewart's house appeared untouched. Next door, half of the Lewis's house was missing. The other half leaned to the left precariously. Smoke rose from the ashes where Paul's bedroom was before Elysium struck.

In the distance, grey smoke snaked to the sky. Destroyed homes dotted the landscape in every direction. Paul's legs shook. He stumbled. Despair came heavily upon him like he'd strapped on a weighted vest in the gym. His stomach dropped to the ground and left him empty inside. He knew he would never live in his home again.

"You okay over there?" Mr. Stewart held an arm out to help Paul balance. Paul refused. "Okay," Mr. Stewart said, "let's survey the damage. Maybe there's some people who need our help."

Mr. Stewart was the first to move. He locked the bunker door as Paul and Jude stood in place, paralyzed by the scene. When Mr. Stewart walked between the two houses, Paul and Jude followed.

Heat radiated from the smoldering rubble of the Lewis's destroyed home. A foot-wide hole in the middle of the house caught Paul's attention. The others didn't notice, so Paul kept walking. *Safety in numbers*, Paul thought.

When they passed the Clarkes' home, Paul sprinted away.

"Where are you going?" Jude shouted into the communication system.

"I need to check Devan's house."

Paul ran as fast as he could in his protective clothing, but his heavy boots made for slow progress. He ran past an unfamiliar family loading their car with luggage. *If they made it, there will be others*. Paul picked up his pace. *Devan's going to be okay.*

He dodged a series of small craters in the road and stopped dead in his tracks. Devan's house was gone. The only remaining piece was the mailbox that read Jones. Paul lifted his booted foot and kicked the mailbox as hard as he could. He fell to his knees on the broken driveway. Fear gave way to sadness, then a wave of optimism.

Their car isn't here! Paul realized. *They got out. Devan is okay.*

Jude's voice broke into Paul's headset. "Paul, can you hear me?"

"I'm at Devan's house."

"How is it?"

A car crept by. The unfamiliar family looked at Paul. A grave-looking man drove a confused looking woman and a small girl. The adults showed no emotion, but the girl waved from the backseat. Paul raised a hand and smiled.

The car slowly swerved in, out, and around craters. As they rambled away, the earth shook beneath Paul. It was an earthquake, but his focus turned to the loud crunching sound coming from the car that had just passed him. Without warning, the car lifted off the ground. Paul blinked and questioned what he was seeing as the car levitated higher than a leaning power pole. It wobbled, leaned left, smashed against the ground, and bounced back onto its wheels.

Behind the car, a rock the size of a coffee table rose into the sky.

Paul screamed for help. "A family's hurt!" he cried.

Jude replied that they were coming. In the meantime, more rocks—asteroids from Elysium—came up from the ground and floated into the sky. It reminded Paul of a hot air balloon festival in New Mexico, but these weren't hot air balloons.

Some asteroids were as small as golf balls. The biggest was the size of a small truck. Countless others were in between. Rising from crumbled houses and craters, thousands of Elysium fragments ascended to the sky.

Paul followed the floating rocks into the sky. They littered the skyline like a million small, brown hot air balloons.

Jude and Mr. Stewart arrived and ran to the car. The driver stumbled out, blood pouring down his face. Paul scurried to help.

Moments later, the family sat on the side of the road as Mr. Stewart administered homeopathy and bandaged their wounds. Paul fetched water and Jude helped disinfect scrapes and cuts.

"Thank you," the driver said. "I hit my head pretty hard. I'm seeing a bunch of blurry things in the sky."

His daughter shielded her eyes and peeked at the sky. "I see them too, Daddy."

Thousands of small rocks hung 200 feet overhead. The rocks kept their distance from one another, suspended in midair like a huge asteroid belt.

"Do you think they'll stay up there or fall back down?" the woman asked.

"No idea," Mr. Stewart replied, "but I think they're moving."

Paul focused on a small cluster of rocks. Mr. Stewart was right. The rocks moved slowly, like clouds. Paul was exhausted and sweaty. His HAZMAT suite stuck to his body. He tapped Mr. Stewart and pointed at the family on the ground.

"Is it safe to take this off now?" he asked.

CHAPTER 13
FINLEY

❦

Why did you have to come pick me up?"

Finley fumed. Another evening ruined by her mother.

"Finn!" Denise said, while backing the car out the driveway. "We've been kicked out again."

"What?" Some of the edge fell off of Finley's voice. "Why didn't we get notice?"

"They gave us notice three months ago."

Finley caught the sharp whiff of whiskey as her mother put the car in drive.

"For God's sake, Mom! Are you drinking and driving?"

Last time this happened, Finley was put into foster care for six months. For six months, Finley listened as they quoted Bible verses and Lee's manifesto. She tolerated their incessant talk about the US empire and their duty to serve within it. During those months, Finley was forced to go to church. The people there encouraged her to serve God and country, insisting she didn't have to turn out like her mother.

One group openly prayed that Finley's foster family would get legal custody. Finley cringed.

When Denise got out of rehab, Finley vowed to never go back into foster care. That meant stopping her mother from driving during her drinking benders.

"I'm not over the limit yet, Finn."

"Pull over or I'll—"

The car slowed to a stop. Denise switched seats with Finley and took another sip out of her coffee cup.

"Denise Matthews," announced her watch. "Blood alcohol level is point zero eight. It is now illegal for you to drive. We strongly encourage you to refrain from drinking anymore this evening."

"That jerk left me."

"Jerk?" Finley resisted the urge to floor it. "I didn't even know you were seeing someone."

Her mom shrugged and held her coffee mug up to her lips. "Brian."

"Your boss?" Finley chewed on a fingernail. "Wait—all the promotions, the new car—it's all because of . . . Do we have to give the car back?"

"Brian said I can keep it."

"Well, we're gonna need it since we just lost our apartment."

"So long as I don't tell his wife."

"He's married?" Finley's heart sank. Her mother was such an embarrassment. Sleeping with another woman's husband again. She hated her life sometimes, but there were logistics to deal with right now. "What about our stuff?"

Her mom pointed to the backseat. "I packed your

suitcase. Everything else we had was on credit. Brian promised he would pay off our debt once he left his wife." She cried softly. "But he decided to stay with her."

Finley drove slowly, not knowing where to go. She refused to cry. *I can't go to Beth's— not tonight at least. Maybe her family will be feeling better tomorrow.* She maneuvered around a piece of tire in the middle of her lane. *Chase is out for the night, but I couldn't take Mom to see his family. What a way to meet your boyfriends' parents. "Hey, I'm Finley, and this is my mother, the drunk."*

Flashing blue lights in the rearview mirror interrupted Finley's thoughts. Finley placed her hands on her lap as the authorities took control of their car through the network. She sighed as her car pulled to the side of the road. The driver's window lowered itself as the policeman approached.

"Denise and Finley Matthews?" he asked.

"Yes, sir," Finley replied.

Denise leaned over Finley's lap. "Hey Robert," she said. "Good to see you again."

"Hey, Denise." Disappointment spread across the officer's face. "Can you confirm you've been the passenger for the last fifteen minutes?"

"Sure have. I had a little too much, so I had Finley drive. We're celebrating new beginnings." She winked at the officer. "What time you get off, Robert? You can join us if you want!"

Finley choked down her gag reflex.

"No, thank you. I want to get home to my wife and kids." The officer viewed his watch screen and tapped the roof of the car. "This is registered to a Brian Petersen. Why are you driving it?"

"Brian was my boss. He gave it to me as a parting gift for a job well done."

The officer shifted from one foot to the other. A call came across the CB radio clipped to his shoulder. "Give me a moment," he said. "Let me give Mr. Petersen a call."

Finley turned to her mom and raised her hands in surrender.

"Don't worry, honey." Her mom dabbed her lips with a napkin. "Brian will tell him the same story, and Robert will probably register the car over to my name. It'll save me the job."

Finley rolled her eyes. As her mom suspected, the officer updated the registration for her.

"Thank you, Robert." Denise touched her watch to accept the registration. "Now to Charlotte, North Carolina and new beginnings."

Finley bit her tongue until the officer was back in his patrol car. Three beeps indicated that she had control over the vehicle again. She shifted to drive.

"What the hell, Mom! What do you mean we're going to Charlotte?" She took two deep breaths and eased off the gas. "I'm not staying with Aunt Brooke again. I've got school tomorrow!"

"You have to drive me there tonight, sweetie. They're expecting us." Denise rolled her window down and weaved her hand up and down in the wind. "Where else are we going to stay? And . . . Brian asked me to leave town."

"There's no way I'm transferring schools." Finley pulled over. The car's gentle hum was the only sound. "It's too late anyway. We can't drive five hours—not this late at night."

Denise put a finger on her head. "I'll tell you what," she said with a smile. "Drive me to Charlotte tonight and keep the car the rest of the semester. Drive it to Atlanta tomorrow, stay with Beth, and finish up the year. By Christmas, everything will be fine, and we'll figure something out."

Finley bit her lip. *Life with Beth could be fun.* "What if her family isn't okay with it?"

"They will be. And even if they're not, you can ask another friend from the soccer team. I'm sure one of them will give you a place to stay. Tell them I got a new job in Charlotte."

Do other parents ask their kids to lie for them?

"Besides, there's no point in hanging around here. I don't have the credit for a hotel."

Finley looked sideways at her mother. *She always has a plan when things go wrong*, Finley thought. *If only she used her good looks and cunning for good instead of drowning her sorrows with a bottle. Not my battle though. And the car . . .*

"Okay," Finley said with finality. "But first—coffee."

***

Her mom began the same talk Finley had heard a thousand times over. How she was going to change and get her life back on track, how great of a daughter Finley was, and how hard they'd had it after Finley's father left. Finley didn't have the patience tonight, so she made the excuse that listening to music would help her stay awake. She turned on the radio, and her mom fell asleep within minutes.

"Why are you such a mess?" she whispered to her sleeping passenger.

Both their watches beeped simultaneously. The dashboard screen lit up at the same time, indicating a government announcement. Finley swiped the announcement away. She did the same thing ten minutes later.

Finley squirmed in her seat. Her large coffee was long gone. She pulled off the Greenville exit to hunt for a bathroom. A new train station for the Streamline rail system appeared inviting. Lights reflected off the tracks as Finley pulled into the empty parking lot.

Finley rushed to the front entrance, leaving her sleeping mother behind. The lobby doubled as the reception area for a hotel, but it was completely empty. There wasn't even a worker at the front desk. She spotted the restrooms in the back corner.

Relieved and ready to get back on the road, Finley noticed a man now at the front desk.

"You got here fast, honey," he said pleasantly.

"What do you mean?"

"You're here to be first in line to get on the Streamline to the SafeCity, right?" He rubbed his elbow. "I don't think we'll get one stopping here tonight though."

"I just needed the bathroom. Me and my mom are heading to Charlotte. She's in the car, and we're—"

The man walked around the counter. He kept his eyes trained on Finley. Finley withered at his gaze.

"You don't know, do you?"

Finley shrugged. "Know what?"

"Any minute, there will be thousands of people trying to get a room in this hotel and a place on the next train outta here." He wiped his brow. "Elysium is heading for us."

Finley waited for the man to laugh. He just stared at her.

"It's all over the news." He pressed his watch. Nothing happened.

Finley's watch was also blank. Behind her, another man burst into the lobby, shaking a bunch of papers in the air.

"The network's down!" he shouted. "We've got to register people with pen and paper. I don't even know if we'll have enough, and there's no way we can check credit scores. It'll be first come, first served."

Finley hadn't moved since the second man ran into the room.

"Looks like you're first in line." The first man waltzed back behind the counter. "Perfect timing for a bathroom stop, wouldn't you say? Better get your mother."

Without thinking, she ran outside into the parking lot to get her mom. Finley's heart beat hard as people flooded the station. Some drove, others rode bicycles, and even more ran on foot. They carried and dragged luggage and held children in their arms. Many wore pajamas. All looked frightened.

Finley hammered on the car window. She flung open the door and shook her mom frantically.

"Get up!" she yelled. "Get up!"

Finley yanked the bags from the back seat and supported her mom as they made their way back into the lobby. The smell of whiskey lingered on Denise as the two of them followed the throngs of people into the station entrance.

A woman began screaming at a man who bumped into her.

"Watch out! I'm carrying a baby here and trying to hold onto my four-year-old."

"Sorry, ma'am," he replied "Someone else pushed me."

The two receptionists tried to get the crowd under control, but it was all too much. The once-empty lobby was now packed and pulsing with terror. At the front counter, Finley signed for a room, explaining that her mother wasn't feeling well. She was so glad they weren't scanning watches, because they would never have been accepted with her mom's current credit score.

"Room 613, building C," said the first man she met earlier. "Head straight there. The door will be open. Lock it behind you as soon as you get in."

Finley draped her mom's arm around her neck as a team of Freedom Fighters entered. The crowd grew more frantic for a moment, but the sight of the new EN-99s settled them down. In the parking lot, an FF barked at two citizens who were fighting for a better place in line.

Finley exited the rear lobby doors to the station platform. Four uninviting, identical, adjacent concrete buildings ran on either side of the track, which ran through the center of the complex. Each building was six stories high with identical black doors evenly placed. A set of exterior stairs ran up the sides.

The Streamline rail system was developed to connect the empire like never before. Hovering trains moved up to 250 miles per hour and never touched the track. Even though the train system embodied the best in modern magnetic technology, the hotel was lackluster at best. The government rushed the job in case another empire attacked and the SafeCities couldn't house everybody. This was the hotel's first night at capacity.

Finley led her mother to one bed and dropped her bags on the other. She rushed to lock the door behind them as a voice came over the loudspeaker. All rooms were occupied. No one else could check in.

The boring grey room smelled of disinfectant. Two twin beds with maroon bed sheets lined one wall. On the opposite wall was a modest desk and chair. A door at the back of the room led to a bathroom.

Finley sat at the edge of her bed, holding her head in her hands. It felt like only five minutes had passed since she pulled off to use the bathroom. If driving her mom to Charlotte wasn't enough of a shock, now Elysium was heading toward the earth. She took a deep breath as her mom lay down on the bed.

"Should we leave?" her mom asked.

Finley shook her head.

Her mother sat up, caught her balance, and went toward the door.

"I just want to see what's going on," she said.

Finley held her head as her mother opened the hotel door and disappeared into the corridor. When Finley joined her, her mother leaned over the railing, looking up. Others were doing the same. Hundreds crowded the railings like fans at a sporting event.

Elysium had changed. When Finley last saw it with Paul, it shone the same bright white light. But it was much bigger now, and there wasn't a single rock. There were two of them, surrounded by thousands of smaller specks of light.

The man's voice returned over the loudspeaker, encouraging everyone to return to their rooms. "You may choose to leave if you wish, but you cannot return if you leave. Elysium is estimated to make impact in twenty minutes." As if an afterthought, the man continued: "Join us as we pray for protection and that God would use this to smite our enemies. More information will follow. God bless you all."

FF soldiers paced each terrace, commanding compliance. Within minutes, the corridor cleared. Finley collapsed on her bed. Her mother stared at the wall, her make-up smudged from crying.

"I love you, sweetie."

"I love you too, Mom." The words rang hollow. Finley worried her mother would notice.

"I know it's been hard on you having me as a mom, but I've—"

Finley waved her off.

"It must have been hard raising me alone." *Please don't apologize that I never had a father.* Finley wanted to hide and avoid her mother's oft-repeated lines.

Instead of recalling past hurts and making false promises, Denise got up and hugged her. Finley hugged back. She longed for the feeling of a mother's embrace. But Finley felt like she was hugging a friend from school who was having a bad day.

"We'll be okay, Mom. Really, we will. You should try to get some sleep."

"I'll try." Her mother held her daughter out to get a better look. She wiped a tear. "It's not like we can do anything else. Besides, if Elysium hits us, dying in my sleep isn't a bad way to go."

145

Finley nodded.

"And—" her mom hesitated. "If you want, we can . . ."

"What is it, Mom?"

"You don't have to," Denise said, "but I think we should
. . . pray."

Finley cocked an eyebrow in question.

"Well, I'd rather face death trying to be right with God,
and . . . and . . ."

"Go ahead, Mom."

Finley bowed her head and closed her eyes as her mom
knelt beside the bed.

"God," her mom started, "I know I've made a lot of bad
decisions, but you see my heart and you know I love hard.
And like that man said on the loudspeaker, we pray that you
will save us and rain snares upon the wicked. Use this—um,
use this meteor thing to bring judgment on the evil empires
of the world."

Does Mom really believe that? Finley cringed. Her mother
finished her prayer. Finley's thoughts immediately went
elsewhere. *I should have kissed Paul.*

With that, she went to the bathroom to get ready for
bed. When she came out, her mom was fast asleep. A bottle
of sleeping pills was open on the bed.

"What the hell!" Finley shouted. She picked up the bottle
and read the label. "Mom, you were hooked on these years
ago. What are you doing!"

Finley watched her sleeping peacefully without a single
care in the world. It wasn't fair she could escape from the
reality she hated. She wasn't worried about being a good
mom, losing her job, the end of the world. Nothing. A small

146

voice whispered in Finley's mind: *Take one.*

"Might as well sleep good if I have to spend my last night on earth stuck in here with you." Finley couldn't believe the words coming out of her mouth. *No, I can't. I can't end up like her.* Finley pictured herself ten years from now, a drunken mess without any job or family. *But why should I stay up all night afraid, crying and all alone while you get to sleep?*

She picked up the bottle and took a closer look. The instructions recommended two tablets. She poured four into her hand. Without giving herself time to change her mind, she threw them into her mouth and swallowed them all in one go.

"Thanks, Mom!"

She kicked off her shoes, took off her bra from under her shirt, threw it on the floor, and climbed under the covers to dream of running away with Paul Lewis.

***

Finley's mouth was dry. Light shone through the window. They hadn't been hit—yet. Denise wasn't in her bed. The network was still down.

Stepping onto the terrace, Finley was met with the sounds of hustle and bustle. Below her on the station platforms, hundreds of people elbowed past one another. Finley scanned the crowd for her mother.

Behind the opposite building, hills covered with trees displayed dazzling fall color. Finley's heart warmed at the bright reds, sunshine yellows, and pumpkin oranges. Bathed in thankfulness, Finley lost herself in Mother Nature's beauty.

Not five minutes had passed before her moment of tranquility was ruined by Denise's voice,

"Good afternoon, baby." Denise held out her arms. She held two drink cups and a bag of food. "You slept a long time, so I got us some coffee and lunch. Looks like we'll be safe here. We missed the worst of it."

Inside the sterile hotel room, Denise chatted away as though yesterday never happened. She mentioned that part of America had been hit, but she saw this as an opportunity for a fresh start. Finley sipped her coffee as the room began shaking. She held her cup away from her mouth as a little spilled on her blouse.

Denise ran outside and shrieked. In the distance, it appeared that an enormous brown bouncy house was inflating before their eyes. Gasps and screams arose from the platform below as the hill in front of them doubled in size. The beautiful trees catapulted from the ground and toppled down the hill. Birds cried and flew out of formation as a triangular mountain formed.

A cataclysmic boom echoed from the mountain as rocks sailed through the air, some landing mere feet away. Buildings went up in flames and smashed into the ground.

Screams echoed through the air as the masses scurried in all directions on the station platform. A rock smashed through the building opposite Finley. It broke through with a chilling explosion.

Finley struggled to take in the scene. Clarity came with one word.

"Volcano!"

A volcano in the middle of Greenville blasted rocks from

within, scattering them all over the city. Denise grabbed Finley's hand in anticipation of another eruption that never came. Fire crackled and hissed from buildings nearby.

Finley ran to the end of the terrace and peered at the parking lot. The frenzied crowd scrambled to get into the station. FF soldiers pointed their guns in a bid for calm.

"Back down," yelled one soldier, "or I'll shoot!"

A man scaled the fence and rushed the soldiers. A green flash struck the man. He fell to the ground, unconscious.

"Everybody calm down!" yelled the soldier who shot the man. "We have orders to shoot anyone who doesn't comply."

Another man climbed the fence. A green laser put him on the ground.

"They're killing them!" a woman from the crowd screamed.

"He's just stunned," the soldier said. "He'll be fine."

More FF flooded the parking lot. The loudspeaker squealed over the commotion.

"If you are registered in the hotel, please return to your rooms. The first Streamline will be here within the hour. Those who have a ticket will be informed of its arrival."

Finley and Denise stayed in their room waiting anxiously, hoping there wasn't another eruption. There wasn't, but the Streamline didn't come either. Nor did the network come back on. Finally, Denise was allowed to fetch food from the station platform. Waiting in her room, all alone in the silence felt like an eternity. Even though her mom was a mess, Finley longed for her to be close rather than be alone.

Thirty minutes passed before Denise came back with tuna sandwiches, chips, coffee, and water. On a normal day Finley would have skipped a meal like this, but she was famished. She hated tuna. Denise had worked at a grocery store after getting out of rehab and always came home at the end of the week with overstocked tuna.

Sometime in the evening the first train arrived. People piled on board, and then it was gone.

"Must be important people to get on the first train," Finley said.

Her mother took a bite of her tuna sandwich. Outside of their window, an FF soldier fired at civilians on the station platform.

"All civilians to your rooms," he yelled, "or you will be treated as rebels!"

Finley finished her tuna sandwich in silence. Her mother began shaking. She was jittery and talked nonstop. Finley had seen her mother go through withdrawal before—too often to worry.

It won't last forever, Finley told herself. Two hours later, she wondered if she was wrong. Her mother shivered in bed under the covers. Finley's nerves were wearing thin. She rammed five sleeping pills down her mother's throat and forced her to drink. It only took a few moments for the shivering to stop. Her mother passed out, and Finley began crying hysterically.

"I hate you sometimes!" she screamed over tears. The hysterics slowly became sobs, which became a whimper, and then finally, she was left without any more tears to cry. Alone in the silence wishing she had someone to hold her, Finley began to take deep breaths to pull herself back together.

Finley felt a familiar sensation on her wrist. Her watch

buzzed for the first time all day. The screen read *Finley Matthews—D*. She tapped the screen, but nothing changed. She couldn't access her contacts or apps. She pulled her mom's limp wrist from under the covers. It was blank except the words *Denise Matthews—D*.

CHAPTER 14
FINLEY

I f you are awake, please turn on your television."

Obeying the voice on the loudspeaker, Finley clicked the remote control. A holographic screen spread across the opposite wall.

A male and female news anchor appeared on the screen, and a small picture in the top right corner showed a destroyed city. *New York City—Obliterated.* A similar picture replaced it. *San Francisco—Gone.* Finley doubled over in pain at the next image. *Atlanta—Destroyed.*

Another destroyed city appeared every few seconds as the news anchors droned on. New York, LA, San Francisco, Atlanta, Charlotte—all devastated. A scream built in Finley's throat but wouldn't escape. Her throat seized up as tears poured from her eyes.

Atlanta's destroyed! she thought. *Beth's gone. Paul and Chase are gone. My school, my friends, my home—all gone.*

Her mother snored as a world map took center screen. Two red dots marked *Points of Major Impact.* They hovered over the empire of Persia, just below Baghdad, and the Atlantic Ocean, east of Brazil. The news anchors explained that Elysium was hit by multiple nuclear weapons. The impact broke Elysium into two smaller rocks and dispersed millions of smaller pieces that remained on course to impact Earth. Scientists asserted that the only explanation was that the space rock was attracted to Earth's magnetic pull. Impact was and always had been inevitable.

One of the larger rocks devastated the Persian empire. The other started a tidal wave heading for the Southeastern cost of America. Experts expected severe damage. Millions of smaller rocks caused damage across the world but left survivors.

Researchers couldn't identify the elements contained within the rocks. And now, the asteroids were lifting off the ground and levitating, covering the sky.

Scientists dubbed them the Janus rings after those that circled Saturn. The North Janus Ring covered the original United States, North Africa, and China. The South Janus Ring hung over parts of South America, South Africa, and Australia. A CG image on the news showed the two equidistant, circular rock formations moving opposite ways around the globe.

A scientist explained that this phenomenon rendered air travel impossible as metal was attracted to the rocks, which traveled at approximately forty miles per hour. The scientist feared missiles would be pulled toward the meteorites. Other areas around the world were experiencing the same bizarre weather conditions, with sink holes and volcanoes cropping up unannounced.

"There are survivors in Atlanta," reported a pale news anchor.

Finley felt a ray of hope. A male news anchor interrupted the broadcast.

"Excuse me, Michelle, we've got breaking news." Images of Atlanta disappeared, and the reporter took up the entire hologram. "I'm being told that LA and San Francisco were attacked by missiles. We have no confirmation of other cities being under attack, but I am hearing that these two cities suffered missile attacks from foreign enemies. We are unsure who launched the missiles, and no empire is taking responsibility."

The screen flashed to a commercial promoting Freedom Fighters and the new EN-99. President Hudson's voice narrated, praising America with patriotic music in the background and young FF soldiers marching in line, EN-99s in hand. The final clip showed Hudson speaking directly to the camera, calling all Americans to fight the evils in this world.

Finley rushed to the bathroom. She flipped open the toilet lid just before throwing up. A hologram of an auburn-haired FF soldier with brown eyes was on the news as Finley wiped her mouth. The soldier stood confidently in front of the Oklahoma SafeCity.

"Earlier today, certain measures were taken for the good of the empire." A chart appeared beside the soldier. "By now, you should have received a message on your watch that included your name and one of four categories. As and Bs, please make your way immediately to a StreamLine station. There, you will be taken to your closest SafeCity. Cs—you are scheduled to come next. We will alert you when it is time to come to the station."

Perfect, Finley thought. *Our safety is based on credit score.* She burned with anger and then collapsed in despair.

Finley wept.

She sat on her bed crossed legged, head in hands, as tears poured from her eyes until she had no more tears left. Her mom never stirred. Finley wondered if there was anyone left in the world who cared about her.

An aggressive knock from a few doors down yanked her from hopelessness.

"Open up!"

Except for the station lights, it was dark outside.

"I'm here to scan your watches," the soldier announced.

She looked out the window to see FF soldiers in the distance working to recover trapped people from a crumbled building. More FF soldiers pounded on nearby doors.

"Category A," one soldier announced to a neighboring family. "Is everyone in here the same?"

Finley tiptoed from the door without opening it. She shook her mother violently, but it was no use. The sleeping pills were working too well.

"Open up!" the soldier repeated.

Finley turned the handle and peered through the crack. A tall, dark soldier held an EN-99. His eyes betrayed no emotion.

"Hello, sir."

"I need to scan your watch, ma'am."

Finley held out her arm. The soldier swiped a device over Finley's. He frowned.

"I'm afraid you're going to have to leave the station in the morning. Anyone else in the room?"

Finley opened the door wide.

"I need to scan hers as well, please."

"She took some sleeping pills," Finley said. "I'm having a hard time waking her up."

The soldier moved silently past Finley and patted her mom on the shoulder.

"Excuse me, ma'am. My name is Francis Simpson. I'm serving in the empire's FF." He spoke automatically, as if reciting his lines. "You have to wake up so I can give you some information."

Denise didn't move. The soldier scanned her watch and nodded grimly.

"You both leave in the morning. We're making room tonight for people in categories A and B."

When he turned to leave, Finley grabbed at his hand. He froze. Finley yanked her hand away and felt her face flush.

"Why?" she gasped. "Why am I in D? Why can't I go to the SafeCity?"

The soldier's stone face softened. His eyes revealed sorrow. He placed a hand on Finley's shoulder.

"There is limited room at the SafeCities. Is your mother a good citizen?"

"It's not my fault!" Finley shook her head. "I'm seventeen, and my mother's a drunk. Why do I have to suffer because of her?"

"Stay in your room tomorrow," the soldier said, ignoring the question. "If anyone tells you to leave, tell them to find me. I'll do what I can."

156

He turned to leave. With one hand on the door handle, he paused. "Finley, my name is Francis. Can I pray for you quickly?" he asked.

Finley closed her eyes.

"Jesus, there are thousands of people like Finley. Please help me do right by you and make a way for her."

The soldier left without another word.

Any momentary peace she felt from Francis's prayer vanished when she turned to see her mom asleep on the bed. Finley tried to wake her. A prod at first, then a strong push, but within seconds she was shaking her violently. She became exasperated and slapped her mother on the arm.

"Wake up!" Finley screamed. "You're so selfish."

Finley punched her as hard as she could on the arm. It hurt her knuckles from where she'd hit Paul just yesterday. Noticing the sleeping pills beside the bed, Finley remembered the undisturbed sleep she'd enjoyed the previous night.

I should take some. I'll forget everything, she thought, *at least for tonight.*

"No!" she screamed out loud. "I won't end up like you."

The temptation mounted as she stared at the bottle. Impulsively picking up the pills, she rushed into the bathroom and flushed them down the toilet. *We've got nowhere to go. Who's gonna help us? Category D, and it's all her fault. I should have taken the pills. I'm never gonna sleep now. You'll end up like her sooner or later one way or another.*

"Shut up!" Finley yelled to the voices in her mind.

Her stomach started to knot up and she felt sick. Just seconds later she threw up into the toilet again. After rinsing her mouth out in the sink, she went back to bed and turned on the TV for more updates. The same two news anchors were still talking.

"Due to the enormous loss of life in major cities across our great empire, we are now inviting all category C citizens into the SafeCities. Please make your way to the nearest station. For those who do not live close to a station or whose nearest station has been destroyed, there will be pick-up locations identified on your watches."

Finley, emotionally exhausted, unexpectedly fell asleep as the news anchors continued talking.

When she awoke, the two news anchors were giving new updates. They were a bit disheveled, and bags were under their eyes. It was nine thirty in the morning, and Denise wasn't in the room. Finley's belly growled.

Broadcasters confirmed the destruction of the Persian empire. Finley spat as the reporters celebrated and thanked God. A government commercial promoted adhering to new procedures and reminded viewers that the USW was attacked, but no empire took responsibility. For the first time, talking heads referred to the empire as the United States of the World and not just North America. The ad ended with a reminder of the pick-up schedule.

"All civilians in categories A through C, make your way to a station or pick-up point." Finley hung her head. "And do not, under any circumstance, associate with Ds."

Finley sank at the news. *They can't even talk to us?*

She was on her feet, steaming, when her mother burst through the door with breakfast.

"Good morning, sweetie!" She handed Finley her food and set their coffees on a small bedside table.

"Mom, we need to get ready to go." Finley took a swig of her coffee. "We have to leave at eleven."

"Don't worry. We can stay here as long as we need."

"Why would you think that?" Finley eyed her mom suspiciously. "An FF soldier told me last night that we had to leave after the eleven o'clock train."

Her mother busied herself with breakfast, unwrapping Finley's muffin and placing it carefully on a napkin. "Don't you worry about us, sweetie. We'll just stay up here today while people are coming and going, boarding the trains. The general doesn't want you wandering around." She winked at Finley playfully.

Finley drank her coffee and picked at her muffin while her mother talked about the latest news. Rioting and looting had broken out in the city, and reinforcements were arriving on the next train. She encouraged Finley that the FF soldiers were handling it, and she shouldn't worry.

"Did you speak to Francis?" Finley asked. "Is that why we can stay?"

"I don't know any Francis," her mother said, beaming. "Let's just say your mama's still got it."

Finley stared at her mother in disbelief. Her mother swallowed hard. The joy turned to shame.

"I'll be away today," she said slowly. "I'll be spending time with the general and his men this afternoon."

She avoided eye contact with Finley and stared at her hands, which searched for something to do.

"Don't look at me like that, sweetie. We'd be on the streets otherwise. I don't like it any more than you, but it's the only way."

"This general must be a good church-going citizen. So kind of him to help us out." Finley snarled sarcastically. "I need to take a shower."

She walked into the bathroom angrily, slamming the door behind her.

CHAPTER 15
PAUL

⤳

ategory C! What's it even mean?"

"I'm C, too," confirmed Jude.

"A, here," said Mr. Stewart. "Not sure what is means, but if the network is back up, then maybe the TV works again."

As Mr. Stewart hunted for the remote control, Jude swiped and pressed her watch.

"It won't let me call Steve or Mom and Dad." Jude slapped her watch and crossed her arms. "None of my contacts are even on my watch!"

Jude, Paul, and Mr. Stewart ate cold sandwiches and drank milk in Mr. Stewart's house. Like the bunker, the Stewart home was solar powered and a generator was hooked up, just in case. The television flickered on.

"Are any other channels working?" Jude groaned.

Mr. Stewart clicked through the stations, but ANN—American News Network—was the only functioning channel.

It was like watching a movie. Entire empires and cities destroyed by Elysium, missile attacks on American soil, volcanoes, and the Janus rings now hovering in the air solidified that nothing would ever be the same again. They sat in silence, glued to the screen in awe of the images. Each of them realized how lucky they were to still be alive.

Survivors from Florida and Georgia and North and South Carolina attempted to leave before the tidal wave arrived. The lucky ones in Category A were already on a StreamLine, headed to safety.

Mr. Stewart offered Paul and Jude ice cream after dinner. Jude refused. Paul couldn't say no. It was chocolate flavor, his favorite.

"I can't believe we have to get to a SafeCity to reconnect our watches for communication." Jude scowled. "Of all the dirty tricks!"

"How will we find Mom and Dad?" Paul asked.

"We'll have to go to the Greenville station," Jude said. "The Atlanta one's destroyed. What about you, Mr. Stewart?"

"There will be lots of hurting people," he said. "I'm going to stay here and help them."

"Come with us," suggested Jude. "We won't be able to contact you."

"I know," Mr. Stewart said. "They killed the network to keep members of the rebellion from communicating. I'd 'a done the same thing."

"Mr. Stewart, how can you think the government is good?" Paul asked.

"I don't think everyone in the government is good. But," Mr. Stewart said, "I believe God has called America to bring true Christian freedom and democracy to the world. God uses good people and bad to bring about his will. In the end, truth will cover the earth regardless of how many empires believe it. And I'll sit in judgment one day for who I choose to support."

Paul wondered how his dad would respond to Mr. Stewart's comments.

"You look tired, Paul." Mr. Stewart took Paul's empty ice cream dish to the kitchen. "Let's head back to the bunker."

In the night sky, broken rocks of Elysium loomed like rulers of Earth.

Jude only cried for a few minutes as they lay next to each other in bed for the second night. When the crying ceased and her breathing grew heavy, Paul slipped his hand out of hers. He rolled out of bed slowly and walked through the dark into the kitchen.

The gentle hum of the refrigerator seemed so loud in the silent bunker, keeping Paul from thinking. He walked to the top of the stairs in search of silence. He stepped outside into the cold darkness and rubbed his arms.

The North Janus Ring threatened Paul and Earth's other remaining survivors. Paul struggled to focus. The news, the rumors, the events—he wished it would all just go away. He dreamed of a simple life, preparing for Friday's state championship.

"I guess that dream's over," he said out loud to the formations in the sky.

He pressed his back to the bunker door. Certain no one could see him, Paul allowed himself to cry. There were only a few tears and some sniffles at first. But as he thought of family and friends who likely died, the tears came fast and furious, splashing on the ground.

Paul's destroyed home was barely visible through the tears. But something moved in Mr. Stewart's house. Paul wiped his tears furiously. Someone was inside the Stewart home. Whoever it was shattered a piece of glass. Paul held his breath, then relaxed.

Someone was probably hungry, he thought. *No need to be a hero.*

He crept back into the bunker and triple checked every lock. He fell asleep holding Jude's hand, hoping he'd done the right thing.

***

It was settled. Jude and Paul would head to Greenville. But first, they had to join Mr. Stewart to see if his house was clear of last night's intruder. He also had supplies to give them for the trip, and he promised a surprise. At the top of the bunker stairs, Mr. Stewart opened a small door and removed three silver pistols. He handed one to Paul and one to Jude and kept the third.

"Have you ever fired a gun before?" Mr. Stewart asked.

Paul and Jude shook their heads.

"I would prefer you not use them, but there may be a time you need to." He faced the bunker door. "Hold it like this—with two hands out in front of you, elbows locked."

Paul mimicked Mr. Stewart and smirked.

"Mom and Dad don't like guns," said Jude.

"That's because we don't have a good enough credit score

to have them." Paul focused on the white dot at the end of the gun's short barrel.

Mr. Stewart lowered Paul's gun with one hand. "Never point that at anything you're not willing to kill—understand?"

Paul nodded nervously.

"Now," he continued, "you take the safety off like this." Mr. Stewart flicked a button with his thumb. Paul and Jude did the same as Mr. Stewart took a deep breath, unlocked the bunker door, and stepped outside, holding his pistol in front of him.

It was colder outside than yesterday. The smell of smoke hung in the air. Mr. Stewart's house appeared empty.

"It's freezing!" Jude said.

Mr. Stewart shushed her with a finger to his lips. "Come on," he whispered, "let's go look around the house. Pistols up."

They edged toward the house like a SWAT team. Paul's body tensed. The backdoor was unlocked and creaked loudly as Mr. Stewart pushed it open. The lights were on, and broken glass covered the floor. Jude's hands shook as she held her gun in front of her.

"Jude," Mr. Stewart said, "stay here while we go look upstairs."

Jude nodded with wide, fearful eyes.

Paul and Mr. Stewart took measured steps through the living room, images of masked gunmen flashing through Paul's mind. But no one was there. The dining room and the study were the same. Empty.

Climbing the stairs, Paul brushed against pictures of the Stewarts. Mr. Stewart grinned carelessly, standing beside his beautiful, put-together wife and their two boys.

Inside the master bedroom first, Paul's heart stopped. Someone was asleep under the bed covers. The sheets moved slightly, but Paul couldn't make out who or how many people were in there. Mr. Stewart motioned Paul to the opposite side of the bed. He moved cautiously to surround whomever shifted under the covers.

Am I ready to pull the trigger? Paul's breathing sped up as he pointed his pistol at the heap under the covers.

Mr. Stewart pulled back the covers. Paul dropped his gun to his side. A small child was curled up in a ball, fast asleep in pajamas and coated in dirt. He had scratches and bruises all over his face. Paul recognized him. It was Owen, the smallest of the group of neighbors Paul had played football with last Friday night.

Paul choked back tears. *Owen is alone*, he realized. *His parents didn't make it.*

"Hey Owen," Paul whispered, as he slid his gun into his pants and clicked on the safety. "How you doing buddy?"

The boy shuffled and cracked one eye open. Paul patted his shoulder.

"Remember me—Paul Lewis?"

Owen rubbed his eyes and gave Paul a terrified look. He lay stiff for a moment before grabbing Paul's hand. Paul squeezed Owen's hand.

Mr. Stewart placed a hand on Owen's forehead to check his temperature then began patting his body for any injuries. Owen winced when Mr. Stewart patted his wrist.

"I think it's broken," Mr. Stewart said. "Keep talking to him while I take care of it."

Paul asked Owen a litany of questions as Mr. Stewart wrapped a bandage around the injured wrist.

"Do you know where your parents are? Are you all alone? Should we get some breakfast?"

Mr. Stewart handed Owen a pill and asked him to swallow it. Owen obliged and lifted his feet for inspection.

"Sprained ankle, I think." Mr. Stewart held Owen's left foot and moved it through the normal range of motion. "Take him to get some food. I'll check the rest of the house."

Paul carried Owen downstairs and found Jude with her back to the kitchen wall, gun out and arms shaking.

When she saw Paul and Owen, she dropped her weapon. The tension left her face, and she began scouring the kitchen for food. She brushed hair out of Owen's eyes.

"How about some eggs, little guy?"

As she cooked, Jude told Owen all her favorite things to do when she was his age. Owen held Paul's hand and stared blankly. He came to life when Jude put a plate of scrambled eggs and toast in front of him. He ate every crumb and washed it down with orange juice before Jude had time to give Paul his plate. Paul paused with his fork in mid-air. He exhaled and pushed his plate to Owen.

Mr. Stewart slid his gun into his pants as he entered the kitchen.

"Nobody else here," he said. He bent at the waist and spoke in a gentle voice. "Do you know what category you're in, Owen?"

Owen took another bite of eggs. Paul lifted his wrist.

"He's in A," Paul said. "It also says, *Go to downtown Roswell*."

"Mine still just says C," said Jude.

"Hmph," said Mr. Stewart. "Mine also says *Go to downtown Roswell*. They must be picking people up there to go to the SafeCity. When are you planning on leaving?"

"I want to go to Greenville," Jude declared. "We'll drop Owen off downtown. If we get him to a SafeCity, someone will look after him."

"No!" Owen squeezed Paul's hand, driving his little nails into Paul's palm. "Don't leave me."

Paul hugged Owen. "We won't leave you, buddy. You can come with us wherever we go."

Mr. Stewart grinned at the scene. He motioned for everyone to follow him. "I still have a surprise for you," he said over his shoulder.

Two classic motorbikes stood side by side in the garage—a yellow Suzuki DR-Z125 dirt bike converted to electric and a neon green Kawasaki Ninja.

"These were my sons' bikes," Mr. Stewart said. "I feel it's time for them to be on the road again."

"Dibs on the yellow one," Jude called.

"Mr. Stewart, we can't take these. All the memories, and—" Paul ran a hand down the Ninja's seat. "We can just walk to downtown Roswell."

"We're going to Greenville, Paul." Jude squeezed the brake lever. "We can't walk that far."

"Where you go with them is your choice," Mr. Stewart said. "My boys would be happy someone is riding them again."

Paul caressed the handles of the Ninja, as Owen clung to his leg. Adrenaline surged inside him at the thought of riding the bike. He thanked Mr. Stewart and promised they would take good care of the bikes.

"Just remember you've been saved for a purpose, son. So, start acting like it!"

Paul and Owen washed and got dressed in fresh clothes, leaving Jude to ride her motorcycle in circles. When Paul mounted his motorcycle, Jude waved. Her bike wobbled. She quickly put both hands on the handles again to regain her balance.

"Careful, Jude," shouted Mr. Stewart. Then looking at Paul, he encouraged, "Your turn, son."

Not only had Mr. Stewart saved their lives, but now he was giving them amazing bikes he had treasured and not used ever since his boys passed away. Paul climbed on, put his hands on the handles, and felt cooler than he ever had in his life. He paused to take in the moment as a wave of fresh hope stirred within him. He wished Finley could see him now. *Maybe we'll find her*, he fantasized.

Paul started his motorcycle and took a few laps up and down the street. Confident he could keep it upright, he lifted Owen onto the back. Mr. Stewart gave them leather jackets, gloves, and helmets.

"Good luck, Paul." Mr. Stewart shook Paul's hand. Apprehension shone in his eyes. "Take care of Jude and Owen and say hello to your parents for me when you find them."

Jude climbed off the Suzuki and hugged Mr. Stewart. "Our family is so grateful for all you've done for us." She kissed him on the check. "You're a good man."

"Be careful, dear."

Paul and Jude cranked their motorbikes, waved to Mr. Stewart, and took a final look around the neighborhood. Five-year-old Owen held on tight as Paul lurched forward in first gear, with meteorites perched precariously overhead.

And just like that, the only home he'd ever known was behind him in a matter of seconds. They were driving away from the security of the bunker, into the unknown. But for the moment, all Paul could think about was how cool he looked on his new Kawasaki.

CHAPTER 16
PAUL

Y ou're going the wrong way, Jude."
They'd just exited the neighborhood and were already going the wrong direction. Paul repeated his message through the helmet's communication device.

"We have to check on Steve."

Jude hadn't mentioned Steve for two days, and Paul avoided talking about him.

They drove down once-familiar roads that looked very different. Two out of three buildings were burned down or half destroyed. Fallen high rises left so much rubble they had to backtrack multiple times, weaving in and out of holes left by asteroids.

The few people they passed on the streets looked dazed and confused. As they turned the corner leading to Steve's house, Paul slowed his bike and let Jude go first. Somehow, Steve's house was upright.

Jude parked her bike in the driveway and ran through the front door.

"Steve!" she screamed. "Steve! Are you here?"

Paul calmly dismounted and helped Owen down. Jude continued screaming, panic increasing each time she called for Steve. Owen snuggled against Paul.

"Don't worry buddy," Paul said. "She's just looking for a friend."

A few minutes later, Jude dragged herself out of the house.

"He should have come," she said. "He's gone. Why didn't he come get me?"

Paul placed Owen onto the motorcycle and set his hands on the handlebars.

"He might have come for you," Paul said. "If he did, he would have seen the damage and thought—Well, we were in the bunker, so he wouldn't have found us."

"You're right." Jude nodded vigorously. "He's probably already at the SafeCity. He's definitely in category A. He's safe, isn't he? I'm sure he is. He's fine. He has to be . . ."

Paul reassured his sister. Together, they turned toward the motorcycles. Owen twisted the handle on the Ninja and made exaggerated motorcycle sounds. Jude held Owen on the back of the bike as Paul climbed in front of him.

"Is your friend not home?" Owen asked.

"He's already gone to the SafeCity," Jude said. "Maybe we'll see him when we get there."

"Will my parents be at the SafeCity?"

"We'll look for them." Jude's voice quivered. "When we get there, we'll look for your parents. Okay, sweetie?"

The smell of smoke grew. Paul maneuvered around a fallen stop sign and stopped. Flames and thick, black smoke

172

poured out of nearby buildings, as if the meteors just hit. The buildings that weren't on fire bore the telltale signs of looting: broken doors and shattered windows.

Owen squeezed Paul tightly as they crept through the area cautiously. Paul's heart fluttered as two people emerged from a grocery store in hooded sweatshirts and masks. They pushed carts overflowing with food and other items. One glared menacingly at Paul and Owen.

"Keep riding, Paulie," Jude said through the helmet headset. "People are going to want these bikes."

In downtown Roswell, shops and restaurants had gaping punctures where meteorites smashed through. Some of the taller buildings looked ready to topple over. A large crowd surrounded a Lee memorial, which was guarded by a dozen uniformed Freedom Fighters.

Jude drove toward the soldier. Paul tailed her. Twenty-five yards away, a soldier aimed an EN-99 at them. Paul and Jude hit the brakes and raised their hands.

"Stop," yelled the soldier, "don't come any closer!" He wore a distinct red armband and signaled for two other soldiers to handle the newcomers. Paul and Jude kept their hands in the air and straddled their bikes as they approached. A red dot rested on Paul's chest.

"Who are you," asked the lead soldier, "and where are you going?"

"We're trying to get to Greenville," Jude stammered. "To—to, to find our parents."

"Who are you?" came a harsh response. "Hands in the air!"

"I'm Paul Lewis, a sophomore at Roswell High. This is

my sister, Jude. She's a freshman at Georgia, and Owen is our neighbor. He's only five."

"Take off your helmet," commanded the soldier. The soldier cocked his head as Paul obliged. "I know you," he said with a laugh. "You scored that winning field goal Friday night and started the fight."

Paul's heart and muscles relaxed. The soldier seemed friendly enough.

"The Milton player started the fight. I was just defending myself."

"Sure, Lewis," replied the soldier, as he motioned for the others to lower their weapons. "I think you guys are better off getting on the bus coming here then heading to Greenville. And if your parents are at Greenville, they'll be heading to the same SafeCity."

Paul brushed the front of his jacket.

"We're leaving on the next bus as well," stated the soldier. "Once we're out, it'll get pretty dangerous."

"You're leaving, too?" asked Jude.

"You have no idea what's going on, do you?" The soldier tapped his watch face. "Almost everything in Atlanta is destroyed. Closer to the city, you'd be lucky to find a building still standing. Roswell's one of the only places not completely obliterated. We were told to stay here—a very important family needs protecting. It's essential that they get to the SafeCity unharmed."

Owen whimpered. The soldier took a knee.

"Hey, buddy," he said. "I'm General Hunter. You're gonna be okay. Let's get you on this bus."

General Hunter scanned Owen's watch. He scanned

Jude's watch and Paul's watch and frowned.

"I'm sorry, but we're taking As right now," he explained.

"What about the kid?" Paul asked.

"He's with A," General Hunter said. "He can get on the bus. If there's extra room, we'll get you two on. Otherwise, get to Chattanooga as fast as you can. The StreamLine there may be taking Cs."

"But our family's in Greenville," Jude said. "Can't you turn on my network—just for a minute—and let me speak to them?"

"Active volcano in Greenville right now. And no, I can't turn on the network." General Hunter chewed on the inside of his cheek. "We're only allowing civilians in a SafeCity to communicate through their watches. Refuse to go to a SafeCity, and you're considered an enemy of the state, just like people in category D."

As if the floating rocks weren't enough, there were rebels and a blossoming civil war. To top it off, Paul's parents and sister were probably in a city with an active volcano.

Owen scooted up on the bike seat to scrunch up against Paul's back. "I don't want to get on that bus if you don't," he whispered.

"Please join the crowd," General Hunter ordered. "It's safer there."

Jude and Paul pushed their bikes toward the fifteen-foot, white marble statue of Stacey Lee. Her face was solemn. She pressed the Bible and Declaration of Independence to her chest with her left hand. Her right hand held the manifesto in the air. The same monument was in every town and city across the empire.

This one looked different from when Paul last saw it. It was covered in fresh spray paint—an act of treason. Black paint across her eyes made her look like a raccoon or bandit. Red across her chest spelled *REBEL* and curse words Paul heard his dad say when he was really angry.

"Owen, is that you?"

Paul jumped at the strange woman's voice. A middle-aged brunette ran toward them, her brown winter coat flapping behind her.

"Owen Simmons," she said. "Where are your parents?"

Paul positioned himself between the lady and Owen.

"We don't know," he said. "Who are you?"

Owen reached toward the lady.

"I'm his schoolteacher, Miss King," she answered softly. She hugged Owen and rubbed his back.

A large grey bus turned the corner, as a crazed looking man sprinted toward it from a desolate building. The bus's brakes squealed as a flash of green light shot out from it, hitting the man. He fell to the ground, lifeless.

"Hold your positions, soldiers!" General Hunter held up one hand. "Keep the civilians surrounded."

The FF surrounded the group. There were nearly sixty civilians, which now included Paul, Jude, and Owen. Green flashed from the windows of the moving bus. One after one, the lasers took down anyone who appeared from the surrounding buildings wielding guns of their own. Within seconds, the previously empty street had dozens of unconscious bodies strewn across it.

"The rebels fell back," General Hunter bellowed. "Hold the line and ensure the senator and his family get on first."

The bus doors swung open, and an FF soldier stood guard beside it. Another FF soldier pushed through the crowd, helping a grey-haired man toward the bus. Paul recognized the senator.

Someone shouted. As if on command, the crowd forged ahead and rushed the bus. Pushed from behind, Jude fell into her bike and toppled to the ground. Owen's teacher clenched Owen as Paul shoved people away to reach Jude.

Paul helped Jude to her feet. A lady tripped beside them, but the crowd pushed forward. Paul yanked the disheveled stranger to her feet, and she got carried away with the crowd. A man attempted to force his way on the bus, but the FF soldier guarding the bus sent the man flying backward with a kick to the chest.

"Category A first," the soldier shouted. "Then if we have room, Bs can get on." He unholstered his EN-99 and fired a green shot into the air. "Sort out these civilians, Hunter. This is not how Americans act."

The soldier guarding the bus scanned his watch, then flipped a switch on his gun. He looked across the tops of the crowd and shouted: "Turn your guns from stun to kill!"

A chorus of "Yes, sir" rang out from the other soldiers.

The soldiers scanned watches frantically, allowing some to board the bus, forcing others to wait. One man tried forcing his way on the bus and got punched hard in the face by the lead FF soldier. A red flash was followed by a blood-curdling scream. A civilian flailed on the ground for a moment and then stopped moving. Blood pooled around his body.

Miss King covered Owen's eyes. "Are you coming?" she asked.

"We can't get on," Paul explained. "But Owen can. He's with A."

Miss King reached under Owen's armpits to pick him up, but Owen twisted away. Miss King plead for Owen to join her.

"I want to stay with Paul."

"Any other As?" yelled a soldier.

"We're in A!" Miss King said. She tugged at Owen's arm.

"No!" squealed Owen.

Paul grabbed Owen's hand with both of his.

"You need to go, buddy." Paul's throat seized. "It's not safe here."

Jude put her arm around Paul and watched Owen and Miss King climb the bus stairs. He quickly wiped away the single tear from his cheek that he couldn't hold in.

FF soldiers climbed on next, and General Hunter was last, his body hanging out the door. The bus rumbled to life.

"Hold the bus!" General Hunter yelled.

He stepped out and commanded the others to squeeze in tighter. There were too many people on the bus. It was almost impossible to squeeze in any tighter. General Hunter lifted two young girls onto the bus who seemed to be without parents.

"We're ready now!" he yelled. "Let's go!"

"General Hunter, get back on the bus. That's an order!"

Ignoring the command, General Hunter pushed the girls deeper into the bus and closed the doors behind them. He slapped the bus twice and took a step backward. The bus pulled away, turned the corner out of sight, and left the remaining crowd in silence. After a few moments, Paul heard quiet tears coming from the lady he had just helped up after she'd fallen. He scanned the faces in the crowd and wondered how many loved ones people had lost since Elysium hit.

A raw hopelessness permeated the atmosphere.

General Hunter stood with his shoulders back and his chest forward. He held his EN-99 by his side and addressed the quieting crowd.

"We're going to stick together. We'll head for Chattanooga."

Paul wondered if General Hunter had family waiting for him at the SafeCity. Trust surged within him toward this man who had just sacrificed his space on the bus to save two young girls.

"It's going to get pretty dangerous out here," General Hunter continued. "We can't stick around. Let's move."

General Hunter stepped forward as the burst of a gunshot rang out. Paul flinched. General Hunter collapsed. A small hole in the center of General Hunter's forehead poured red. The air filled with screams and cries. The crowd ran in all directions as more gunshots sounded.

"Get on the bikes and go!" Jude yelled. They jumped on and without any time to put on their helmets, drove off at top speed.

"Stop!" someone begged as Paul rode past the crowd.

"No one move!" a rebel yelled.

Paul's heart raced as he sped away. Bullets whizzed past his head, as he went faster and faster. In a few moments the screaming faded.

They pulled off the road and ducked under a cluster of trees on the highway entrance ramp leading to the

Chattahoochee River. There was no one around. With his heart beating fast, his breath heavy, Paul walked through the line of trees and looked to the muddy river below. He pictured Owen clinging to his hand, a look of sheer terror in his eyes. Paul held back a scream. His stomach wretched, and he vomited.

"We did the right thing, Paul." Jude slid down the trunk of a tree. "We'd be caught by those rebels if we'd kept him with us."

Paul wiped his mouth. "Or Owen would be here with us."

"Yeah," Jude said. "Or we could all be dead."

Something splashed in the river. A blue crane pushed off the shoreline and flew low over the water.

"Those were the last FF soldiers in Atlanta," Jude said. "We need to get out of here. Greenville or Chattanooga?"

Paul watched the crane and shrugged.

"Vote on the count of three," Jude proposed. "Right hand for Chatt, left for Greenville."

Jude counted to three. Paul raised his left hand.

"Greenville it is."

Most things were taken, but the looted store had some useful items. Paul and Jude grabbed food, wool hats, face coverings, and sunglasses. They jumped on I-85 heading to Greenville and opened up the throttles on their bikes. The number of cars dwindled as they got farther from the city. No one was heading in the same direction as Paul and Jude.

They're the smart ones, Paul thought. *No one in their right mind would travel toward an active volcano.*

The cold air didn't sting with his hat and face covering,

so Paul pushed his bike to its limits. He reached one hundred miles per hour at one open stretch but couldn't keep that pace. Jude was uncomfortable going that fast, so Paul repeatedly sped up only to slow down as Jude caught up.

On either side, the trees became denser as they made their way toward Greenville. But no matter how fast or far they went, the meteorites hovering above in the sky reminded Paul of his reality. He feared for the people left in the clutches of the rebellion. Guilt gnawed at his insides for leaving Owen with Miss King.

They stopped a few times to use the bathroom and eat some of food, which gave Jude time to scold Paul for going too fast.

"Do you think they could be in one of those cars that passed us?" Paul asked Jude.

"The worst that can happen is we don't find them and turn around and go back to Mr. Stewart."

"I thought you'd want to get to a SafeCity to see Steve."

"I do," Jude said. "But first we need to find out what happened to Mom and Dad."

They never stopped for long since they were both eager to get to Greenville as soon as possible.

In different circumstances it would have been thrilling to ride motorbikes on the open highway.

Paul tried to enjoy the surrounding scenery of the trees and meteorites floating above his head, but images of Owen being carried away and Hunter taking a bullet to the head haunted his thoughts.

What's happening to all those civilians who couldn't get on the bus? I hope Owen makes it to the SafeCity okay.

Paul tried to block the thoughts out of his mind, instead imagining arriving in Greenville and seeing his family.

After hours of riding, the sky readied for dusk as Paul and Jude reached the outskirts of Greenville. The newly formed volcano rose above the North Janus rings. Smoke billowed from the top, as the volcano gazed intimidatingly over the city. The streets were empty and there was no sign of meteorites. Despite the lack of meteorite damage, many shops were obviously looted.

Following signs for the train station, Jude and Paul reached a roadblock. They cruised to a stop twenty feet away and raised their hands to the FF soldiers who aimed guns at them. Having guns pointed at them was becoming a new normal.

A soldier approached them. Jude explained their story and offered her watch. The soldier scanned Jude's watch, then scanned Paul's.

"You two are very lucky," the soldier said. "I've just been told to not let any more people through. The trains are already at full capacity for tomorrow. Follow the signs to the station and register at the front desk. But first—"

The soldier went through everything Paul and Jude had. He confiscated the pistols Mr. Stewart gave them, stuffing one in each of his back pockets.

"Follow the signs to the station and register at the front desk. Another car came in just before you, so you'll be next in line after them. Love the bikes by the way."

"Thank you," Jude said.

Then he lifted the wooden barricade to let Paul and Jude through.

The buildings beyond the barricade were nothing like those on the outskirts. Smoke trickled out of smashed windows and bullet-ridden walls. The station's parking lot was full of burnt-out cars. They parked their bikes near the entrance and went through the reception doors. Paul stopped to get his bearings as a young girl ran toward him.

"Paul, Jude—you're here!"

CHAPTER 17
PAUL

Hope jumped into Paul's arms. His mom gave him a tearful hug, while his dad hugged Jude. Jude burst into tears and Hope launched into contagious laughter. An unfamiliar couple with black skin and graying afros grinned as they watched. Hannah waved them closer.

"Paul, Jude," she said, "this is Mr. and Mrs. Cook. We wouldn't have made it here without them. They're our traveling family."

Mr. and Mrs. Cook smiled, their gleaming teeth matching a fresh bandage around Mr. Cook's head. Paul shook their hands.

"Pleased to meet you, son," greeted Mr. Cook.

"Pleased to—"

Suddenly the earth began to shake, and Paul and Jude froze in fear. Paul instinctively grabbed Mr. Cook's arm, who placed his hand on top of Paul's. As suddenly as the ground began shaking, it stopped. Paul quickly let go of Mr. Cook's arm, feeling a little embarrassed.

"I had the same reaction when I felt the first one," Mr. Cook said.

"No you didn't," his wife joked. "You fell down the stairs!"

"Well, that's true." Mr. Cook put his hand behind his wife and sighed. "Your parents were the ones who helped me."

"Welcome to Greenville StreamLine station." An FF soldier with salt-and-pepper hair combed to the side broke into the conversation. He was a serious-looking, middle-aged white man with a strong jaw line covered in black stubble. As he stood up, his six-foot-two frame and broad shoulders were intimidating. "We'll have everyone evacuated by tomorrow morning. No need to worry about the tremors. Don't worry about the rebels either. We've taken care of them."

A vase of bright red roses gave a splash of color to the reception desk. Paul imagined handing the flowers to Finley.

"The final train leaves tomorrow morning. Your arrival brings us to full capacity. God must have a great purpose for you. We are just about to close the station for tonight. After tomorrow there will be no more trains operating in the whole of the Southeast. I'll need to scan your watches to make sure none of you are category D."

The soldier moved from behind the reception desk to scan their watches. He started with the Cooks.

"Brent and Lucille," the FF soldier said. "We're honored to have the parents of another FF soldier with us." He handed them a bag. "Please wear the uniform in this bag when leaving tomorrow. There's also some food in there for you. You'll be in building B, room 312."

"Your family will be in building C, room 427," the soldier announced, scanning the other watches and presenting a bag to each.

"We'll have a run through of the boarding process tonight at seven," he said. "This being the last train, we don't want to risk leaving anyone behind. And as a reminder, you cannot take anything with you to the SafeCity."

Paul's dad groaned. He took off his backpack to show a travel-size tea kettle, tea bags, sugar, cream, and mugs. Paul laughed.

"Can we at least have a cup of tea in the room tonight before we go?"

"You may keep it for tonight. But everything you need will be provided at the SafeCity," the soldier said. "Even tea bags."

When he scanned Paul's watch, the soldier's eyes lit up.

"Paul Lewis—sixteen-year-old athlete, huh?" He thumbed past a few screens on his watch. "You may have the makings of a Freedom Fighter."

Paul stood a little bit taller and pushed his chest out. His family and the Cooks eyed him.

"Paul's too young to fight." His father's voice was thick.

"According to our President, Paul is capable of speaking for himself. The new law allows young men his age to serve," the soldier stated. "If he so chooses, he can stand with his brothers and sisters to advance freedom and democracy throughout the world."

"Democracy!" Paul's dad spat. "I don't think those category D's out there are liking democracy much at the minute."

Paul's mom grabbed her husband's hand. "Not now, John," she whispered.

The soldier looked at his watch.

"John Lewis, you came to this beautiful land one week before your country went to war." He rubbed his chin. "Did you desert your country in its hour of need?"

John stared at the soldier in silence

"You're lucky to be staying here with us tonight," the soldier continued. "You barely made category C. If it weren't for your wife's good credit, your entire family would be category D. If you so desire, you are welcome to leave and join the rebels. We are perfectly capable of taking care of your family for you."

Paul's dad looked away from the soldier. He mumbled an apology as his shoulders slumped in defeat.

"As you know, sir, our son is an FF soldier and isn't fighting for a democracy that speaks to its citizens like that," interrupted Mr. Cook.

"Come on, John. Let's go," Hannah encouraged, pulling John away. His shoulders slumped and he looked defeated.

"Sorry, sir," he mumbled. Paul hated seeing his dad give in like that, but what else could he do?

"I should think so," the soldier said to John. Then turning to Mr. Cook, he cautioned, "I think you ought to realize that when an empire is at war for which God and ideology the world will follow, that empire does not consider being polite to potential rebels a priority. Are you friends with potential rebels, Mr. Cook?"

The atmosphere was tense. Mr. Cook looked directly at the soldier. Without missing a beat, he spoke assertively.

"Our beautiful country was founded by supposed rebels if I'm not mistaken. People of my color," he said, "were given freedom by so-called rebels. As you know, soldier, history doesn't remember leaders who oppressed certain rebellions kindly. And I'm a friend of the truth."

The soldier seethed.

"I think we'll be going to our rooms now." Mr. Cook turned and led the group away.

"Mr. Lewis," the soldier called after them, "We've already had to dismiss a few people today. Please don't give me any reason to dismiss your entire family. And your son has great potential. I'd hate to see that wasted." His sinister grin grew. "And one other thing—you will all address me as General Clark from now on."

As they left, a lady walked through the lobby smelling faintly of alcohol. She followed General Clark into an office with no windows.

The station platform was filled with people milling about and FF soldiers standing guard. A train track ran through the center of what was four identical buildings. One of the four was now a cavernous pile of rubble.

The Greenville station was on a train line that stretched across the entire US. It started in Raleigh, ran through Charlotte, onto Greenville, and then through Chattanooga, Memphis, Oklahoma City, Albuquerque, Las Vegas, and finished by splitting in two—going to San Francisco and LA. There were other lines that connected to this mainline from cities such as Atlanta, Birmingham, and Dallas.

This was one of two mainlines that spanned America from east to west. The other, in the north, went from New

York to Seattle. There were three north to south lines from Quebec City to Miami, Vancouver to Mexico City, and down the middle of the country, Winnipeg to Houston. This high-speed rail network had only been around a few years and ran completely on magnets and electricity. It reached speeds of up to 250 miles per hour. Paul had never been on the StreamLine before and was excited to know what it felt like.

The Lewises and Cooks said goodbye.

Hope hugged Mrs. Cook. "See you soon, Grandma Lu."

On the far platform, everyone wore grey pants and long-sleeve shirts. Some looked puzzled and shocked, holding hands with family members. Others chatted eagerly with Freedom Fighters.

At room 427 of building C, Hannah held her watch to the door handle. The door clicked and opened automatically. Inside the room were two twin beds and a couch. The room had been used the night before but not cleaned. Paul closed the door and relaxed. Jude and her mom embraced.

"Let's get cleaned up," Hannah said. "Then you two can tell me everything that happened."

Dinner was a cheese sandwich, sliced apples, chips, and water. Paul and Jude shared their story of the last couple of days in Atlanta. Paul's dad put the kettle on for tea. He flicked on the TV and turned the volume up. He motioned them all to silently join him on the bed he sat on.

"Why?" asked Jude.

"This is a government building," he explained. "After what happened in the lobby, it wouldn't surprise me if someone is listening to us."

189

He then launched into their own story. He explained that they ate dinner with Grandma on Monday night, watched Elysium from her balcony, and went to the motel at the bottom of the mountain like usual. When they learned Elysium turned toward Earth, they stayed put. Following an uneventful night, they thought Elysium had missed them. They soon realized their mistake.

"The earth started to shake while we were packing the car in the morning," John said. "Then rocks started to fall. One hit our car and just missed your mother."

John lowered and talked faster as he described rocks striking the motel. They ran for cover, stumbling when rocks from the volcanic explosion struck nearby. Hope suggested they follow a stream and duck under the bridge.

"She saved the day," Hannah said. "And you'll never guess what happened next."

Paul's dad took the electric kettle, poured water into five cups, and dropped a teabag in each cup.

"Well?" Jude asked. "What happened?"

John stirred his tea and looked thoughtfully at the steam rising from it. "A fighter jet flew by us," he said, "and crashed into the forest."

Hope crossed her arms. "That's not all, Daddy!"

"Just as it flew past, the pilot ejected." John paused. "I ran over to see who it was."

"Ran?" Hannah said. "When you finally plucked up the courage to go, you did not run!"

"Okay, okay—maybe I wasn't running, but I was in shock. When I first saw him, I hardly recognized him with his long beard and scruffy hair. He hadn't washed for days."

190

"Just tell us who it was, Dad!" Paul demanded.

"Gizmo."

Jude gasped. "Giz—"

Hannah clasped Jude's mouth with her hand.

Paul recalled the day his granddad and Gizmo came to watch one of his soccer games. Paul was only thirteen but still remembered it vividly. He was playing for Roswell Santos u15s in a championship game in North Carolina. He'd played well all weekend, but the final game was tough. He scored the game's opening goal, a free kick from just outside the eighteen that hit upper ninety.

But the other team was much stronger and faster.

A big, ugly player—number six—gave Paul a hard time. He knew Paul's dad was British, so he mentioned it every chance he got.

Paul kept his cool early on, when his team was winning. But the other team kept playing dirty. Kicking, elbows in the head, and number six actually spat on Paul. He wanted to punch him, but he was at least a foot taller and had fifty pounds on him. The referee was giving Paul no protection.

"Are you serious, ref!" Paul screamed out after another late tackle. "Aren't you gonna call any of these fouls?"

The referee gave Paul a yellow card for dissent. It was just like the football game last Friday night.

Paul's throat seized up, his bottom lip started to shake, and the first tear dripped down his cheek, which he quickly wiped away with his muddy sleeve. Feelings of sadness and hurt were overtaken with anger and hate.

A few moments later his chance emerged. Number six, who had been giving him a hard time, was just about to receive the ball from a pass. Paul knew he wasn't strong enough to hurt him by pushing, so he ran full speed and jumped into the tackle, knowing he had to keep his cleats down unless he wanted a second yellow card. As his first foot left the ground, the hatred became even stronger. He decided to make him pay. Bringing both feet off the ground, cleats up, Paul smashed right into his ankles.

Crack!

The brute screamed out in pain. Parents and players rushed the field, and chaos ensued. A parent from the other team called Paul a Brit coward. "Just like your dad!" he yelled, frothing at the mouth.

When everything settled down, Paul got a red card. John took Paul away from the field to wait in the car park. Number six left in an ambulance.

Paul's granddad and Gizmo watched the rest of the game together. The final score was one-nil. Paul's goal won them the game.

"You got the game winner, son," Paul's granddad said, "but I think it best for you to leave before all those parents come over."

"Thanks," Paul said under his breath.

"I'm going out of town for a while," his granddad said. "Won't see you until Thanksgiving, son."

Paul hugged his granddad, then turned to shake Gizmo's hand.

"Nice one, soldier." Gizmo winked and grinned.

A few weeks later, Paul saw Gizmo again. This time, it was at his granddad's funeral. That was the last time he'd seen him.

"His jet had been hit by one of the rocks from the volcano, so he had to eject." John continued his story. "He was pretty banged up, so I had to help him to his feet. We knew we couldn't go back to our motel, so we looked for the nearest house, which happened to be the Cooks."

Jude asked where Gizmo had been since Granddad's funeral.

"Says he's been locked up in the Pentagon," John said. "They've had him working on those new weapons."

"The Cooks were so nice to us," Hope piped in.

"Wait!" Jude interrupted. "Why was Gizmo on a jet? Where was he going?"

"I'll get to that in a minute," John promised. "Turned out, Mr. Cook fell down the stairs and banged his head during the earthquake. Mrs. Cook was petrified. She stood on her porch pointing a shotgun at us!" The group laughed at the memory. John went on. "She came round when she realized we weren't dangerous. And after Gizmo came out of his daze, he helped Mr. Cook. They were so grateful to have us there, they decided to take care of us."

John came and sat back on the bed as the tea brewed.

"Gizmo was in a rush to find your grandma. He'd stolen the jet from the Pentagon and—I see that look, Paul, but you have to believe me. The rebels orchestrated the whole thing. Gizmo drove up the mountain and got Betsy from the retirement home. By the time Gizmo and your grandmother were back at the Cooks', they'd torn off their watches and cut out their chips."

Hannah covered Jude's mouth, stifling a shout of surprise. Once her mom removed her hand, Jude spoke in a near-whisper. "We saw the rebels in Atlanta. They're killers. They shot an innocent FF soldier who gave his space on the bus for some young girls."

"And wasn't Grandma in group A?" Paul asked. "She always went to church, and Granddad was friends with President Hudson."

"That was a long time ago, sweetie," Hannah replied. "And yes, Grandma was in A, but she joined the rebellion anyway. We knew she had been keeping some things from us, but we never knew the whole story."

John took over the storytelling again.

"We spent the evening talking about the rebellion, and they asked us to join. They wanted to break our watches and cut our chips out. The Cooks wanted nothing to do with it and we wanted to find you guys, so we said no. Next morning when we woke up, Gizmo and Grandma were already gone. They didn't even say goodbye. I'm not sure if they're delusional."

Hannah looked like she was about to cry.

Hope smiled through her loss. "That's when Mrs. Cook said she would be my grandma."

"The Cooks have been incredibly kind to us and fell in love with Hope. We drove here together and arrived just before you. It took longer than expected, but I won't tell you that story. We were hoping to get more answers here and find out how to communicate with you."

Paul and Jude had questions they wanted answered, but John put his hand up as they were about to speak.

"Not now, kids. We can talk a little later." He stood back up and began fixing the tea. "It's a very British thing to do during a crisis. To simply put the kettle on and have a cup of tea," he explained in his very posh British accent. "It's therapeutic to the soul, believe it or not. Who's having sugar?"

Paul held up two fingers, Jude one, Hannah zero, and Hope held up four fingers with a huge smile.

"You know two's the max, boo." John laughed and began scooping the desired amount into each person's mug.

When Hannah wasn't looking, John scooped three spoonfuls of sugar into Hope's mug and gave her a wink. She smiled with delight. Then, to top it off, he pulled out a pack of chocolate biscuits from his bag. They all loved chocolate biscuits.

"Turn off the TV now, babe," he asked Hannah, and she did. "The world can be falling apart all around you, but if you're with people you love and have a warm brew in your hand, you can forget all about it for just a moment."

He handed each person their own mug one by one and looked them each in the eye.

"You don't even have to speak."

Paul sat on the edge of the sofa watching his family as he held a warm cup of tea in his hands. He sipped silently; it was still a little too hot, but it felt nice. Nobody spoke. Complete silence except the sound of sipping and the occasional crunch of a biscuit. John was right. This was a moment of priceless tranquility in a world of chaos.

CHAPTER 18
FINLEY

Wrapped in a towel, Finley came out of the bathroom to an empty room. Her mother was out meeting some of her new uniformed "friends." Finley dreamed of being back in school for a normal, boring Wednesday. Instead, she was living in a hotel room with her mother, who was once again degrading herself.

The room shook. Finley counted to fifteen, and the tremor stopped. They came every hour now, like clockwork.

Through the window, black smoke rose from the volcano and danced around the floating rocks. On the station platform, thousands of people lined up to board the train that would arrive shortly. Finley changed her clothing, applied a little makeup, and ambled onto the open walkway. She leaned over the rails as category A and B citizens prepared to board.

Mixed emotions stirred within as Finley surveyed the scene. *Do I really want to be on that train with those people?* she wondered. *Churchgoers, Hudson lovers, USW-for-all people?*

Eager children held hands with parents, husbands and wives smiled at one another or managed pleasant conversations with Freedom Fighters. A young teenage girl hugged herself and trembled. A middle-aged man came up from behind and wrapped his arms around her. The girl snuggled into him. *Her father*, Finley realized. *Unconditional love. Maybe I do want to be on that train. I'd want my children to have a father like that. Chase could be that father.*

The train approached from the west, a huge, white bullet gliding soundlessly down the track.

"Please step aside and let the arriving FF disembark. Then you may proceed to your assigned seating," announced the loudspeaker.

As the train stopped, screams rose from the parking lot outside the station hotel. Finley ran to peer around the corner. Thousands of people outside the station pleaded to get on the train. FF soldiers lined the fence, which was recently topped with barbed wire.

The train stopped. Hundreds of FF soldiers poured out of the train onto the platform and marched through the lobby and into the parking lot. The remaining soldiers cleared the platform, allowing waiting civilians to board. Moments later, the train was whisked away, back in the direction it came from.

A lot of movement began happening all at once, and Finley could see everything from her vantage point. The newly arrived FF, taking orders from General Clark, set off into different areas of the city in small units. Finley saw Francis, the soldier who had been so kind to her last night, leave with one of the groups.

197

A new group of civilians, who had been camping outside the station waiting to get in, flowed in from the parking lot. The loudspeaker crackled to life. An authoritative voice announced four more trains would run today to take citizens to SafeCities. The next train was set to arrive in ninety minutes. A and B categories had priority.

A and B? Finley wondered. *What chance have I got?*

Ninety minutes later, another train arrived. FF soldiers exited, pushing and pulling large cargo boxes. After the train departed, the soldiers opened the boxes on the empty platform. Thousands of food packages and articles of folded grey clothing spilled out. The soldiers carried away the goods as another load of civilians filled the station.

Finley returned to her room to lie down. Five minutes later, her mother pushed open the door.

"Hey honey," she gleamed. Her hands held food and grey clothing. She dropped the items onto the bed and began sorting through them.

"New clothes?" Finley asked. "For us?"

"We have to wear them when we go to the SafeCity." Denise tossed a bag to Finley.

"The general said we can board the last train, we'll be leaving with him tomorrow morning."

The room trembled, echoing Finley's internal sentiments.

"Is that really a volcano," Finley said, "or just a mountain?"

"The general said it's a volcano. He said some have erupted in other cities as well."

"And when we get to the SafeCity, will you be moving in with the general?" Finley's eyes pierced her mother. "Guess I'll be on my own."

"No, sweetie." Denise dropped her head. "The general doesn't want me to acknowledge him from the moment we step on the train. If anyone—me, you, the general, other soldiers—if anyone mentions anything he said, there would be severe discipline." She handed Finley a food packet with a cheese sandwich, apple, packet of chips, and bottle of water.

Finley ate fast. Denise didn't eat. Just sat with her shoulders hunched, looking at her feet.

Finley squeezed onto the bed next to her mom, so their shoulders touched.

"So," she said, "we'll get to start a new life at the SafeCity?"

Denise sat up.

"That's right, sweetie. A new life and a new me."

Finley gave an unconvincing smile. Despite the optimism in her voice, Finley's mom was still the same tragic woman. Finley excused herself to take another shower. Her hair was still wet from the first one, but she needed to think. Her mother yelled about a growing rebellion while Finley let the water warm. According to General Clark, it was primarily led by people in category D.

"All the Ds can't be part of it," Finley said, sticking her head out of the bathroom. "And besides, what if the Ds aren't wrong? And aren't you forgetting, we're D as well!"

"Not for long," she promised with a wink.

As Finley slipped in behind the shower curtain into the warm water, Denise yelled entering the bathroom. "Do you really think those rebels are right to fight against the government, the church, the destiny of America?"

There was a new harshness to her voice. Finley popped her head around the shower curtain to respond.

"What's gotten into you?"

"I told you—it's a new life when we get on that train, Finn. I'm getting right with God." Denise softened her voice. "I'll be back. Gotta get us on that train."

"You don't think God will mind you being with the general all day if you're gonna get right with him tomorrow?"

"Goodbye, Finley. You'll thank me one day."

Finley swallowed a scream and finished her shower. She dried off and tried on her new grey clothes. She immediately regretted it. They were dull and a size too big. Despite hating the style, she wondered why she didn't get a big grey parka like some people she'd seen on the platform.

Gunfire.

Finley's body jolted. She jumped to her feet and rushed out the door as something exploded.

She ran to the end of the terrace. Dozens of cars in the parking lot were on fire. The FF engaged civilians in battle.

"The rebels," Finley said. "It's real!"

Red and green lights flashed as the FF soldiers kept their backs to the station in defense of the entrance. The rebels answered with machine-gun fire emitted from nearby buildings. Civilians tried to scale the fence but fell back as soon as they made contact.

They've electrified the fence! Finley gasped.

The FF soldiers made way for civilians to enter the lobby. Finley almost threw up when she witnessed a woman trip and get trampled on by civilians fleeing the burning cars and rebels. A second huge explosion sent people and shrapnel flying. Finley covered her mouth and cried.

The gunfire from the rebels was much louder than the

zapping noises coming from the FF soldiers, so it seemed like the rebels way outnumbered the FF. She had never seen people killing each other before. Her heart was now palpitating as her hands began to shake at the thought of the rebels storming the building and taking control. She backed toward her sixth-floor hotel door.

"Train approaching!" echoed the loudspeaker. "Stand back to allow FF soldiers to get off first before entering the train."

Hundreds of soldiers rushed from the train to the battle. Civilians pushed their way onto the train. Anyone not in grey clothes was prohibited from boarding, but some civilians snuck past the soldiers.

Rebels hurled rocks over the fence at the train, then peppered the side with gunfire. FF fell beside civilians to bloody deaths.

The battle continued as the train rocketed off, leaving hundreds of civilians waiting on the platform. In the parking lot, the FF soldiers worked together, picking off the rebels one by one. The FF inched forward as the rebels' gunfire slowed. The trained military was too much for them. Rebels were running away without firing as it appeared they were getting low on ammo. FF offered no mercy. With an unlimited source of ammo, they shot even those who raised their hands in surrender. They moved into the city and set fire to any building occupied by rebels.

A dark calm covered the station. FF soldiers surveyed the parking lot. They put out fires, provided menial first-aid, and gathered dead bodies. Two soldiers carried a third to safety. The injured soldier groaned. Multiple bullet holes in his body left bloodstains on his white uniform. Finley's heart raced. It was Francis, the soldier who prayed for her.

"Please head to your room," ordered a voice over the loudspeaker. "Do not exit unless told to do so by a soldier."

Finley moved toward the steps to speak with Francis, but it was no use. Dozens of families ran toward Finley, desperate for an open room. Finley turned and slipped into her room and locked the door.

She slid down with her back to the door, breathing heavily. Her cries turned to sobs. She let out all her fears and frustrations. She sat alone, paralyzed with fear and lost track of time.

After a long moment of silence, the door banged against Finley's back.

"Finley?" Denise said through the cracked door. "It's me. What are you doing at the door, sweetie?"

Finley let her mother in and took a cup of coffee from her. The two sat on the bed, as Finley's mother stroked her daughter's hair.

"Have you been crying, honey?" she asked. "The FF took care of all those rebels. Besides, the general said we were never in any real danger, and the next train will be here soon."

As if on cue, a voice over the loudspeaker called all remaining category B citizens to the platform. Finley and her mom pressed against a window and watched thousands of people stream toward the train in their grey clothes. The loudspeaker rang out a second time, commanding category C citizens to wait at their doors.

"Some will be chosen for this train," explained the voice. "Others will leave tomorrow morning."

Finley and her mother hurried onto the walkway, as FF soldiers chose C citizens at random to get on the platform. Soon, the platform was full. One man, still waiting at his door, argued with a nearby FF soldier. He walked toward the soldier, shouting threats. When the FF pointed his EN-99 at the man, the man froze with his hands in the air. Slowly, the man walked backward to his room and closed the door.

The day's final train disappeared, and the platform was empty again. As disheartened citizens moped back to their rooms, the loudspeaker continued sounding off instruction.

"All citizens left at the station must have their watches scanned for assigned positions on tomorrow's train. We will run through the boarding process at seven tonight," stated the voice, "and everyone must be present. There is very little room left on the train, and some people are still arriving. If you need dinner, please make your way onto the platform within the hour."

***

Finley and her mother donned grey clothes for dinner. Finley glanced at the parking lot. The bodies had been moved. A few burnt-out cars remained, and smoke spit sporadically from nearby buildings that once housed rebels. FF soldiers stood guard, but most kept their EN-99s holstered.

Soldiers scanned every citizen's watch before dinner. Finley was shocked to discover she and her mother had moved up to category C. Her mom winked and held a finger to her lips.

After dinner, the tremors continued as Finley and her

mother strolled along the platform. It was the first time she had been allowed to stroll freely on the platform. Finley stood in the last rays of sunlight as the sun began to set. Beyond the station's barbed-wire fence, parts of Greenville were lit from continuing fires. The North Janus rings moved overhead, blocking the sun for brief moments as they passed by.

"How are you ladies doing tonight?" A tall, dark, handsome FF soldier grinned confidently. He stood on the other side of the fence and was only a couple years older than Finley.

"Good, thank you," replied Denise. "If you don't mind me asking, why are we practicing boarding tonight?"

"The last train comes tomorrow. There's only one, and it's a little smaller than the others." He kicked a piece of debris. "We're completely full, and all of us soldiers have to get on as well. Can't leave anybody behind."

"Why don't they send some more trains?" Finley asked.

"Trains are limited," the young soldier explained. "Elysium took out a lot of the Southeast, and a tidal wave affected a lot of Florida. Experts expect all these volcanoes to erupt within two weeks. Maybe sooner. But don't worry"— he wiped his forehead—"we'll be long gone by then."

A man and his wife walked past, pulling at their young son's sleeve. The soldier stepped closer.

"I've been in training at the SafeCity for the last nine months," he said through the fence. "Once you get used to being underground, you'll love it. Everyone believes in America's calling down there. We're all in it together!"

The soldier raised a fist and walked away, whistling a tune to himself.

Denise turned to Finley. Her face soured.

"I learned some things today from the general," she said. "I don't have time to discuss it, but you can't tell people you were best friends with Beth. And we can never speak out against Hudson."

Finley's eyes welled up with an odd mixture of anger and tears. *How can she make me deny knowing my best friend? It's because she's Muslim. This isn't right.*

Denise looked away.

"Not now," she said. "I have to see the general. Let's meet here at six forty-five. We can't be late for the boarding practice."

Finley sighed through a hug and walked with her to the lobby. When her mother walked away, Finley left to go back to their room.

"I love you," Denise shouted after Finley.

Finley kept walking without responding and went back to her room to rest.

"Finley!" Denise stood at the entrance of their room. "You fell asleep. Boarding practice starts in five minutes. Hurry up!"

Finley wiped the drool from her mouth and slipped on the grey parka her mother held out to her. It was nearly seven. The pair went to their assigned spot on the platform and waited. Finley stood on a blue circle marked 12C. Her mother stood on 11C. The numbers on the floor had been painted on with spray paint.

A man called for quiet over the loudspeaker. He then announced the order of operations for the following morning. Everyone would be called from their rooms fifteen minutes before departure. They were to walk in an orderly manner to their assigned spots. The call would come between eight and ten in the morning, so all were to be ready early. With it being the last train and the threat of the remaining rebels, things had to go like clockwork.

"It will be a tight squeeze," the man continued, "so move in as far as you can and leave seats for the elderly, women, and children."

A few lines away, Finley met a familiar face. His eyes caused Finley's heart to skip a beat. Butterflies danced in her stomach.

"Paul!"

CHAPTER 19
FINLEY

In complete shock, Finley turned her head to look at her mom's back unable to believe he was really there. Was she hallucinating? She turned back to look at him, and he was smiling back. Her heart raced with excitement as they gazed at one another. Finley couldn't hear the instruction from the loudspeaker anymore. It had become white noise, totally eclipsed by the longing to run over and be with Paul.

Emotions of hope burst within Finley as she imagined spending her life with Paul. He had survived. He was standing on the platform next to her. They would be heading to the SafeCity together tomorrow. She was convinced it was fate, that he was the one. Her smile grew bigger coming from deep within her. He smiled back, and Finley knew he was feeling the same as she was.

The crowd began to disperse, and she lost sight of Paul for a moment. Just before she began to panic, he was there, standing in front of her.

"Paul!" Finley wanted to throw her arms around him and

hold on to him, but she held back, waiting for him to speak.

"Hey, what's up?"

After hearing his voice she couldn't hold back. Finley flung her arms around him and closed her eyes.

"I thought everyone was dead," Paul said. "The news said Atlanta was totally destroyed. I thought I'd never see—"

Finley stepped back. "We were lucky to survive."

A man and woman approached Paul.

"My family's here," Paul said. He introduced his mother, father, and sisters to Finley.

"I recognize you," John told Finley. "You're on the soccer team, right? You've got a good engine on you."

Finley thanked John and introduced her mother.

"I'm guessing you two would like to catch up," said Hannah. "You can't go far, but—"

"Be back by nine thirty," Denise interrupted.

Finley's heart raced as she and Paul walked hand in hand, communicating silently. *I'm so happy you're here. I like you. Like, really like you.*

It was completely dark now, the dim station lights were all that guided their path. Once out of the crowds, Paul stared at the burning buildings sprinkled in the distance. Finally, they spoke and swapped stories about how they got to Greenville station. When they'd both finished, Paul asked what category Finley was in.

"D." Finley lowered her head. "Well, we were. My mom made a deal with the general and got us moved into C, but I don't want to talk about it."

"As long as you can come to the SafeCity with me tomorrow," Paul said, "I don't care."

"What do you think about all the categories and stuff?" Finley asked.

Without saying a word, Paul grabbed her hand and lead her away down the side of the platform. Being led by Paul Lewis down a dark, unlit path made Finley forget about meteorites, volcanoes, selfish parents, and a civil war. Anticipation pulsated within her at the thought of being completely out of sight of anyone. It felt like she was a real high school girl again. They went down a little ditch close to the fence.

"Don't touch it," Finley warned. "The fence—it's electric. I saw a man try to climb it and he was electrocuted. He flew back ten feet."

Paul pulled Finley closer, away from the fence that was topped with barbed wire. It was completely dark, and they were totally alone. Finley thought for a second they might get in trouble for being so close to the fence.

"I don't know, I don't feel like I can trust either side. I've seen rebels kill FF soldiers, but I know the government doesn't like my dad either," Paul whispered. "Have you heard from Beth? Seen anyone else from home?"

"No." Finley's breathing sped up. "I messaged her that we were going to Charlotte. I don't think she's . . ."

Finley pushed her face against Paul's chest, hiding her tears. Paul squeezed her against his body. Guilt about Chase and fears of Beth getting shot by an FF soldier constricted Finley's throat. She cried harder.

So much for a romantic night, she thought.

Finley's chest quivered. Paul sniffled. A tear fell from his eye as he tilted his chin down to look at Finley through the dark. She never imagined Paul Lewis crying. She'd seen him start two fights in just the past week and loved how fiery he was. Seeing him cry like this, however, and hearing how he spoke about Owen earlier, made her like him even more.

"I made myself a promise," Paul said, his lips inches from Finley's "If I ever got the chance to kiss you again, I would."

Yes! Finley screamed to herself. *Please do it!*

"But," he said, "I feel like I should just hold you."

Finley melted in Paul's arms. Her tears dried to the rhythm of Paul's heart.

An FF truck drove down the street. Its lights flashed across Finley and Paul. Finley awkwardly untangled herself from Paul and stepped out of the small ditch. Suddenly, Paul grabbed her hand. With one motion, he wrapped one arm around her waist and the other around her shoulders. He spun her toward him and kissed her on the lips.

Finley kissed back as their bodies pressed together. She wrapped her arms around him and squeezed. She had never been kissed before; her heart raced but she didn't even have to think about doing it the right way. It came naturally.

When Paul released her, Finley realized she'd been holding her breath.

Paul laughed. "I couldn't miss my chance again."

Finley gave Paul a final quick kiss, then draped her arm in his. They walked across the platform as the truck that had startled them moments earlier backed through a guarded gate. The gate closed and the truck parked against the platform. Three Freedom Fighters leapt from the truck. One spoke into his watch, summoning three more soldiers who walked down the platform from the hotel. The FF who arrived on the truck departed toward the train station, leaving the other Freedom Fighters standing guard.

"Hey!" shouted one of the guards. "You're not supposed to be down here. Get to your rooms. It's almost curfew, and we've been told to shoot anyone who defies the rules."

Paul hurried Finley away. Out of eyesight of the soldiers, they slowed to a walk. For thirty minutes, they strolled up and down the platform talking about school, friends, sports, and what life would be like living underground.

"I like you," Paul said. "But Chase—I don't want to do him wrong if he's alive."

"Chase is a really nice guy," Finley said. "I'm sure he'll make some girl really happy one day, but it won't be me."

The station lights reflected off Paul's eyes. Finley let go of his hand as they approached the lobby.

"Wait here," Paul said. "I have an idea."

A moment later, he returned from the lobby and handed Finley a single red rose. Finley held the flower to her nose.

"Stole it from the general. Serves him right for making my dad look like an idiot," Paul said. "Probably good if you keep it in your pocket though. He won't miss it by the time we leave tomorrow, but probably best he never finds out."

"It smells wonderful." Finley said, placing it in her pocket. Even though she was nervous about having a stolen rose, watching Paul take it made Finley feel even more special.

CHAPTER 20
PAUL

All of the Lewises were asleep—expect Paul. He dropped to the floor and banged out fifty push-ups, then looked outside. The Janus rings hovered in place. The volcano continued pulsing black smoke.

The ground trembled. A family of four—a tall man leading two small children by hand, followed by a disheveled woman—walked by the window. A surge of adrenaline pulsed through Paul's veins. No one was supposed to be outside until ordered.

Paul tapped the window lightly. The man eyed Paul and put an index finger against his puckered lips, pleading for Paul to stay quiet.

Rebels? Paul wondered. *Will they find Grandma and Gizmo? Should I join them?*

Quickly as they arrived, the family vanished. Paul turned on the television and muted the volume. ANN came up first. Paul flicked through the channels. All showed a black screen with a yellow digital number in the bottom right corner. Paul clicked once more. A man talked quickly in front of a ruined city. Paul turned on the subtitles and pulled open the curtains slightly. A growing sliver of light stretched across the room.

"I'm standing on the edge of Long Island, overlooking the East River at what used to be Manhattan. All you can see is rubble. Fires rage in certain parts of the city, and the smell of death is everywhere. There are no survivors that we know of."

Paul's parents and sisters stirred in their beds.

"What's this, Paulie?" John asked.

Paul motioned for his dad to watch as the man continued.

"If anyone sees this, you need to believe me. This was not Elysium, nor do we believe it was from another empire. The rebellion believes these attacks came from within our own empire. New York, LA, and San Francisco were all rebellion strongholds and are reporting the same thing. As ANN is reporting, Elysium did hit. To our knowledge, most of Persia is believed to be gone. If there are any rebels near a volcano, leave immediately. The government is holding back information, and those volcanoes will erupt within forty-eight hours. Do not go to the SafeCites if you value your freedom. We contacted someone who escaped from one, and they said anyone not conforming to their policies will be—"

The screen went blank. Jude was beside her dad.

"We have to go," she said. "That's where Steve will be—at one of the SafeCities. How can you trust that guy anyway? He could be anyone. The government wouldn't bomb their own cities. That's insane!"

Hope climbed out of her own bed and climbed in with her mother.

213

"We need to be ready for the train in one hour," John announced. "We're at the mercy of the volcano if we don't."

Paul followed his dad into the bathroom and shut the door behind them.

"I just saw another family leaving," Paul said. "We can do the same thing."

John shook his head. He opened the bathroom door. "Give me a minute first, son."

Hope pulled the curtain wide. "What's that man doing in the other building Mommy?"

A man in the building opposite their own left his room wearing black pants, running shoes, a blue hoodie, and a baseball cap. He slung a backpack over his shoulders and dashed toward the stairs.

An FF soldier met him and motioned him to stop. The man juked to the right and was met with a red laser dot on his face. The young man spun and sprinted in the opposite direction. A flash of green light struck the man in the back. Hope and Jude gasped. The man stumbled onto the railings and fell over the side, dropping four stories to the ground. Hope screamed. Paul yanked the curtains closed.

Paul could hear his heart beating.

"Attention," stated a man over the loudspeaker. "There has been an unexpected change. The train is arriving in thirty minutes. Please come to the platform immediately."

"Come on everybody, hurry up," John ordered.

"That guy's dead," Paul shot back. "We should get to choose if we stay or go!"

"Too late." His dad peered out the window. "The FF are all over the platform."

"Can we not take a vote?" Paul asked.

Hope sobbed.

"Everyone get ready," John said. "It's time to go."

CHAPTER 21
PAUL

Paul hated that they were walking out the door to get on the train but knew he had to stay with his family. He had no other option. He couldn't run away with a volcano about to erupt. Following his parents and a stream of people, they entered the outer stairwell as Finley and her mother scurried down the stairs next to them. The chaos grew distant for a moment as Paul relived last night's kiss.

"You OK?" Paul asked quietly.

Finley shook her head.

"There were rebels on TV this morning." Paul lowered his voice. "They said the government destroyed some cities."

"My mom keeps saying they're helping us, but I don't like the feeling of it." Finley grabbed Paul's hand. "I still have the rose in my pocket."

Once they were on the platform, Paul promised to find Finley once on the train. Finley thanked him with a kiss on the cheek before parting.

By the time he was at his designated spot, all of his

family's eyes focused on him. John looked at Paul like he'd just scored a game-winning kick. Jude's huge grin caused her eyes to nearly squint closed.

"Paulie," she squealed as Hope and John laughed.

Hannah, on the other hand, was stoned faced.

"Do any of us know this girl?" she asked. "Where's she from?"

"Oh, come on, honey—let him be."

"She's our friend, Mom," Jude said. "She came to our house when you were at Grandma's."

"What!" cried Hannah. "Did she stay the night?"

"Five minutes until departure." The voice over the loudspeaker sounded robotic. "There will be sixty seconds to get on board before the doors close and the train departs. Refusal to comply with procedure will not be tolerated."

The FF milled through the crowd, ensuring everyone was in the proper, assigned position. Most were polite, but a few were harsh. One who was a few years older than Paul pushed people around, forcefully placing people in their exact positions.

A dirty group of six men and six women arrived and worked their way into position. Despite their obvious exhaustion and lack of personal hygiene, they carried an air of importance. FF soldiers surrounded them.

"Where's the general?" a new arrivals shouted. "We want on the train."

A young, aggressive soldier pointed his gun at them.

"You can't show up one minute before departure and get on," he yelled. "We should leave you deserters here to burn with the mountain."

The young soldier looked over his shoulder with confidence. When he looked back, an EN-99 was trained on his chest. The man who asked for the general held the gun steady.

"Nobody move!" General Clark waded into the crowd. "Officer Fendel, that is no way to speak to our guests. These brave men and women infiltrated the rebels, knowing it may cost their very lives. With God's protection, they've completed their mission and made it back here to leave with us."

The young officer holstered his gun.

"And a last-minute change of plans." General Clark sneered. "The seven people who arrived late last night will have to wait behind. There is no longer enough room on the train for everybody now that our spies have returned safely. What a shame."

General Clark stepped lightly on the platform, stopping in front of Mr. Cook and Paul's dad. He gave a sinister look. "Here they are," he said. He spoke quickly to Officer Fendel, the young soldier, then whispered something to him. The general saluted Officer Fendel and waltzed away as the train approached.

"You cannot get on that train," Officer Fendel told the Cooks and Lewises. "If you attempt to board, I will shoot you."

"You can't do that!" John protested. "What's going on?"

"If you speak again, I'll shoot."

People piled onto the train, and the doors closed. Paul craned his neck for Finley.

"Don't move, boy!" shouted Officer Fendel.

The train jolted to life. Between two large men, Finley pressed her distraught face against the glass. Paul wanted to raise a hand toward her but thought better of it. She waved good-bye. Paul watched, motionless.

"Don't worry," Officer Fendel said. "There's another train coming."

"Another train?" John said. "I thought—"

"You thought what we wanted you to think."

"How old are you, son?"

"It's Officer Fendel to you, and I ain't your son." Officer Fendel held up his gun. "I used this on someone this morning, and I'm more than happy to use it again. Especially on someone with coward's blood."

"We don't want any trouble, Officer," said Hannah.

"I think it best if you put the gun away," Mr. Cook said.

Officer Fendel tightened his grip on his EN-99. Mrs. Cook prayed under her breath. Hope buried her face in her mom's grey clothing.

"You don't really want to do this," Mr. Cook insisted, edging closer to the officer. "You weren't made to hurt people, son."

A green flash sent Mr. Cook flying across the platform. Mrs. Cook ran to her husband, screaming. She dropped to her knees and put his head on her lap.

"Don't call me son," Officer Fendel shouted. "And don't worry, he's not dead. It's only set to stun."

As Mrs. Cook whispered to her husband, Officer Fendel flipped his thumb and fired a red laser at a set of stairs near the end of the platform. The stairs collapsed.

"Now it's set to kill."

John crouched beside Mr. Cook and rubbed Mrs. Cook's back. Suddenly—

Crack!

John dropped next to Mr. Cook. Blood trickled down his face. Officer Fendel wiped the handle of his EN-99 and waved his gun from side to side.

"If anyone tries anything," he stammered, "I'll kill ya!"

Paul watched Officer Fendel walk down the platform to open the back of the truck that had arrived late last night.

"You okay, Dad?" Paul knelt next to his dad.

John turned over and mumbled with a forced smile, "Your mum hits harder than that, mate. I'll be fine." But as he touched the top of his head his hand came back covered in blood. "Find something to help wrap it up, will you?

Hannah ran into one the bedrooms on the platform floor behind them and came back with some white pillowcases. As they were trying to figure out the best way to wrap John's head, Paul noticed an FF soldier he'd not seen before coming from the back of the truck, pushing a rectangular wooden box on a dolly. The FF logo was emblazoned on the box that was six feet long, three feet high, and three feet wide. Officer Fendel whistled nonchalantly as the soldier pushed the box down the platform past the Cooks and Lewises.

The new soldier looked curiously at the remaining citizens. "I thought we were supposed to be the only two left?"

"We were," Officer Fendel said. "General told me to leave them here or shoot them. Set it in the middle of the platform. The train will be here any minute."

The second soldier wheeled the wooden box as a train

roared toward them from the east—the first to come from that direction.

Paul looked at his father, whose hand was coated in blood from his head. Suddenly, a red laser flashed in Paul's peripheral vision. The FF soldier that had come from the back of the truck collapsed and fell to the ground dead. Hope screamed as Paul instinctively jumped up from the ground to rush Fendel. He had barely turned around when Paul thrust himself forward with his leg raised, kicking him in the chest. Fendel stumbled back and fell off the edge of the platform onto the track. Jude screamed as Fendel landed on the track just as the train was arriving.

"Quick!" Paul pointed toward the station. "Everyone in there!"

Jude and Paul helped John stumble into the room. Hope shook Mrs. Cook, who cried on her husband's chest. Paul grabbed Hope.

"We got to go, Grandma Lu," Hope plead as Paul carried her away.

They dove into a tiny apartment. Paul slammed the door shut and pointed at the open window overlooking the station platform. Hope scurried to her mom, and Jude held her dad's hand as he lay on the bed. Blood soaked through the pillowcase wrapped around John's head as a makeshift bandage.

The train stopped, and its doors slid open. The Lewis family was scared to even breathe loudly as they listened through the open window.

"Who are you?" asked a soldier with a deep Southern accent. "Where's Fendel?"

"My husband and those boys got into a scuffle," Mrs. Cook said. "One of them fell on the tracks. The other got shot along with my husband."

"Looks like you've done our job for us then, ma'am. We would have had to kill Fendel anyway." The soldier kicked the crate softly. "No one's allowed to know about this here weapon. Any other folks on the platform, ma'am?"

"No," Mrs. Cook said. "We were the only ones."

A green light flashed, followed by a second.

"Okay fellas, let's get this weapon on."

Two soldiers exited the train and wheeled the crate past the unconscious Cooks. A group of soldiers, hidden by the darkness inside the train car, laughed before the train listed away.

For a moment, all was quiet. Then an explosion rattled the walls and open window.

The volcano! Paul thought. *It must have erupted!*

Paul ducked and covered his head from rock and debris.

An eerily long minute passed. A cry escaped from Jude. Paul looked from the broken glass mirror to the bed sheets on the floor to the filthy bathroom. He covered his nose against the smell when he heard a growl.

"I'm still here, you filthy scum!" A red light flashed outside the window. A door to a nearby room blew open. "You didn't kill me! You've got coward's blood—you can't kill me!"

Smoke and dust from the blast seeped into the Lewis's room. Officer Fendel roared.

"Eeny, meeny, miny, moe!"

Another room exploded with a flash of red.

Paul peeked out the window to see Officer Fendel hobbling toward their room. He bled from the right side of his head and held an EN-99 in his right hand. His left arm hung limp, and he dragged his left foot along as if rendered useless.

Paul snuck into the adjoining room, hoping to blindside Fendel when he walked through the door. Fendel banged on the door where the Lewises cowered.

"I know you're in here," Officer Fendel yelled, "and I'm going to kill all of you."

He pushed through the door and headed for Paul's family. As he dragged his way toward them, Paul jumped out from behind the adjoining door, landing on his back. Paul wrapped his arms around Officer Fendel's neck.

Paul was able to relive every detail and thought that raced through his mind in the following moment—a moment that would change his life forever, a moment that would separate his entire life into two sections: before and after his first kill.

The room went silent except the heavy beat of my own heart. I gripped my arms tighter and tighter around his neck and grappled my legs around his waist. His gun fired up in the air. A piercing zap! The room went red. The ceiling caved in from above, and I heard the gun drop to the floor. Fendel grabbed my arms and tried to pull himself free, but I gripped even tighter around his neck.

I felt a burning pain in my forearms as Fendel stuck his fingernails deep into my skin. The pain was excruciating, but in that moment, something took over me that felt almost like an out of body experience. Time slowed down. Through the smoke I could see my mom and sisters huddled together, coughing from the dust they had just inhaled, frozen in sheer terror. The drum of my heart beat was loud. I felt the blood pulsating through my veins slow down as each muscle screamed for more oxygen.

My arms, forearms, legs, and hands burned with pain from gripping so tight. Any moment now I was sure to lose my grip. I couldn't hold it much longer. About to give up and let go, my muscles suddenly locked up and pain ceased.

My muscles became like stone, and even if I wanted to let go, I wouldn't have been able to. I felt Fendel's lungs gasping for breath. His throat and windpipe seized up as my arms grew tighter and tighter around his neck with every passing second. I was like a boa constrictor squeezing its prey. Each time Fendel gasped for breath, I squeezed a little tighter.

My senses became heightened in every way. Fendel wore too much cologne. I felt sweat drip from his nose onto my arm. My dad lying on the bed turned his neck and made eye contact with me. Blood stained the side of his face.

Surely, he can't last much longer. I'll be responsible for his death. He deserves it though; he was planning to kill my family. But he's probably only eighteen or nineteen. Does he have a family? Does he have a girlfriend? Where's Finley? She's on the train.

Hundreds of crystal-clear thoughts raced through Paul's mind in mere seconds as he continued to squeeze Fendel to death.

And then, it was over. Officer Fendel's fingernails released their grip. His knees buckled, and he fell backward. Paul braced himself for impact. The fall knocked the wind out of him. Paul panicked. He couldn't breathe, and a dead officer was lying on his diaphragm.

Calm down, he told himself.

After three tries, he took a small breath. Then came another, a little longer and deeper. Finally, he took a full breath. Oxygen rushed through his body. Someone grabbed Paul's forearms. His pale-faced dad looked at him with a blood-stained pillowcase around his forehead.

Blood dripped from the scars left by Officer Fendel's fingernails. Paul pushed his dad away and climbed to his feet.

Outside, Mr. and Mrs. Cook lay on the floor. Above the opposite building, black smoke rose from the volcano. There was no sign of lava. It didn't erupt.

To the west, fire and smoke billowed from the train track. A train car engulfed in flames lay in shards.

The crate, Paul thought. *That weapon—it exploded along with the train!*

He collapsed on a nearby bench—the same one he sat on with Finley last night.

Will I ever see her again? He stared at his shaking hands. *What if her train was blown up as well?*

Paul folded his arms and smarted where Officer Fendel sliced his nails into his skin. He leaned forward and vomited between his legs, onto the platform. Tears splashed down his cheeks as reality set in. He'd taken another man's life.

CHAPTER 22
FINLEY

The doors opened, and Finley looked to Paul. He wasn't moving. Finley's mom got on and took her seat alongside a middle-aged lady who had a small child sitting in her lap. Finley was trying to figure out what had just happened since those people showed up on the platform as the FF ordered her onto the train. She was desperate to make sure Paul was on but couldn't see him as more people piled on. Bodies crammed in one after the other, squishing Finley. She frantically pushed her way to the window. She started panicking and her chest tightened.

She pushed past an overweight man, his body odor offending her nostrils. He wouldn't budge an inch to let her through, and he mustn't have showered for days. She finally got to the window and saw Paul, still on the platform with his family and the Cooks.

Why's he not on the train? I need to get off.

The doors closed. The FF soldier on the platform blew his whistle and the train began to move.

Finley wanted to scream but all she could do was wave goodbye. Paul stood stunned, immobilized. Suddenly the train jerked, taking off at great speed. Finley stumbled into the lady behind her.

"Ouch," she gasped. "Weren't you listening? You're supposed to hold on when we first move."

Finley didn't care; all her focus was on Paul. But the train sped off and she could no longer see him. In a few moments the city of Greenville was far behind. She was moving away from the only person in the world she wanted to be with.

Finley swiped her watch, but it was useless. The screen read *Finley Matthews—C.* There was no way to call Paul.

"Where are you going, Finn?" yelled Denise.

Finley ignored the question and pushed through the crowd. Men eyed her as she squeezed past them. Passing a kind-looking gentleman with a toddler in his arms, Finley stopped.

General Clark spoke to the group who spied on the rebels. His salt-and-pepper hair shook as he spoke. His green eyes, strong jawline, and kind smile intimidated Finley.

"I'm glad you made it back," General Clark said to the spies. "The Lord was with you."

"Everything went as planned, sir," one of them replied.

Finley was too anxious to be polite and interrupted the conversation.

"Excuse me, sir."

General Clark looked at Finley. "Yes, young lady," he said. "What can I do for you?"

Finley hesitated. The general stooped down so that his ear was near her mouth.

"I'm sorry to interrupt," she said, "but my friends were left at the station. What's going to happen to them?"

"Oh, them?" The general straightened to his full height. "We have a small train arriving there soon, the last one from the east coast. Your friends should be joining us at the SafeCity this evening."

Finley's chest swelled with joy. "Thank you, sir," she said, wiping away a tear. "That boy is a school friend."

"That boy has promise," General Clark said. "And if I may ask, what is your name?"

"Finley, sir. Finley Matthews."

"Finley?" General Clark's smile turned to disgust. "Is your mother Denise?"

Finley nodded timidly.

"Your mother is a very kind woman," the general said. "She really cares about you." He gave Finley's body a once-over, causing Finley's skin to crawl. "Are you an athlete? You're in pretty good shape. The FF love to see athletes join up."

"I play soccer, sir."

"Well, a young, pretty athlete like you would be a credit to the FF."

Finley wanted to rip his eyes out so he'd stop smiling at her the way he was. *What a dirty pervert. He thinks I'm like Mom.*

"I hope to see you sign up for FF training during registration at the SafeCity. Maybe you'll even find a husband. Many young FF soldiers are finding love following this devastating time."

Finley almost vomited in her mouth. Sensing she should be amiable in front of the crowd, all she did was smile back.

She accepted his handshake and held on for an uncomfortably long time before whisking away to her mother.

She went and found a standing spot next to Denise and spent the rest of the trip thinking about greeting Paul at the SafeCity when he arrived later that day.

God, I hope he arrives. I don't know what I'll do if he doesn't.

CHAPTER 23
PAUL

There was no pain. No remorse for taking a life. Paul closed his eyes and took a deep breath, listening to the crackling fire from the destroyed train.

Still on the bench, he heard the rumbling volcano behind him. The rocks of the Janus Ring loomed overhead, slowly moving across the sky. But Paul could think only of Finley.

Will I see her again? he wondered. *Will she still want to be with me—an FF killer?*

He sat silently, alone with his thoughts until a loud shout from behind interrupted his grievous solitude.

"I can't believe it. Paul!"

Numb, Paul craned his neck. Grandma Betsy stood on the other side of the tracks. A familiar looking man was beside her, but Paul couldn't place him. The man dropped down the platform and crossed the tracks. Paul stayed still. He didn't wave, stand, or speak.

Am I hallucinating? he feared.

The man put a hand on Paul's shoulder and looked

into his eyes. Something glimmered there—a comfortable familiarity.

"Great to see you, soldier. The rest of the rebellion will be excited to meet you."

Paul reached for the right words. Only one came.

"Gizmo?"

"Are your parents here?"

Paul didn't answer. Gizmo shrugged and scanned Paul's body from head to toe with a handheld device.

"You've got some pretty nasty scratches on your arms, and you're a little disoriented," Gizmo said. "But other than that, you're fine."

Paul moved his mouth but nothing came out, as Gizmo applied ointment to his wounds.

"Impressed with that device, eh?" Gizmo motioned to the device he used to scan Paul's body. "It's a new invention of mine. It lets me do a full body scan and instantly notifies me of any injuries or illnesses. Pretty handy, eh?"

Paul closed his mouth.

"You're healthy as a horse, by the way. Here," Gizmo said, "take these."

Paul held out his hand and caught what looked like a batch of homemade pills. As he determined what to do with the pills, someone screamed his name.

"I can't believe you're here!" His grandma held Paul's face in both her hands. "I'm so happy to see you. Are you okay? Where's the rest of you?"

She wrapped Paul with a huge hug. He didn't hug back.

"Aren't you glad to see me?" she asked.

"He's fine, Betsy." Gizmo dropped two more pills into

Paul's hand. "He just needs a bit of space."

Soon, the rest of Paul's family arrived. Hannah and Hope ran to Betsy, crying. John, helped along by Jude, stumbled out of the apartment. John's head was covered in blood, and he carried an EN-99.

"Come on, soldier," Gizmo told Paul. "Let's go find out what's happened."

Gizmo helped Paul to his feet and guided him toward John and Jude.

"It's great to see you both," John said as Gizmo went to work applying oils to John's head. Then he pulled an assortment of homemade pills from his pocket and stuffed them down John's throat.

"What happened?" Gizmo asked.

"Brent and Lucille first," John coughed through the pills. "They were stunned by the new weapon."

Within seconds, Gizmo was on his knees helping the Cooks as Hannah explained why they didn't get on the train. John tried making his way to the Cooks, but he nearly fainted.

"You need to sit down, John," Betsy encouraged as she walked over to look in the room where Fendel lay dead. "One of these rooms will have a bed in it."

"No!" screamed Jude, not wanting Betsy to go in and see Fendel lying dead on the floor. "Not that one. Try the one down there."

Betsy came back and helped Jude guide John to a clean room with no dead body. Soon, the Cooks were on their feet and heading into the apartment. Just before they entered the room, someone shifted on the other side of the tracks.

A beautiful dark woman stood between two strong men. Gizmo waved.

"Are there any Freedom Fighters left?" the woman asked.

"No," Gizmo said. "At least we haven't seen any. I need to take care of these guys for a moment. They've been through a lot."

The woman nodded, and the three strangers split up. They moved in and out of shadows, seeking any remaining sign of life—friendly or otherwise.

Hannah led Paul into a room and sat him next to Jude on a couch. Across the room, John rested on a bed, his feet propped up on a pillow. The Cooks sat on another double bed, the effects of the EN-99 slowly wearing off. Gizmo and Betsy entered with food and drink.

After Hannah told their tale, Grandma Betsy shared her reasons for leaving Hannah and John at the Cooks' house.

"I knew you would try and talk me out of going with Gizmo," she said unapologetically. "I didn't want to put you in a situation where you had to watch me leave."

Hannah looked at the floor. Tears filled her eyes.

"After you left, we went down into the bunker," Gizmo said. "I put together a little communications device to get in touch with the guys who helped me escape the Pentagon. We made communication with my rebellion connections, and they told us to meet the rebels in Greenville who were planning to move to the base in Atlanta. Once you left," Gizmo said softly, "Betsy got pretty upset. She hated the decision she had to make."

Gizmo stopped long enough to let his last comment sink in. No one replied, so he continued.

"Anyway, we set off on Mr. Cook's motorcycle on the back roads towards Greenville. Once in Greenville, we met up with the rebels."

"And the train?" Hannah asked, a vein becoming pronounced on her forehead. "Who blew up the train?"

Gizmo sighed. "The rebels," he said. He dropped his head and his voice along with it. "And me," he admitted. "We got word about a very dangerous weapon on board, and we were given orders to stop it at all costs."

"The tip was right," Hannah said. "I'm glad we weren't on the train though."

"But we could have been!" Jude gasped. "And you"—she looked in horror from Gizmo to her grandmother—"you would have killed us!"

Hope nudged her sister. "But we weren't on the train," she said calmly. "Why did all the category D people get left behind, Mommy?"

Hannah rubbed John's arm and gazed out the window.

"What's wrong with people in category D?" Hope asked. "Are they bad people?"

"No," Hannah said. "Most of them are like you and me."

"It's time you learned what was left out of your history books at school," Betsy said. "It started a few years after your mother was born."

Betsy and Mrs. Cook took turns speaking. They explained that it all started when children who didn't receive certain vaccinations weren't allowed in school. People thought it was a good idea, because they wanted their children safe and healthy. Then parents who didn't vaccinate their children saw their credit scores drop. Governments around the world

234

tracked citizens to determine if they helped or hindered society.

"I honestly thought it was a good policy," Mrs. Cook said. "There had been some horrific pandemics, so we believed what they told us—that if we didn't follow the rules, millions more would die from diseases."

The policies expanded and became stricter. If someone didn't recycle or buy certain products, that person was seen as hurting the world. That's when the government normalized basing credit scores on how you lived your life. China developed the concept, but the rest of the world soon followed suit. When these ideas came to America, government officials had to present it carefully. After all, the country was founded on freedom. So, the officials swore citizens had the freedom to choose without repercussions. They said credit scores made it easier for those who wanted to stay safe and healthy to steer clear of those who were hurting society.

"I lost friends over it," Betsy said. "Moms shunned other moms who refused vaccination. Families didn't want their children playing with unvaccinated kids, and vice versa. Some people thought it was evil to take the vaccines."

Betsy went on to explain that what the governments really wanted was power. They sought control over the people. They introduced the network with free watches and internet, and people loved it. People were so smitten with free technology that they overlooked the dangers. Almost overnight, everything everyone did was tracked on the network.

"All for the safety of America, of course," Mrs. Cook added.

But the move did make the country safer. Criminals couldn't escape the network. They were put in prison and crime almost vanished. Then Stacy Lee became president and added religion to it.

"That's when I started to worry," Betsy said. "But there was no going back."

Catholics had good credit. Initially, so did most mainline Protestant churches, Mormons, and Jews. Islam was considered a threat to society, and any practicing Muslim lost credit. Leaders quoted studies that showed people who regularly attend religious institutes are less likely to commit crimes and more likely to have healthier families.

"Why didn't you tell us this before, Grandma?" Jude asked.

Betsy's face dropped. "It became dangerous to talk bad about the government, and you never knew who was listening in. Besides that," she said, "life was good. I'd never seen such prosperity in all my life, and I liked it."

"Same here, sister," Mrs. Cook agreed.

Mr. Cook sat up. His eyes were clear, and it seemed the effects of the EN-99 were gone. He coughed twice before speaking with a croaky voice.

"We turned a blind eye," he said. "You have to forgive us, children. There was so much good happening. Lee did amazing things for the Mexican immigrants who came to our country. Then she freed millions of slaves from the drug cartels. And after our army defeated them, Mexico asked to join the US. Lee's manifesto was unfolding before our very eyes."

The effect was instant and unquestioned. President

Lee was upheld as the savior of the world, and her writings became sacred. Once Canada joined, even the naysayers became swept up in nationalistic pride and glory. The Cooks were so enraptured with President Lee and her vision for the USW, they encouraged their son, Tyler, to join the Freedom Fighters.

"But since Hudson got into power and the threat of war began growing," Mr. Cook said, "we started having concerns."

He explained how Hudson convinced people he was helping Muslims by sending them back to Persia and inviting all Christians to live in America. His word became truth, and if you didn't vote for him, you were labeled unpatriotic, and your credit dropped.

"So, is everyone in the government . . . evil?" Hope chewed on her nails. Tears pooled in her eyes.

"No, not all honey." Hannah snuggled Hope. "There are some wonderful people in the government."

"Your granddad believed in America and democracy up until the day he died," said Grandma Betsy. "When Gizmo showed up at my retirement home two nights ago and told me how Tommy died, then all my suspicions were confirmed."

"What do you—" Jude said. "How did Granddad die?"

Betsy looked at her daughter. "You haven't told them, Hannah?"

"We've been pretty busy trying to stay alive, Mom! And we didn't want to worry them."

"Kids . . ." Betsy shuffled uncomfortably and cleared her throat. "Your grandfather didn't die of a heart attack. We think he was poiso—"

A knock came at the door. The pretty woman who shouted from across the tracks earlier marched in without waiting to be invited. Anger lived in her eyes, and an automatic rifle was slung over her shoulder. She wore a blank tank top revealing light brown skin and tattooed arms. Her jet-black hair was spiked and shaven on one side. Black cargo pants and boots covered her legs.

"The whole station looks clear," she said. "Who are these people?"

"This is Betsy's family. They didn't make it on the last train and are lucky to be alive by the sounds of it," replied Gizmo. "Everyone, this is Shay. She's heading up the revolution here in Greenville. She was in touch with those who helped me at the Pentagon."

Paul's tally of traumatic events kept piling higher. The family he saw secretly leaving the station, the man shot on the walkway, not getting on the train, saying bye to Finley, killing Officer Fendel, the train blowing up, sitting with Gizmo and Betsy, and Granddad being poisoned. And now he was in a room with a rebellion leader.

"Why weren't you on the train?" Shay asked. "Are you Ds as well?"

"No, we're not." John propped himself against the wall. "We were the last in line for the train because we arrived just last night. A bunch of people showed up unexpectedly this morning, and the general put them on in our place."

"What did these people look like?" Shay asked.

"There were seven of them, I think." John shrugged. "All dressed kind of like you guys."

"It must have been Kelvin and his crew. I knew I shouldn't

have trusted him!" Shay slammed her fist against the wall. "Mark thought they might be spying on us. This means we have to move quicker. They might be back to finish us off."

"What do you mean, back to finish you off?" Jude piped.

"Kelvin came to us the other day, saying he'd been kicked out of the station. He wanted to know what our plans were. He was an old friend of mine from school, so I trusted him. He left just before they came."

"Left before who came?" John asked.

"The FF."

"What did you tell him?" asked Gizmo.

"Too much," Shay said. "I told him how many people we had and that we were heading to Atlanta to get to base."

"Did you tell him where the base was?"

"No, but I told him our gathering places throughout Greenville. That's how they knew where we were." Shay walked across the room and grabbed Jude's forearm. "We have to get these watches off them now! Get the chip out of their necks as well, Gizmo. Pronto."

"Excuse me!" Jude yanked her arm out of Shay's grip. "I don't want mine taken off. How will Steve find me?"

"We haven't got time for this," Shay said. "Get it off now or else!"

"I don't know who you are, young lady," John said. He braced himself against the wall and closed his eyes against the dizziness. "But you can start by speaking to us with a bit more respect."

"We're at war," Shay spoke through gritted teeth. "The government will know exactly where we are if you keep that on. We need to get to Atlanta. We've got limited transport, and there's an active volcano that could erupt any minute. We haven't got time to debate. You can take it off yourselves, or I'll take it off for you."

"My boyfriend's a Freedom Fighter," Jude shouted. "He'll come get us."

"Like those FF pigs who've just been blown to kingdom come on the last train?" Shay pointed in the direction of the train, then pulled a knife from the strap around her thigh and grabbed Jude's forearm.

Jude struggled against Shay. A green light flashed, and Shay collapsed. Paul turned to his father, who held Officer Fendel's EN-99.

"Green's just a stun, right Gizmo?" he asked calmly. "I don't care who she is. She can't threaten us like that."

"Yes, green is stun." Gizmo bent down and pressed his ear against Shay's chest. "But you shouldn't have done that. She's the commander of the rebel forces in Greenville. And she's right. You need to take off your watches or we're all in danger."

Jude pulled her arm against her chest. She tucked her wrist under her shirt, hiding her watch from view. The two men who accompanied Shay on the platform earlier stepped into the room gasping for breath. John pointed the EN-99 at them and told Paul to grab Shay's gun from beside her. Paul obeyed but felt like he was moving in slow motion. He grabbed the gun and pointed it at the two strangers.

"What's going on, Gizmo?" asked the bigger of the two.

"They're with me, Mark." Gizmo held Shay's wrist and counted her pulse. "Seems we've had a little misunderstanding."

"What's wrong with Shay?" The shorter man trembled as he spoke.

"She'll be fine in about twenty minutes," Gizmo said. "In the meantime, everybody needs to take their watches off—now."

"We need to discuss this as a—" John started.

"Keep them on," Mark said, "and we're all dead. End of discussion."

"They're not coming for us." Jude pointed at Gizmo. "They only want him."

"Last night, the pigs started setting fire to any building where Ds were gathered." Mark clenched his fists. "They shot anybody who tried to escape."

"I don't believe you," Jude cried. "The Freedom Fighters protect us!"

"They don't protect us," the smaller man said. "They protect you."

"I wish it wasn't true," Betsy said, "but it is. I saw it with my own eyes."

Hannah thrust her arm out. "Take mine off, Gizmo," she said. "Please."

"Dad, they could be lying!" Jude shouted.

"Why would your grandma lie to us, princess?" John spoke dejected. "We've all known it could lead to this."

"I don't believe them," Jude pouted.

"Shut up, Jude!" Hannah screamed. She had reached her tipping point. Gizmo snapped off her watch and rubbed her newly bare wrist. "I know you think you love Steve, but you're letting it turn you into a fool. All of you, line up. Now!"

Paul hadn't heard his mom shout like that for a long time. Along with Hope and Jude, he silently obeyed. John raised an arm to make his watch easier to remove.

One by one, Gizmo cut off each person's watch with a pair of sharpened pliers. When Gizmo approached Jude, tears fell from her eyes. Still holding Shay's gun in one hand, Paul reached toward Jude with the other. Jude squeezed Paul's hand.

"Okay, that's the easy part," Gizmo said. "Now for your chips. Who wants to go first?"

Gizmo pulled out a small surgical knife. Hope cuddled up to Hannah, Mr. Cook put his arm around his wife, and Paul stood speechless, holding Jude's hand.

"Go on then, I'll give it a go," John said in an overly cheery voice. "It can't be that bad if Betsy had it done."

"I wouldn't be too sure," she answered back. "It won't kill you, but it is going to sting."

Gizmo washed John's neck and the surgical knife with a disinfectant wipe, then stuck the knife into the top of John's neck under his left ear. Blood rushed out as John groaned. All his muscles tensed then relaxed when Gizmo tossed the chip to the floor. He handed John a drink and put a hand on the EN-99.

"Oh no you don't, mate," John said warily.

"You need to lay still. You've already lost a lot of blood." Gizmo placed a cotton ball in John's hand and guided it to his neck. "Apply pressure here for five minutes and you'll be fine. Now," he said, "who's next?"

Gizmo wiped his hands and the knife with a new disinfectant wipe. In a few minutes, both Cooks had been de-chipped. Mrs. Cook passed out during the procedure, but she insisted she only closed her eyes.

The gravity of the moment weighed on Hannah. She cried as Gizmo removed her chip, mourning that her family would never be a part of normal society again.

Hope was bravest of all. She'd been pricked and prodded with so many needles in the hospital that she barely flinched. She even thanked Gizmo and asked if he was doing okay.

Jude sat on the couch while Paul held her hand. She squeezed hard when the knife pierced her skin, pain mixed with sadness.

"You're last, soldier," Gizmo announced.

Paul stood beside the couch, cradling Shay's gun. Gizmo pierced Paul's neck with a swift motion. Paul remained still, gazing forward and wondering why he felt no pain. Sitting down beside Jude, Paul applied pressure against his neck to stop the bleeding. The chip clattered to the ground at Paul's feet, reduced to a piece of trash.

"Mark, you and Logan take these chips and watches down to the tracks and throw them in the fire," Gizmo ordered. "They'll come soon to check what's happened."

Mark and Logan—the shorter man—gathered all the chips, watches, and disinfectant towels. Gizmo turned to Shay, who was starting to wake up. He put a pillow under her head and gave her a drink. In a few moments, she was awake and coherent. She knew her name, where she was, and why she was waking up on a dirty floor.

"I'm sorry for shooting you earlier," John said, "but I couldn't let you do that to my family. We had no idea who you are."

She shot razors at him with her eyes. "It's been a crazy week for all of us."

John asked how many rebels were in Greenville.

"Yesterday, we had thousands," Shay said. "This morning, one hundred and thirty-five, but many of them are wounded."

Gizmo peeked at the incision on John's neck. He pushed the cotton ball back in place and went to inspect the Cooks' incisions. As he did, he told Shay they needed to get to Atlanta.

"Looks like you're all gonna be fine. No infections, and I managed to keep the cuts very small," he said positively.

"I don't want to be around when the volcano goes off," Shay said. "Or when the FF show up." She looked around. "Where are Mark and Logan?"

"They should be back any minute," Gizmo said. "They're throwing the chips in the fire."

"That's good," Shay said. "They'll presume you all died on the train. On your feet then, let's go."

Mark and Logan ran into the room. Mark, the bigger of the two, held his hand, which dripped blood.

"Chips are burnt to a crisp, Gizmo. Commander Shay," Mark said, "are you okay?"

"I'm fine," Shay said. "What happened to your hand?"

"The flames jumped out at me as I threw the chips in," he said. "No big deal. I wanted to make sure they all got in there."

Gizmo pulled a small bottle from his bag and shook it hard onto his palm three times. He gave some pills to Mark, instructing him to take them immediately to help with pain and blistering.

244

"Okay, let's move out," Shay commanded. She turned to Jude, who crossed her arms. "You coming princess?"

***

Walking from the Greenville station to meet the remaining rebels felt like an out-of-body experience for Paul. He maneuvered around crumbling buildings and burnt-out cars, unsure whether the fires still raging or the eerie silence with the occasional rumbling of the volcano disturbed him the most.

High above, the meteorite belt hovered in midair.

Paul felt like he wasn't the same person. He'd never noticed the chip in his neck before. But now that it was gone, it felt like there was a gaping hole in his neck.

Guess I'm a rebel now? he thought. *From football hero to murderous rebel in a week!*

Paul had been in a few fights at school. But any time the fight got serious, a parent or teacher would step in and stop it. This morning was different. No one stepped in. It was kill or be killed.

Shay took her weapon back from Paul as they left the station, so John handed him the EN-99, instructing Paul to never switch the gun to kill mode. Holding the EN-99 was a strange sensation for Paul, like an extra limb attached to his body. The longer he held the gun, the more he felt attached to it. He felt his body's energy merge with that of the weapon.

Fendel needed to die, Paul told himself. *He would have died on the train if I hadn't killed him anyway. I couldn't just watch someone kill my family.*

245

Shay, Mark, and Logan led the group, followed by the Cooks, the Lewis family, and Gizmo. Paul brought up the rear, EN-99 at the ready. The pace was slow to accommodate the Cooks and Lewises who were still recovering. Hope held her grandma's hand directly in front of Paul.

"Thank you," Hope said over her shoulder. "If you hadn't stopped that man, we'd all be dead. He was evil."

Paul wondered if Officer Fendel was evil or if he was just obeying orders. A sharp burning seized Paul's throat as he realized he hadn't had a drink all day. "I need a drink," he said.

The group made a beeline for a store in the distance. Smashed windows, busted doors, and tipped-over shopping carts welcomed them at the entrance.

"Looks like we're in luck," Shay said. "Let's get some shopping carts and take as much back to the others as we can."

They went off in different directions to gather any available food, drink, or clothing for them and the rebels they were on the way to meet. Paul, Hope, and Jude stuck together.

At the back of the store Paul opened the glass door to grab a bottle of orange juice. The power had been turned off days earlier, but the juice bottle still felt cool. Paul grabbed a bottle marked "No pulp." Liquid ran down the side of his mouth and onto his clothes as he gulped the juice down. The burning in his throat instantly subsided.

Lowering the bottle to catch his breath, he grinned at Hope, who drank a carton of chocolate milk. Jude sipped a cold caramel latte and dropped dozens of them into her cart.

"I'm starving!" Hope giggled and wiped her mouth with her sleeve. "Let's eat some candy before the adults find us."

CHAPTER 24
PAUL

The Lewises, Cooks, Gizmo, and Grandma Betsy pushed filled-to-the-brim grocery carts behind General Shay toward a white and grey, nineteenth-century house. The windows were broken, and the paint peeled off the sides. Two broken bay windows opened out on the street. Silhouettes of people moved around inside. On the porch, a man glided back and forth on a porch swing with his eyes half open. He jumped to his feet as they approached and turned his rifle on them.

"Easy, soldier," shouted Shay. "There's no more FF in Greenville for now. We're safe for the time being."

"Yes, ma'am," replied the man. "Sorry for dozing off. Long evening."

"It has been for all of us; we need to get moving though. We've brought food and supplies. Once we've eaten, we need to move out. There's no one to stop us from leaving now. Let those inside know we've got food and supplies."

Suddenly, dozens of people piled out of the house,

helping themselves to food from the shopping carts.

"Bless you," a sleepy older lady said as she grabbed some bread.

Shay placed a compassionate hand on each shoulder as her wary soldiers walked past to get food. She encouraged them to eat quickly. They needed to cross the river in case the volcano blew.

Mr. Cook raised an eyebrow. "Why haven't you left sooner if you believe the volcano will blow?" he whispered.

Paul edged closer to hear the answer.

"Some tried and were turned back," Shay said. "Everyone here is category D, so we couldn't get on the train. After ERA attacked the station, they received orders." She gave a knowing smile to two young men who bit into a piece of stale bread. "Dispose of all Ds."

"ERA?" Paul asked.

"Extreme Rebel Alliance," Shay said. "People who hate the government and want to bring it down. They've been around for five or six years, but it's illegal to even talk about them."

"Is that—" Paul started. "Is that what you are?"

"If your watch is gone and your chip removed, you are too. But last night, the FF killed even those still wearing their watches." Her voice caught in her throat. "I watched children die."

She spat on the ground and rubbed the spittle into the dirt.

"I heard the rebels attacked first," Jude said.

"They've been attacking our freedom . . ." Shay sneered. "Your freedom! For years! We can't go anywhere without it being known. Our music, education, and religion are all censored."

Grandma Betsy gave Shay and a warm embrace.

"You're on the right side of history, General Shay," Betsy said. "The night is always darkest before the dawn, but the Lord has had enough of these lies."

"Thank you, Betsy." Shay forced a smile and pulled away from Betsy. "But I'd prefer not to bring God into this."

A young boy approached Paul. He pointed at the gun Paul carried.

"Isn't that an EN-99?" the boy asked. "Are you part of the FF?"

Emboldened by the boy's question, dozens of others peppered Paul with questions. Paul gave part of the story but spared them the gory details.

"Well," said an old man who patted Paul on the back, "I'm glad you're on our side."

Paul bristled at the comment. *I'm not on anyone's side*, he thought. *I just want to be at the SafeCity with Finley.*

Someone yelped. The ground trembled and quaked with more power than usual. Shay stood on the porch steps and cupped her hands.

"Okay people, we're moving out in ten minutes," she said. "Once we're on the other side of the river we'll figure out the best way to get to Atlanta. We are not coming back. Only bring the necessities you plan on carrying to Atlanta."

Small groups stood huddled on the road, awaiting orders. John draped a limp arm over Paul.

"Looks like we're going back to Atlanta, mate."

Paul looked at his father. There was still blood on his face, but the bleeding had stopped. Whatever Gizmo did worked.

"Think you can get to Atlanta in your state?" Paul asked.

"Course I can." John stood as tall as possible. The effort caused him to squint in pain. "But I heard once we get out of this area, they should have cars we can get in. FF didn't burn them all up. "

"Those soldiers aren't all bad men." Mrs. Cook stood behind them, a tear in the corner of one eye. "Our son is one of the best men I know."

Yeah, but would he shoot these families if he was ordered to?

The look on Mrs. Cook's face indicated that Paul didn't think the question. He mumbled it out loud without realizing.

"No," she said, "he wouldn't. This is not Christianity."

"Well, everything I've heard about Christianity tells me I should be building this empire like those FF soldiers."

"Jesus is the only way to heaven, Paul. The only way to have your sins forgiven." Mrs. Cook explained. "Some people don't do a good job of representing him. They make Jesus into what they want him to be."

"So will the real Jesus let me into heaven if I reject the one the FF follow?" The shock of killing a man was wearing off, and Paul relished the bitterness of each word.

Mrs. Cook dropped her head a moment. When she raised it back up, she admitted she didn't have an answer. Paul smirked.

"I don't like this empire building stuff anymore than these ERA fellas," John said, "but not everyone who follows it is evil. Mr. Stewart supports their ideals, and you wouldn't be here if it wasn't for him."

251

"So the ERA people are wrong then?" Paul gripped the EN-99 tighter.

"What do you think?" John asked, encouraging Paul to look around.

Paul turned to look at the people surrounding him. Men, women, and children of all ages and ethnicities. They wore dirty clothes and huddled together on the road. They were many things, but they didn't seem a danger to society.

The earth convulsed. The crowd screamed and pointed to the volcano. To their horror, bright orange lava flowed down the mountain in every direction.

The group of misfit soldiers began marching toward the bridge to cross the river. Unfortunately, the volcano was the same direction. As the ground shook, Paul wondered if they should be walking the other way. Lava poured out, breaking the volcano at pressure points and allowing more lava to burst forth. His stomach knotted up.

Hannah caught up to Paul. She took one look at his face and knew what he was thinking.

"The other side of the river is the safest place if that lava keeps coming down. To get there, we have to go this way," she said. "We'll head west at the station to cross the bridge. I wish we could use these cars, but without the network, they're useless."

They pushed forward, walking toward the erupting volcano, the molten lava, and possibly their deaths. Older people and young children couldn't walk as fast, and some were injured like John and were moving at a snail's pace. Paul turned to look at his dad. He was leaning on Gizmo, who helped him along. Paul waited up to walk beside them. They seemed much calmer than how Paul was feeling.

"Gizmo was really close to your granddad you know, Paulie," John broke the silence. He didn't like quiet and was always starting conversations.

"I remember you coming to one of my soccer games."

"Yes, I did," Gizmo laughed. "You got sent off for fighting."

John chuckled as Gizmo continued.

"Your granddad wouldn't tell you to your face, but he was very proud of you that day."

Paul remembered breaking the kid's leg and the brawl that followed with both sets of parents. "That boy was a lot bigger than you. Tommy said he saw something very special in you that most people didn't possess anymore."

"And what's that?" Paul asked.

"Conviction. You'll do what's right, even when the crowd doesn't."

Another small eruption snapped Paul back to the reality of the present peril they faced. He spun in circles until he spotted Jude.

"Jude," he shouted. "The bikes! They're not on the network!"

Jude and Paul ran ahead of the bedraggled rebels. The EN-99 slapped Paul's back as he ran. He pulled the strap tight against his chest and held the butt with his right hand.

"How fast can you go, Jude?" he asked in between pants.

"I'm going as fast as I can, you idiot!" she gasped.

"I'll just stay with you then." Paul acted like he could have gone faster but was happy to use Jude as an excuse to slow down.

The bikes were where they left them. Lava was now throbbing from multiple areas on the mountain. It was going to be a race against time to get everyone safely across the bridge.

"I'm going for my jacket and gloves," Paul shouted.

"Get mine too!"

Paul pumped his legs up the last flight of steps, grabbed their jackets and gloves, and rushed out of the room. Jude handed him a water bottle in the parking lot. Paul downed the water and flung the empty bottle to the ground. They put on their jackets and gloves and simultaneously put on their sunglasses.

Jude looked at Paul and smiled. "Let's go save the day, little bro."

They sped down the road, the wind cooling their faces after getting sweaty from the run. When they reached Shay, she waved them on.

"To the back!" she shouted. "Pick up the children first."

Paul twisted the throttle on his motorcycle to reach the children and injured at the back of the group. Hope stood next to Hannah, breathing heavily. She hadn't walked this much for years, and it was obviously taxing for her heart.

"Get on, Hope," Paul demanded.

"No," she said weakly, "let the younger ones go first. I'm fine."

"Hope," Paul shouted. "This isn't the time to be a hero. You need to get on. Your heart—you can't keep going like this."

Hope smiled and took another step forward. "My heart is strong," she insisted.

Paul gave up on his little sister and loaded up a lady and a small child on his bike. The three of them made it across the bridge in just under four minutes. The engine roared on the trip back, which took less than half the time.

Three trips in, the gap between Shay and the stragglers increased. Those at the front had picked up their pace, eager to escape the volcano. But the injured got progressively slower. The heat from the volcano was draining everyone's energy.

Finally, it was Hope's turn. She swung her leg over the seat as a loud explosion sounded. Paul jumped at a small volcanic eruption spitting out of a hole in the ground twenty feet away. Coal-black smoke surrounded the lava bubbling from the hole. The small hole released an intense, suffocating heat.

"Mom," Paul shouted. "You get on too."

Hope and Hannah wrapped their arms tightly around Paul. Confident in their ability to hang on, Paul sped away. Jude loaded Grandma Betsy and another child on her bike. The mountain poured rivers of lava like something out of *National Geographic*. Paul knew anything in the lava's path would be destroyed.

Every able-bodied person ran at full speed as Paul zoomed past on his way to the bridge. Shay had stopped walking and stood in the middle of the group, shouting for everyone to move faster and patting them on the back as they passed by.

As soon as Paul dropped Hope and Hannah off on the other side of the bridge, he sped off without as much as a goody-bye. Jude followed.

The faster runners had now reached the other side of the

bridge as Paul and Jude drove past. The runners hunched over trying to catch their breath as they frantically yelled for the others to hurry up. One man carried a small child on his back. He put the child down at the head of the bridge, then turned back to help others.

There were more people in the group now, their caravan almost double its initial size. But there weren't just people in the group. Animals ran beside and behind the caravan. Dozens of dogs, cats, skunks, and turkeys followed the crowd, their instincts compelling them to cross the river to safety.

Small volcanic eruptions exploded up from the ground sporadically around the group. Paul and Jude weaved in and out of the smoke rising from the holes as lava gurgled to the surface. At the back of the crowd were John, Gizmo, an old man, and a limping middle-aged woman with two kids.

"Where's everyone else?" Paul shouted.

"Taken by the lava!" Gizmo said. "They're gone."

Paul patted the back of his motorcycle seat and motioned for his dad to climb on.

"No," he said. "Take her—Jackie and her kids. Take them first."

Jackie's eyes were all terror. Goosebumps ran down her brown skin, and her black hair bounced in a messy bump. *She looks so healthy!* Paul fumed inside.

"But, Dad—" Paul idled his motorcycle next to his father.

John pushed the bike away. "Jude will get me when she gets here," he insisted.

Paul tilted the bike toward the stranger and her children.

"Get on," he growled.

256

Jackie set one child against Paul. She put the other on her back and climbed on the bike, clinging to Paul. The bike threatened to tip over with each move, forcing Paul to weave carefully and slowly to maintain balance.

Through the smoke, he spotted Jude's bike on the ground. Jude was next to it, holding her ankle. Scratches marred her face. Paul drove toward her.

"Keep going," she said. "I hit some lava and fell off. Drop them off and come back for me."

At the bridge, Shay helped the kids off the bike. Jackie jumped off and fell to the ground. She moaned and grabbed her leg. Paul looked away and sped off toward Jude.

As he arrived, fire erupted nearby and lava pooled in the street.

"Get on!" he shouted.

"Go get Dad!" she yelled through tears.

"Shut up and get on!" Paul yanked her onto the bike. He raced across the bridge, passing Shay who was helping Jackie. He threw Jude to the ground by Hannah, Hope, and Grandma Betsy. Hundreds of people milled around aimlessly, staring at the scene on the other side of the river. Paul sped over the bridge.

"It's too dangerous now!" Shay waved her arms at Paul. "You can't save everyone!"

Paul swerved to avoid Shay and rode into blinding smoke. On either side of the road, buildings were on fire. The heat choked Paul, the smoke made it nearly impossible to see through his sunglasses. He moved methodically, dodging lava potholes and debris that cluttered the street.

He yelled for his father but got no response. Then—

"Over here, Paulie!"

Paul drove toward the voice through the haze. Gizmo covered his mouth and coughed. John sat on the street curb. The old man Paul didn't know crouched over them both.

"I can only carry two," Paul said. "Sorry, Gizmo—you'll have to run."

"He can't," John said, pointing at Gizmo's leg.

Paul looked down. Gizmo's left leg oozed blood. His pants were burned off at the knee.

"Got hit by some volcanic rock," Gizmo explained. "I can barely walk."

Paul reached out to help his dad get to his feet, as the lava crept toward them.

"We need Gizmo," John said. "Without him, there's no way we survive. He's the brains and the healer. Take him, son."

"I'm the eldest and the biggest burden to the group," the old man said, coughing. "Just look after my little Daria. She's my granddaughter, the little redhead you gave a ride to just now. We lost her parents last night. She has no one else."

Paul pictured Owen being dragged away from him in downtown Roswell. He wouldn't let that happen to another child.

"ARGGGGGGHHHHHHH!"

Paul dropped the kickstand on the bike. He dismounted and approached the group of three men.

"I can make it, Dad. I'm the fastest one here. I can make it." Paul rubbed his gloved hands together. "It's the only way we all get out of this alive."

"What are you—" the old man started.

"Just get on!" Paul said. "I'm running for it."

"No! I won't allow it," John said. His eyes plead for Gizmo to back him up. "Gizmo, tell him."

A small eruption splattered to their left. Lava seeped ever closer.

"He's right, John," Gizmo said. "He can make it. He's the only one who can."

"Damn it!" Paul shoved his gloves into his dad's hands, then sprinted away toward the bridge.

Twenty yards in, his legs felt like lead, and his muscles burned like the fires around him. The heat from the fire and lava singed his skin. He gagged in the smoke. Doubt crept into Paul's mind, but he focused on putting one foot in front of the next. *I need it now more than ever*, he thought. *Time to put all those night runs to use.*

Explosions behind him reminded Paul of the Sunday school story of Sodom and Gomorrah. He pictured Lot's wife looking back at the burning cities and turning into a pillar of salt. *Don't look back, Paul*, he told himself. *Run your hardest and you'll be at the bridge in five minutes.*

Behind him, the river of lava flowed ever faster, nipping at his heels. Paul felt its heat and pushed forward when every cell in his body screamed for him to stop.

A light rumbling sounded, and then John, Gizmo, and the older stranger were by his side. The trio of grown men squashed on a single motorbike matched Paul's pace and encouraged him to keep moving.

Paul's legs ached and burned. His heart raced, and his lungs longed for fresh air. Sweat poured down his face and made his jacket cleave to his torso. Paul gripped the EN-99 tighter and pushed through the fatigue. *I'm not going to stop*, he reminded himself.

"Not too long to go—bridge is just ahead," John shouted. "Bike's about to die though. We have to speed up. We'll wait for you on the other side."

The motorcycle's taillight faded into the smoke. Paul ran toward the bridge's crossbeams that came in and out of view. Exhausted, Paul was flooded with an overwhelming feeling of loneliness. The heat exacerbated the problem, causing his legs to wobble.

Paul slowed to a walk, pulled his shirt over his mouth, and breathed in deeply. Lava burst through the road at his feet, knocking Paul to the ground hard. He peered behind him, where the lava followed his path. Paul pushed against the ground, but he couldn't move. His energy was depleted.

His mind fogged over. He wanted just a little rest time. His eyelids grew heavy as another lava explosion blew up in front of him. But for Paul, there was no sound. He didn't hear a thing. The world was calm.

Paul sighed and closed his eyes. *I'll be fine*, he thought. *What was I even worried about in the first place?*

Through the haze, a voice cried out and cut through Paul's mental fog. The voice jolted Paul from his doldrums. He opened his eyes.

"Paul! Why are you wearing that big coat? It's too hot to run in that!"

Finley Matthews stood in front of him. Wearing the same clothes she had on during the summer scrimmage: black soccer shorts, red sports bra, and white socks to her knees. Her hair was pulled back. Sweat lined her brow. She was smiling at Paul, almost laughing.

"Take off your coat," she said, "and I'll race you to the bridge."

Paul rubbed his eyes. *It can't be her*, he thought. *She left on the train. This isn't real.*

"Come on, Paul," she said, "there's no time outs in soccer."

Finley gave Paul her beautiful smile as her sparkling brown eyes blinked. She reached a hand out. Paul took it and pulled himself up. She leaned against his weight and helped him sit up. He unstrapped the EN-99 and took off his coat.

Lava lapped at a parked car ten feet away.

"We're skins." Finley winked.

Paul ripped off his shirt and started towards the bridge.

"Don't forget the gun, silly."

Paul turned back and grabbed the EN-99. He started to thank Finley, but she was gone. He squinted in every direction, but no Finley. He strapped the gun over his shoulder and ran toward the bridge with newfound energy.

I've got this, he thought. *I can make it. Thanks, Finley.*

Paul peeked behind him. He'd put some distance between himself and the lava now. He slowed to a jog.

"Over here, mate!"

John and Gizmo waved joyfully from the other side of the bridge. Paul stepped onto the bridge relieved to have made it when the earth shook even more violently. His heart sank as the bridge split down the middle and crumbled into the river below.

CHAPTER 25
PAUL

For a moment, panic coursed through Paul's veins. Then hopelessness took its place. He stared in disbelief at where the bridge once stood and was struck with an urge to drink something. His tongue stuck to the roof of his mouth. He tried to swallow the spit in his mouth, but the attempt only stung his throat. He licked his lips, but that only got more ash into his mouth. Even the sweat on his face felt dry.

Dust rising from the collapsed bridge combined with smoke and fire blocked Paul's view of the other side, where John and Gizmo, Hannah and Hope, Jude and hundreds of others gathered in safety. Paul eyed the muddy river below.

It's only thirty yards wide, he guessed. *Could I swim it?*

The lava stream rippled toward him. It would be on his heels and in the river below in a matter of minutes.

Finley, he thought, *I know you're in the SafeCity but you somehow saved my life by showing up here. If you feel like it, now would be a great time to show up again.*

Below, the collapsed bridge formed a small dam, and he saw his chance. If he went quickly, he might be able to get across the river before the rubble washed away. Paul slipped and slid down the steep, muddy embankment toward the river's edge. He held branches and roots to avoid tumbling headfirst into the large riprap, while maintaining a death grip on the EN-99. Branches and thorns whipped him as he passed, scraping his bare back and arms.

Across the river, John and Gizmo cheered him on as the dust cloud cleared. Fueled with new hope, Paul forged through a cluster of brambles to the embankment. He was covered in mud. Blood seeped from cuts and scrapes on his chest, back, and arms.

The water rose rapidly as Paul climbed onto the precarious, collapsed bridge. Stepping carefully from one huge concrete boulder to the next, he repeated his coach's mantras to settle his nerves. River water sprayed Paul's face, washing away some of the ash and dirt and stinging his wounds. He opened his mouth to let the water spray into his mouth, only to swallow a mouthful of bitter water.

Fifteen feet to the other side, the rushing river tugged at the floating debris—sending parts of his perilous road to freedom downstream. The water poured over the rocks and covered Paul's trainers. He jumped the last few feet and lunged onto the dry embankment as the water swept over the last piece of the bridge.

Paul scrambled to his feet, as the water swallowed up his temporary bridge. On the other side of the river, trees turned to ash. Lava fell into the river and hissed violently.

"Dad, Gizmo!" Paul yelled. "I made it!"

He grabbed hold of roots and slowly pulled himself up the muddy embankment. His adrenaline spent, making it to the top felt like an impossible task. He inched his way up and collapsed at the ridge. There was no welcoming committee. He wasn't greeted by his family or Gizmo. He was greeted by an eerie quiet.

Paul poked his head over the ridge. The group of weary rebels were gathered in a large circle. They sat just past the tree line, silently staring at the ground, surrounded by a small group of FF soldiers. The soldiers pointed EN-99s at the rebels, keeping them in place. The group Paul had just helped get to safety now looked terrified, fearing for their lives.

Jackie, the woman with the hurt ankle, snuggled her two children. There were two army jeeps behind the FF soldiers each holding a driver, bringing the total number of armed soldiers to eight. Shay lay prostrate and unconscious in front of an FF soldier dressed in his battle uniform. A red mark on his sleeve indicated he was a soldier of high rank.

The soldier kicked Shay's limp body. "Does anybody else want to question me?"

No one moved. A boy whimpered, and a woman shuddered.

"Good," the soldier continued. "Now, listen carefully. All of you are going to help us repair some damaged roads and bridges. If you comply and work hard, you will not be charged with treason. Show even a hint of disobedience, however, and I will happily get rid of you."

He raised his EN-99 and blasted a nearby tree to emphasize his point. The laser was red.

"In case you're unaware, you are all prisoners of war." He toed Shay's boot. "Cuff this one up and put her in the jeep soldier."

Two soldiers cuffed Shay and folded her limp body into the back of the Jeep. She made a slight squeaking sound.

She's still alive. Paul breathed a sigh of relief.

"What will happen to her?" Mr. Cook was on his feet and taking tentative steps toward the cluster of soldiers.

"You only speak when you're spoken to, D!" the soldier scoffed. "She'll be taken and tried for treason. Then publicly executed. There is no room for apostasy or idolatry in our new world."

"I don't think a free democracy should execute people for not believing in what they believe." Mr. Cook took another step forward. "I love this empire, I'm a category A citizen, and my son's an FF soldier."

"Well, category A citizen, you're part of the rebellion now, which means I have to treat you the same as these other dissidents." The lead soldier raised his gun at Mr. Cook, who raised his hands. "You're considered a threat to the destiny of God's coming empire." He moved toward Mr. Cook and hit him across the face with the back of his hand.

Now, Mrs. Cook was on her feet. She stomped in front of the crowd.

"How dare you talk about God's empire and hit an innocent old man," she yelled. "Shame on you!"

She faced the FF leader. The soldier hit Mrs. Cook the same way he'd hit her husband. She dropped down next to him. Paul had a good vantage point, about twenty five yards away up a little higher, still behind the tree line. Lying on the ground, he wasn't worried about being seen.

Suddenly, a man with a strong, athletic build ran at the FF soldier, but he wasn't fast enough. A flash of green dropped him instantly.

The soldiers picked up the Cooks, pushed them to the side of the road, and shot a single red laser at each of them. Paul's stomach knotted up, and his eyes widened. Mr. Cook crumpled to the ground, then Mrs. Cook followed.

Paul froze. Time stopped. The sweet, old couple that had helped his family get to Greenville station were dead. After a few reactionary gasps, silence consumed the atmosphere as the soldiers turned to face the crowd again, aiming their weapons at them. The anger boiling inside Paul quickly turned to hatred.

Still shirtless, muddy, and bleeding, Paul stood to his feet holding his EN-99. Right hand on the handle, index finger on the trigger, left on the front hand guard to steady his aim. He was shaking as he looked down the front sight trying to concentrate. Paul had never shot a gun before.

Should I turn it to kill or just stun them? Either way I'm probably going to die.

He was about to push the button to kill mode when Hope stood up and screamed. She was quickly pulled back down by Hannah.

"Bring that child to me," screamed the lead FF.

A soldier began walking through the crowd toward Hope. Paul had to act. Hatred for the man who murdered the Cooks and the instinct to protect his family flooded his entire being. A rush of emotions flowed through his body and somehow he knew they were flowing into the EN-99.

Paul looked down the gun and took aim at the lead FF soldier. He pulled the trigger, a red light flashed from the end of the gun, and Paul watched as if in slow motion as the laser traveled toward the man he hated. The soldier dropped to the floor.

I didn't turn it to kill.

The five other soldiers turned to look at Paul. Without thinking he fired five shots in quick succession without any real aim. It all happened in a split second. Each shot seemed to have a mind of its own as they each traveled through the air to their intended targets.

Paul had never had any firearms training in his life, and his dad hated guns. There was no way he could get six for six from this distance, but each FF dropped to the ground as the red shot hit them straight in the chest. Paul saw movement in the two jeeps and fired two more shots.

Zap! Zap!

Eight for eight. Two more dead.

Paul walked out of the tree covering and scanned the area for more FF. Something moved to his left. He aimed and fingered the trigger.

"Paul!"

Hope ran toward him, her arms open wide. She embraced Paul and wept. He let the gun fall to his side.

"It's okay," Paul said. "You're safe now." He looked down at his EN-99, which was still set to stun.

CHAPTER 26
PAUL

One by one, ragged rebels approached Paul. They shook his hand and thanked him with shaky voices. A smile hid Paul's desire to be alone. He may have saved the thankful rebels, but he also killed eight more people—soldiers whose names he never knew, whose faces he never saw.

A group of male rebels dragged the dead bodies near a building and stripped them of their weapons. The man who got shot earlier for defending the Cooks led the small group of rebels. Paul watched the group callously tug weapons from the dead soldiers' hands, strip them of their armor, and discard their bodies in an alley.

Across the river, Greenville burned. Lava engulfed every surface. Smoke twisted and spun in the wind.

Hannah, John, Jude, and Hope left the crowd to bury the Cooks. Paul stayed put.

It's my fault, he told himself. *I should have acted sooner. I could have saved them.*

Hope snuggled into Jude and wiped her nose with her sleeve.

That will never happen again, Paul vowed. *I'll never let another innocent person die at the hands of the FF. I'm shooting first from now on.*

Walking to the edge of the collapsed bridge, Paul mulled over the recent killings in his mind. He wondered why his gun malfunctioned. He purposefully set it to stun, but it killed those soldiers. And despite his lack of skill, every shot hit exactly where he wanted it to.

At the edge of the bridge, a slight breeze made a thin opening through the heavy smoke. For a moment, Paul took in a clear view of the burning city of Greenville. He eased himself down on the bridge and sat in silence, legs dangling over the edge, EN-99 resting on his lap. In the distance, the volcano hiccoughed a last bit of lava and released a long, steamy sigh. Smoke rose beyond the levitating rocks above, the rocks that Paul once couldn't take his eyes off but barely gained his attention now. The bright orange, molten flow mesmerized him as it hit the river, sending off small, white wisps of steam.

He sat silently for some time, wanting to be left alone but at the same time hoping someone would check on him.

Footsteps sounded gently from behind. General Shay lowered herself to the bridge beside Paul. She shook her head and spoke, focusing her eyes across the river.

"I'm indebted to you," she said. "I would have been killed if you hadn't stepped in. You have saved us all today."

A flame sprung up on the other side of the river and quickly dissipated.

"You're welcome." Paul whispered.

"We won't move out until you're ready. But the sooner we take cover in the trees, the better. The news of these FF deaths will spread quickly, and we don't want to be here if reinforcements arrive."

"*When* they arrive," Paul responded.

He pinched a palm-sized rock and flung it into the steaming river below. It disappeared in the water.

"We can go now." Paul stood up and gazed at the fires blazing in downtown Greenville. "I don't want to see anyone else die today."

He turned around to see Gizmo standing beside Mark and Tyrone—the two men from the station earlier this morning—and the athletic man who carried so many kids on his back across the bridge. The same man who charged down the FF trying to defend the Cooks. They each patted their own EN-99 they'd taken from the FF Paul had killed.

"Thank you, Paul." Mark tilted his head to force eye contact. Paul caved, and Mark gave a sad smile. "You're a real hot shot with a gun, aren't you?"

Paul looked away, and his face grew hot.

"We're so glad to have you with us, bro," Tyrone said with a voice like a coach. "We need more men like you."

"I'm Chad." The athletic-built man stepped forward. "We've not met officially, but I'm amazed at your courage and character. Your aim's pretty good, too. I feel a lot better knowing we have men like you on our side."

Paul brushed the ash from his hand and shook Chad's. His grip was strong, but his eyes were kind.

"How old are you?" he asked.

"Sixteen," Paul replied. "I saw you run by with those kids on your back earlier. Pretty impressive."

"Well, it would have been nice to have another bike. You and your sister didn't look like you wanted to share." Chad smirked and brushed dirt from his shoulder. "Looks like you're a natural-born soldier. We could do with a few more people like you."

Am I one of them now, part of the rebellion? I didn't even want to take my watch off this morning. I just want to be with Finley at the SafeCity. I didn't want any of this.

The group watched Paul in expectation, leaning forward to hear whatever he had to say. No one had ever taken on the FF and come out on top before. Paul was humbled under their eyes. He felt their expectations, their assumption that he would become some sort of leader. But he wasn't a leader. He was still just a kicker.

Sure, he could take credit for the first kill. He really aimed for that one. But the others?

Pure luck, Paul thought. *Those shots had minds of their own.*

Instead of admitting this out loud, he asked a simple question.

"Is the green bike still here?"

Gizmo pointed over his shoulder. "Yes," he said, "it's back with the group."

"Let's move out then," Shay commanded.

As the group marched away, Gizmo motioned to Paul. He was limping, and the bandage covering his leg was covered in blood. Despite this, he looked better than when Paul picked him up on the other side of the bridge.

They walked together slowly, Paul plodding along to keep pace with the injured genius.

"Paul, I know you still feel like a sophomore in high school, but these people now look to you as a leader," Gizmo said. "I've never seen someone take to the EN-99 as fast as you have."

Paul swallowed audibly, keeping his gaze on the ground in front of his footsteps.

"You're right to be a little nervous. This rebellion is very real," Gizmo continued. "They're creating an army—the government has been working to keep it hidden since President Lee's reign. They squashed it in the early days but it's been growing in recent years. Hudson had become blinded by pride and didn't believe it was a threat. Even if Elysium hadn't hit, the rebellion was imminent. By ignoring the threat, it's been able to grow, becoming much bigger than any government officials realize—or will admit in public."

Paul scratched his ear as Gizmo caught his breath. "So, when did you join the rebellion?"

Gizmo raised an eyebrow and fell back into a slow walking pace. "I should have joined a long time ago, but I wasn't brave enough to leave President Hudson. We had such a good friendship in college." He coughed into his hand and wiped it on his pant leg, leaving a light red smear. "Your granddad was like a father to the both of us. And Hudson was like my brother. I never had a real brother, you know. We'd done so much good together, and it was hard to leave all that behind. I probably should have left after he started to make money from the cancer drug."

"Cancer?" Paul asked.

Even at their slow pace, Gizmo and Paul were nearing the crowds. Shay barked commands from a makeshift platform. Rebel fighters listened with varying levels of attention. Most looked too tired to care what she had to say.

"Yes, cancer." Gizmo ran a hand along a handrail skirting a sidewalk. "It was a horrible disease that used to kill millions of people every year. Can you imagine?"

Paul envisioned a disease that struck like the EN-99: ruthless, precise, unrelenting.

"Harry—who you know as President Hudson—and I came up with a cure just after we graduated college. There were countless types of cancer, but this cure worked for every one of them. To top it off"—Gizmo coughed—"it was something no other cancer medication was."

They were on the outskirts of the crowd now. Paul leaned against a building, as Gizmo put his weight on a pile of cardboard boxes.

"It was dirt cheap to produce!" Gizmo pulled at his hair with excitement.

Paul shrugged. "That's a good thing, right?"

"It was! But Harry convinced me that if we made a profit, we could do even greater things for the world with the money. He was right," Gizmo said. "We did great things with the money, but at what cost to our character? We could have done great things with a smaller profit. Well, I carried on inventing, and he carried on making money. All the while, people were choosing between our life-saving medication and groceries."

"I learnt today that we haven't been told the full story in our history books."

"That's true, unfortunately," Gizmo said. "We used the money to clean up the oceans, to make the oceans self-cleaning organisms. It started when we changed the DNA of clams. The process was excruciating, but the results were great. By the time we were finished with them, those clams were able to recycle the ocean's water, to filter the bad stuff and spit the good back out."

Gizmo continued telling the story. He explained that their invention was met with initial skepticism. Some people thought they were evil for genetically modifying animals. That skepticism turned to praise when the oceans were transformed. "Once the water turned blue again," Gizmo said, "no one was screaming to save the clams."

The invention was such a success that Gizmo and Harry were invited to China. The government officials hoped they could help with China's pollution problems. However, some of Harry's money-focused friends were on bad terms with some Chinese leaders. So, Gizmo went alone.

"I wanted to change the world and help people," he said, "even if my long-time friend had changed course."

"You've been to China?"

Gizmo grinned. "With all that story, that's what stuck out? You're not impressed with my genetically modified clams?"

"What was it like—China, is it as bad as they say?" Paul asked. "We learned in school that it's an evil, atheist empire. Weren't you scared?"

Gizmo tut-tutted after Paul's comments. "I loved China," he said, "but it had some serious problems."

Gizmo explained that the entire country was on the

brink of ruin. The cause? Three billion people—"or rather," Gizmo said, "the waste created by three billion people."

Every street corner, shop, and park in China was heavy with a horrific smell. It didn't just smell bad. It was dangerous. The smells came from bacteria, and where there's bacteria, there is sickness. When Gizmo arrived, many were very sick because of it.

Inspired by the success of the clams, Gizmo turned to a similar solution. He gathered a team of Chinese scientists and genetically modified hogs.

"They turned waste into amazing compost." Gizmo's eyes glazed over at the memory. "Little by little, they ate through the landfills, turning it into compost and manure. It healed the land, and the crops grew wonderfully in the new soil."

With two big environmental advances under his belt, Gizmo was eager to return to his first love: medical research. He joined some brilliant minds and invited Harry to collaborate, but he turned down the opportunity.

The light left Gizmo's eyes. He bit the inside of his cheek and inhaled slowly. "Harry had a new passion," Gizmo said. "Politics."

Gizmo and Harry Hudson went their different ways. Eventually when they had more money than they knew what to do with from the cancer drug, Harry allowed it to be made for next to nothing and became a hero to the public in the process. Gizmo regretted he hadn't done it sooner, but putting it behind him, he dove headfirst into his research. In time, his team discovered how to grow nerves and fix damaged brains. Thanks to their efforts, mental health care became a thing of the past.

"It was a glorious time!" Gizmo exclaimed. "Then it all changed when Harry became president."

Instead of opening doors for Gizmo's research, Harry—President Hudson—wouldn't let Gizmo leave the country. The new president even forbade Gizmo from speaking with anyone beyond America's borders. As a result, Gizmo couldn't share his discoveries with the world.

"I'd learned how to heal the human body, the land, and the oceans. Our team healed almost every disease that had plagued humanity through the centuries, but," Gizmo said, "I couldn't heal the human heart. People were still selfish, greedy, and arrogant. So I set out to discover the unknowns of the human soul."

Paul held up a hand. Gizmo stopped and looked at Paul quizzically.

"Sorry, Gizmo, but what's that got to do with joining the rebellion?"

"Harry stopped speaking to me after he became president, but your granddad encouraged me to go up against Harry. I was terrible in front of a crowd though and didn't stand a chance, so I began researching humanity's greatest problem—ourselves."

Paul rolled his eyes and hoisted his EN-99 overhead with one arm. "And this is what you came up with?"

Gizmo's eyes widened. "Yes," he said with a giggle.

A cat sauntered to Gizmo, his grey fur nearly blackened by the volcanic soot. The cat rubbed against Gizmo's leg, seemingly oblivious that countless creatures recently met their fate across the river. Gizmo bent down to pet the cat that scurried away at the touch.

"The government funded my work," Gizmo continued. "What they didn't know was that my research transitioned from a search for clean, renewable energy to a rather spiritual journey. In a short period, my whole world view, philosophy, and theology transformed." The cat peeked out from behind an overturned trash can. Gizmo waved a finger, and the cat disappeared again. "I discovered how to take all the energy within a human and harness it into a single focus point. I envisioned using this energy to power a house, grow crops, or fly a plane. But when Harry found out about it, he had different plans."

Paul held the EN-99 out at arm's length.

"Yes," Gizmo said. "He wanted to use it for a weapon."

Paul begged to understand how the gun worked, but Gizmo shrugged.

"We don't have the language to describe what we discovered. Some people think it's the soul or matter or the spirit that connects with the weapon." Gizmo flapped his hands wildly in the air. "We know that more than ninety-nine percent of the human body—of everything actually, all the space in between the atoms—is nothing. It's just empty space. What's in that space?" His voice climbed with excitement. "We don't know! But what we do know now is that it's extremely powerful. And I'll tell you another thing," he lowered his voice and looked around to make sure no one else was listening. "That weapon—the EN-99—it doesn't have to be a weapon."

Paul looked at the gun in his hands from all angles, feeling for hidden buttons or compartments. Gizmo told him it was no use, that there wasn't a hidden trigger or switch. The gun's power rested in its power source. The human who held it.

"The law of attraction states that positive or negative thoughts bring positive or negative experiences into a person's life. Sound familiar?"

Paul nodded.

"That's good, because people have believed it for centuries," Gizmo said. "And it's proven that you can control atoms if your thoughts are strong enough."

"Okay," Paul said. "I think you lost me there."

"Have you ever felt you could change a person's thoughts or the atmosphere in a room by your thinking? Or when your will and emotions are stronger than theirs," Gizmo said, "how they kind of override someone else's?"

Paul admitted he'd had the experience.

"It's kind of the same thing. People do what they believe is possible," Gizmo said. "For years, experts thought it was impossible to run a mile in four minutes. Then, someone did it. Once that person broke through that man-made glass ceiling, dozens more followed suite.

"That weapon"—Gizmo stuck out his tongue in disgust at the word—"it's powered by human energy and people's thoughts. The button that lets you toggle between stun and kill changes nothing."

Paul turned from Gizmo to the gun. He studied it, rubbing his hand on the switch. Gizmo put a hand on Paul's.

"The person holding the gun chooses whether he wants to kill," Gizmo said. "The gun simply obeys. Whoever wields this weapon, their desire changes the gun from kill to stun. All the EN-99's power is within the human mind and the energy we unknowingly possess."

That must mean I wanted to kill those soldiers! Paul thought. He pushed the gun toward Gizmo, afraid of what it might do.

"Well," Paul stammered, "why did you make it possible to hurt people with it?"

"It isn't a weapon, Paul!" Gizmo grabbed the gun and raised it overhead. He pulled the trigger repeatedly. Paul flinched, but nothing happened. "See? It's not a weapon! Most people won't believe me, but it's true! The EN-99 is whatever you believe it is. It can be used to make a plant grow. In fact, that's what I was designing it to do. I wanted to harness this untapped energy for good."

"Then how'd it become a weapon?" Paul asked. "Who was the first idiot to kill someone with it?"

Gizmo dropped his head. He handed the gun back to Paul and began pacing nervously, ashamed to admit one of his greatest regrets.

"Wait! You're telling me—"

"I can explain, but it doesn't make it any better." Gizmo raised his eyes to Paul's. "Harry came into the lab one day and told me your grandfather was murdered for helping the rebellion. I lost it. I'd been in the lab for months, and—well, I went crazy. I pointed the device at him and asked if he'd killed your grandfather. He just gave me this sinister, heartless smile. I fired the EN-99, and Hudson became the first casualty of his beloved weapon."

"President Hudson is dead?" Paul covered his mouth.

"No, he's not dead. He'd disguised a man as himself to tell me the news. Harry is many things, but he is not ignorant." Gizmo closed his eyes in pain. "He feared my

279

reaction—rightly so. He watched the whole thing through a one-way mirror glass. When I fell over his body weeping, the real Hudson walked in the room. He slid the weapon from my hands, and his men arrested me."

Harry threated to kill Grandma Betsy if Gizmo didn't comply in moving forward with the weapon. From Gizmo's recollection, half a million EN-99s had been manufactured thus far. All information to make the gun was stored in Gizmo's head and on a single small flash drive that only he knew about—"which I store here for safe keeping," Gizmo said, pointing at his breast pocket.

All other information on the weapon was destroyed when Gizmo escaped the Pentagon the night of Elysium.

"We knew that night would work best," he said. "Everyone was so focused on the asteroid that they took their eyes off me long enough to escape safely and find your grandma."

"Why—" Paul paused and rubbed his forehead. Dirt smeared in odd patterns. "If it's so dangerous, why not destroy all the information? Isn't the risk too great?"

"Believe me," Gizmo said, "I've been tempted to toss it all in the trash. But the greatest thing I discovered on my journey over the last decade is that the human heart can change. I still believe the weapon can be used for good, Paul."

"And you believe you can change the human heart?" Paul tried picturing the football players who taunted him and hated his father becoming his best friends, rolling out the red carpet for the Lewises and a world of D-level citizens. "How is that possible?"

"Well," Gizmo laughed, "let's just say I'm not an atheist anymore."

"Come on, Gizmo—look where religion has got us. You're seriously a Christian now?"

"No, I'm not a fan of religion like that. I'll tell you about it another time, but we really should be getting off the main road."

They walked over to the crowd of people.

"Paul, I've told you more than any other person alive about that weapon. I'm not even sure if the men and women who worked with me in the pentagon know this much. I'm trusting you to keep this a secret for now."

"I will," Paul replied. And he meant it.

CHAPTER 27
FINLEY

Finley watched the world flash by as the StreamLine hovered above the tracks at lightning speed. She imagined holding hands with Paul and walking into their joint apartment at the SafeCity. For the first time since she was a child, Finley resolved not to let her mother's dark past ruin her own future. If things went well, she would marry someone—Paul, perhaps?—and start a family.

They'd been traveling for around two hours since General Clark had assured her Paul would be following them on the next train. People were becoming restless, and kids were beginning to get whiny.

Suddenly, the never-ending line of trees disappeared, and the train car became enveloped in darkness. They were underground now. The SafeCity must be near.

"Are we here mommy?" an excited child asked.

Finley was excited to see inside the SafeCities. She'd seen on the news that there were places to grow food, thousands of apartment-like homes, hospitals, places to play sports, and training facilities for FF soldiers. The thought of this new normal—a new start—enticed Finley.

The darkness was replaced with a bright light, revealing a huge open space. The train hovered fifty feet over a bridge. Acres of farmland stretched as far as the eye could see. Corn grew in one plot, orange trees in another. Some fallow plots of dirt were being plowed by machines driven by humans wearing green jumpsuits.

Breathtaking! Finley thought. *And it's all underground!*

Workers in the field looked up at the train and gave joyful waves. The anxiety, fear, and helplessness that gripped the train turned to hope and excitement. Children giggled and waved at the tiny people below. Parents cried tears of joy.

The train moved quickly into another tunnel and popped out in a smaller area. The train now rode closer to the ground. Passengers gawked at hogs—hundreds of them—eating piles of trash.

"The waste hogs!" shouted a young teenager.

Dozens of huge conveyor belts delivered trash from every corner. Mounds of trash were built and then diminished as the pigs moved from one pile to the next.

"Look at those pigs go—it's just like they said," the teenager continued. "The waste hogs eat the trash, turn it into fertilizer, then eat more. Amazing!"

A pair of bright green tractors sputtered into view and began piling up manure created by the waste hogs. They pushed the manure toward the farmlands.

After passing through another dark tunnel, they arrived at what looked like a shopping center. It was smaller than the last two areas, and thousands of people in different-colored jump suits moved leisurely from store to store. Many stopped what they were doing and waved at the passing train.

The fourth area brought them fifteen feet from the ground. Hundreds of uniformed FF soldiers—broken into a dozen or more units—saluted the passing train, an impressive show of power.

After one more tunnel, the train eased to a stop. The doors opened, and the passengers piled out as quickly as possible. Denise grabbed Finley's hand as they made their way onto the platform. Three steps away from the train, the flow of human traffic halted.

Following some murmurs, the crowd quieted in anticipation. A female voice called out over the loudspeaker:

"Welcome to Tennessee SafeCity. Before you go any farther, please listen to the following instructions. We understand you have had a long journey, so anyone who needs a restroom will find them to your left."

A handful of adults holding squirming children moved toward the left. The voice continued.

"We are so happy you have made it safely to your new home. We understand many of you have had a very difficult week, but be encouraged—your new life starts now! We are going to help you find your calling as we rebuild our great empire and continue to move toward fulfilling the destiny of this great land. The first thing you must do is register. Scan your watch, and you will be given food and water. You should then wait until your name is called. You are the last group of citizens to arrive, and we're pleased to have you bring our city to maximum capacity. We pray blessing and prosperity over you and your families. USW for all."

"And for all, freedom and life!" the crowd responded collectively.

Finley responded half-heartedly. Her mind was elsewhere. General Clark promised that Paul would be arriving within a couple hours. Until then, Finley could think of nothing else.

The crowd inched toward a full body scanner, the same kind Finley remembered from the one time she went in an airport as a child. She and her mom had flown to Uncle Greg's wedding in California. Everyone had fun, but the fun didn't last. Uncle Greg divorced Aunt Sherri three years later, and Denise never spoke to her brother again.

Denise walked through the scanner without incident. Finley followed.

"Welcome Finley Matthews," said a calming female voice attached to the scanner. "We're so glad you are here to build our nation even stronger than before. USW for all."

Finley continued toward Denise as her watched buzzed. Finley looked down.

620.

"I'm the same, honey," Denise said. "Six hundred twenty. They'll call us as a family, I guess."

At a set of big double doors, a sweet-looking older lady in a jumpsuit handed Finley and Denise a bottle of water and a small bag of food.

"Welcome to your new home," the old lady said kindly. "Please find a place in the next room and wait for your number to be called."

Finley took the food and followed her mother into a huge waiting room crowded with thousands of people. Finley slouched on a seat next to Denise. She rested her head on the back of the chair, closed her eyes, and imagined greeting Paul when he arrived.

***

"Six hundred twenty," a strong male voice spoke out over the loudspeaker. "Six hundred and twenty, please report to booth F. Denise and Finley Matthews, please come to booth F."

Denise nudged Finley on the shoulder.

"Come on, Finn," she said excitedly. "That's us!"

Finley rubbed her eyes and yawned. Around her, hundreds of people wore the same boring grey clothes. She stood up and wondered if Paul had arrived.

The room was eerily quiet.

"Over there." Denise pointed at a big purple F hologram. They walked over, hand in hand, and pushed through the temporary door into a little makeshift booth. A mousy young lady waited. She sat behind a small black table with two empty chairs, one for Finley and the other for Denise. Her black hair was pulled back, her green eyes sparkled, and she had beautiful healthy-looking white skin. She wore a white buttoned up shirt reminding Finley of a nurse. The lady stood up, walked around the table smiling, and held out her hand,

"Welcome to Tennessee SafeCity," the attendant said as she motioned Finley and Denise to take a seat before returning to her own seat.

With the push of a button, a holographic image sprang up labeled *Vital Information.*

"Please tell me about your journey," she said with sincerity. "How did you go about getting here?"

Finley picked her cuticles. Denise explained how they stayed in the Greenville station and got on the last train via their category C status.

The attendant swiped the air, and the hologram scrolled to a new page. "I see you're residents of Roswell, Georgia," she said. "Why were you in Greenville?"

"We were on our way to see my sister in Charlotte, and we stopped at the station motel in Greenville," Denise explained. "Is there anywhere I can get a real drink round here?"

Finley rolled her eyes. *Here we go again.*

"You're allowed one *real* drink a day—with your evening meal." She swiped three hovering checkboxes and talked while keeping her eyes on the hologram. "We also have people here who can help you live your best life. Would you like me to sign you up for a counselor or therapist?"

"I'm alright," Denise answered quickly. "Thanks though."

"You are both incredibly fortunate," the attendant said. "Roswell took quite a beating, as did all of Atlanta."

"Could you—sorry to interrupt," Finley said, "but could you check where my friends are on your network, please? They got left at the station we just came from."

The attendant smiled and swiped at the hologram. "I would be happy to," she promised, "once I have you and your mother registered."

She pushed a few holographic buttons and scanned their watches. Once scanned, Finley's watch rejoined the network. Delighted, she swiped left and right.

"This isn't right," she said. "My watch must have a bug or something."

"Oh, don't worry," the attendant said. "You'll have plenty of time to learn the new functions once we get you settled in your room. There are some great new apps we picked just for you! But enough about that. Let's walk you to your room."

"Ma'am," Finley said. "What about my friends?"

"Of course. Excuse me. You may each look up two people. We would be here all day if people could search all their friends and family." The attendant threw a new hologram into the air. "So, who would you like to look up first?"

Finley asked where Beth Kahn and Paul Lewis were. Denise gave Finley a harsh look when Beth was mentioned. Finley crossed her arms.

While the attendant searched for information on Beth and Paul, Finley stuffed her hand in her pocket to massage the rose Paul gave her on the station platform. *It's gone!* Finley realized. *It must have fallen out on the train or in the waiting room.* Unconcerned, the attendant pushed the hologram, scanning through the information.

"Looks like Beth is still in Atlanta—alive and somewhat healthy." She flipped through a few pages and paused. "Her blood pressure is high but nothing to worry about. She has been placed in category D and is registered as Islamic."

"She's alive!" Finley said. "The rest doesn't matter."

"I'm sorry, but the rest does matter." The attendant said softly. "President Hudson declared war today. All category D citizens and those who removed their watches have been declared an enemy to the empire."

"But Beth isn't an enemy of the empire," Finley said.

"She—she—she loves America! You have to believe me!"

The attendant swung the hologram to the side and locked eyes with Finley. "I don't decide who is in which category," she said. "I'm afraid your friend—she is your friend, correct?—is in trouble."

Finley shook her head and tapped her watch screen.

"Where have my contacts gone?"

"Your old settings have been erased, and you may not communicate with enemies of the empire unless you desire to be considered one yourself. Your watch will be updated with new information shortly," the attendant explained, "after you register for a job."

Finley hyperventilated. She tried to control her breathing, but it only worsened.

"I can tell you where Paul Lewis is if you want to move on?" the attendant responded robotically.

"Yes please," Finley said through staccato breaths. "Tell me where Paul is. He should be on his way here."

With a puzzled look, the attendant continued scanning the screen. She flipped through five pages of information, then three more.

"I'm sorry," she said, "give me just one moment."

She flicked at the hologram screen past pages of images and microscopic text.

"It seems Paul Lewis was recently at the station you left. But his watch just turned off. We're not sure where he is now." The attendant tucked her hair behind her ear and lifted her watch to her mouth. "I need to report another missing person—family, actually. The Lewis family from Roswell, Georgia, no longer have their watches on. All members of the family—John, Hannah, Jude, Paul, and Hope—are not reachable on the network."

She flipped through two more screens.

"Also," she continued, "the Cooks from North Carolina—Lucille and Brent—are no longer on the network. Neither is Officer Fendel. My data shows the Cooks are the parents of Derek Cook, an FF soldier here at our SafeCity." She abruptly stopped talking into her watch and smiled at Finley and Denise. "Time to show you to your new home."

The weight of the news numbed Finley's senses. She couldn't move.

The attendant acted like it was no big deal. Denise rubbed Finley's back and asked for her opportunity to learn the whereabouts of two people.

"Finley," the attendant said, ignoring Denise's question, "please listen carefully. There are two possibilities when a group of people disappear off the network like this. The first and most likely is that something killed them. This has occurred to millions of people all over the country recently. Since your friend and his family were near an active volcano, that's the most likely. The second possibility is that your friend—and apparently his family—removed their watches and took themselves off the network. I cannot confirm either way. I'm very sorry."

Finley wiped her eyes and quietly thanked the attendant.

"Now," the attendant continued, "it's your turn, Ms. Matthews. Let me find those two people for you."

Finley was desperate to ask more questions but couldn't get the words out.

Are they all gone? Is Paul gone? Jude? Are they dead?

Denise grabbed Finley's arm and squeezed tightly.

Get off me, you drunk whore, Finley thought, slapping her mother's arm away.

Denise spoke a few more minutes with the attendant, but Finley didn't hear anything she said. Finally, they stood up and shook hands. Not cognizant she was moving, Finley followed the official as Denise held her hand. They passed through electronic doors, up stairways, and down corridors. At each turn, everyone they passed smiled and greeted them, despite being complete strangers.

After fifteen minutes, they came to a row of numbered doors spaced ten feet apart. They stopped in front of room G68. The official scanned Denise's watch, and the door slid open. Denise and Finley stepped into a beautifully furnished living room and were encouraged to take off their shoes. A brand-new red sofa and a glass coffee table sat on soft, grey carpet. Finley removed her shoes and let her feet sink deep into the lush carpet.

Finley had never lived in a new apartment. To her right was a small kitchen with a sink, some cupboards, and a small fridge. There was laminate brown flooring and a small dinner table with two chairs inside the kitchen. It was beautiful, but Finley felt no gratitude.

The official pointed to the left and said something, but Finley only heard mumbles. Denise guided Finley into the bedroom with two single beds next to one another. Finley lay down on a bed and stared at the blank grey wall.

Two voices warred within her mind: hope and despair, life and death.

At least I have Mom.

You mean the drunk.

Beth's still alive. She's strong. She'll make it.

Enemy of the state, starving, probably homeless. She probably only has days left.

What about Chase? Maybe he's alive.

His whole neighborhood was probably destroyed. Stop acting desperate for someone who wouldn't even kiss you.

Paul isn't confirmed dead yet. He could be alive.

He's reckless, always getting in fights. He probably joined the rebellion. Besides, he only wants to use you and lose you anyway.

Finley longed for peace, but the voices continued.

I don't fit in here, she thought.

I don't believe in what they believe.

As soon as they find out Mom's a drunk and I hate religion, they'll probably throw us out.

Paul isn't coming for me.

Eventually, the mental effort sent her into a terrible, dark place between nightmare, nothingness, and a poor excuse for consciousness. She lay still, staring at the wall as minutes turned to hours.

From time to time, Denise attempted to speak to her, but Finley never responded. Hours turned to days. Denise slept in the bed next to Finley. Occasionally, Denise rested her hand on Finley's shoulder, stroked her back gently, played with her hair. Once she even sang to her daughter, hoping to elicit a response.

All Finley heard were mumbles, but the melody of her mother's song came to her like a forgotten dream. Every so often tears dripped down her cheeks, but she felt no emotion.

Denise put food beside her, but Finley didn't eat. She

drank a little water here and there that her mother held to her mouth, but then returned to staring at the blank grey wall. Late one day, Finley wasn't sure how many days had passed, Denise washed her down with a damp cloth. The moist cloth was warm and refreshing on her clammy skin.

Despite this, Finley didn't thank or acknowledge her mother. She knew what Denise was doing, but she refused to acknowledge her. Finley was depressed and in shock.

The next day, flashes of logical thought returned to Finley.

Where was Beth sleeping tonight? she wondered. *Is she really an enemy of the empire? And Paul—he's either dead or he destroyed his watch. Either way, there's no way of communicating with him. But there's a chance he could be alive.*

Finley pinched her eyes tight to keep a grasp on the tiny ray of hope she felt—the first in days.

Chase. He talked about marriage. Maybe there is someone else out there who would love me like he did. Or at least like me enough to never leave me or use me. I can't end up like Mom, Finley thought.

As if summoned from a dream, Denise whispered in Finley's ear.

"Finley, sweetheart. Someone's here to see you. Please turn around and say hello. It's been three days."

Finley didn't move. She refused to face reality.

"You'll have to come on in," Denise said loudly. "Let's see if you can get her to speak."

Footsteps came to the head of Finley's bed.

"I'll leave you two alone," Denise said. She left the room and closed the door quietly.

The air conditioning hummed in the background.

Finley's guest took a knee beside her bed.

"Hey Finn. It's me, Chase."

CHAPTER 28
CHASE

Chase was only fourteen when Grandma Anna spoke it out loud. She wouldn't make it much longer—probably not even to the end of the day.

The fresh smell of white Cherokee roses clashed with the stale smell of his elderly grandma who awaited her final breath. She lay motionless, while Chase's mother wrapped her two hands around one of her mother's single, frail hands. Chase and his father stood at the foot of the bed in reverent silence.

The silver wedding ring around Grandma Anna's neck sparkled in the setting sun that shone through the window. Chase's grandma had worn it on a chain since her husband passed away. She slowly lifted a hand and grasped the ring tightly, looked into Chase's eyes, and motioned him to come closer.

Chase moved to his grandma's side.

"The wearer of this ring will bear a child who will usher in new hope to our empire," she said weakly. "In our pursuit of holiness, we've lost our way. The child will bring restoration at a time when the whole world is in chaos. Men would not choose the bride you seek, but it will be his choice."

She pointed a finger to the sky before carrying on.

"This child," his grandma said, "this girl will be stunningly beautiful. Her feet will carry the message of peace with every step. She will hail from a broken family—a prodigal. Find her, Chase. Your heart will lead you."

As Chase struggled for words to speak, his grandma smiled and breathed her last.

ACKNOWLEDGMENTS

T he idea of writing a novel never crossed my mind until my early thirties. Until then, I would have laughed at the idea of being an author. But I guess being married to an amazing actress and musician who inspires creativity has worn off on me.

Macie, you are my best friend. I love all the many forms of artistic and creative appreciation you have brought into my life and our family.

Miriam, my princess—without you, I never would have fallen in love with reading and the joy of getting lost in different worlds. You inspired me to tap into a level of imagination I never knew existed. Your beautiful, kind, and smart personality is scattered throughout the characters in *Implosion*.

Eliana, you are such a powerful person. What you are capable of inspires the underlying message within the pages of this book—that within each of us lies something so powerful that it can change the world. Your love, smile, and leadership qualities are scattered throughout the characters in *Implosion*.

Judah, my son—you were made to change the world. Your powerful emotions and big heart have inspired me on a level I never knew possible. Thank you.

Tiffany, you were the first person to read this book before the first draft was even complete. You gave me a pat on the back in just the right season, which encouraged me more than you know.

Mark, thanks for all the time you spent listening to my ideas and chatting with me about empires, kingdoms, and characters. So many of your ideas have made this story come to life. I am so thankful for your friendship and leadership.

Grace, thanks for giving me new insights and ideas that helped me make some tough decisions on the direction of the book.

Daniel Brantley and Argyle Fox—when I began writing, I was told how important it was to get the right editor. I was convinced after our first few conversations that you were the best guy for the job. Thank you for bringing this story to life in a way that I couldn't.

This book was born from a dream so vivid and real that I didn't know what to do with it. Thanks to my creative wife who convinced me to write a short story from it, which turned into a novel. You can find the dream in chapter twenty-one.

Finally, I want to acknowledge a deep longing within the heart of every person. There truly does exist a kingdom that will satisfy everything your soul longs for. I hope this book will inspire you to seek after it with all your heart, mind, and soul—even when the world tells you it doesn't really exist.